UNFORGETTABLE NOVELS OF THE WEST BY JACK BALLAS . . .

TOMAHAWK CANYON
Cole Mason came to New Mexico Territory looking for a good graze—and found a bloody range war instead . . .

DURANGO GUNFIGHT
Quint Cantrell wants to bury his past. But the Hardester clan wants to bury *him* . . .

MAVERICK GUNS
Clay Mason's brother has been marked for death by a sly killer—but when you take on one of the Mason clan, you take on *all* of the Mason clan . . .

MONTANA BREED
Young Rafe Gunn wanted to look into his family's past. But first he had to look death square in the face . . .

DON'T MISS THESE
AUTHENTIC WESTERN SERIES
FROM THE BERKLEY PUBLISHING GROUP

FURY by Jim Austin
Meet John Fury. Gunfighter. Legend. Where there's trouble, there's Fury.

THE HORSEMEN by Gary McCarthy
The epic story of a frontier family's glorious dream, raising horses in the untamed West.

NORTHWEST DESTINY by Bill Gulick
The award-winning author's acclaimed trilogy of white men and Indians bound by blood.

DESPERADO by B.W. Lawton
On the razor's edge of the law, one man walks alone.

TEXAS LEGENDS by Gene Shelton
The incredible *true* stories of the West's most notorious outlaws and heroic lawmen.

Westerns by Giles Tippette
The new star of the classic Western novel, Tippette captures the American dream in the saga of the Williams clan.

Westerns by Richard Matheson
Winner of the Spur Award for Best Western Novel. Look for *By the Gun, The Gunfighter,* and *Journal of the Gun Years.*

Westerns by Jack Ballas
His fiction tells the gut truth of the old West in all its raw action and glorious, hardfisted notions of swift vengeance and six-gun justice.

MONTANA
BREED

JACK BALLAS

J

JOVE BOOKS, NEW YORK

MONTANA BREED

A Jove Book / published by arrangement with
the author

PRINTING HISTORY
Jove edition / March 1994

All rights reserved.
Copyright © 1994 by Jack Ballas.
Excerpt from *Texas Horsetrading Co.* copyright © 1994
by Charter Communications, Inc.
This book may not be reproduced in whole or in part,
by mimeograph or any other means, without permission.
For information address: The Berkley Publishing Group,
200 Madison Avenue, New York, New York 10016.

ISBN: 0-515-11337-9

A JOVE BOOK®
Jove Books are published by The Berkley Publishing Group,
200 Madison Avenue, New York, New York 10016.
JOVE and the "J" design are trademarks belonging to
Jove Publications, Inc.

PRINTED IN THE UNITED STATES OF AMERICA

10 9 8 7 6 5 4 3 2 1

To Gary Goldstein, my editor. He gave me my chance, taught me, and guided me. As long as there are editors like Gary, the traditional Western will persevere.

And to the Berkley sales representatives, who have through their tireless efforts presented my books and gotten them on bookshelves. Without people like them, no author would succeed.

CHAPTER
ONE

Rafe Gunn shifted the candle to better light the safe dial. Lightning flashed, water dripped from weathered eaves, and wind whined, sighed, and whistled around and through cracks in walls and window frames. A chill ran up his spine, and he snapped a glance over his shoulder.

Twenty dollars, just twenty dollars will be enough to get me out of here, he thought, hoping there was that much in the old safe. Even in this year of 1862 wages were more than the three dollars a week his uncle paid him. He'd not been able to save much of it.

He had watched his uncle open this heavy, green steel box for years. Every time his Uncle Thaddeus opened it, Gunn strained his eyes to see the numbers dialed. He had long ago committed them to memory.

A gust of wind buffeted the storefront. The old building creaked in protest. Gunn held his breath. If caught, he could never prove the money was owed him.

He and Thaddeus lived over the store. If his uncle came downstairs, Gunn might have to kill him. He shuddered at the thought, but had made up his mind he would do it if he had to.

Sweat beaded his brow. The cold rain of this New York night did nothing to stop the nervous sweat pouring from him. One more turn of the dial to the right and he twisted the worn handle.

He imagined his uncle's palm prints being forever imbedded into the metal. Thaddeus grasped every cent as though it pained him to see it spent for anything.

The first thing Gunn saw when the door opened was a rusty metal box. It had been brown the first time he'd seen it. He

1

remembered his father lying on the bed upstairs, dying of lung fever, handing that very box to Uncle Thad. His words had been "Keep this for Rafe. It's all I leave him, but enough to give him a start." Until now, Gunn had not known where his uncle had kept the box.

He reached in, pulled it toward him, untied the leather thong, and opened the lid. Atop its contents lay a piece of yellowed, brittle paper with "Rafe" scrawled on it.

He opened the folded note and read: "Son, I leave you these few pitiful things that were mine. The money is yours to do with as you will. Use it wisely. I love you, son, as did your mother." He had signed the note, "Your father, Christopher Gunn."

Gunn blinked back tears, for the father he'd known such a short time, and stared into the box.

A slim-bladed knife in a leather sheath rested on top. The leather was finely tanned and beautifully tooled. Gunn remembered his mother doing work like this. He slipped the knife and its sheath into his boot top.

Next he saw a leather pouch, the one his father had worn around his neck. It was similar to others he'd seen the warriors of his mother's Oglala Sioux band wear. Gunn slipped the thong over his head, letting his father's medicine bag rest on his chest.

The rest of the box's contents were more double eagles than he'd ever seen. He stared at them a moment, guessing that more than three thousand dollars in gold coin rested there, and by the words his father had written, they were his.

Staring at his fortune, he didn't hear the stealthy squeak of the stairs.

"What the *hell* are you doing in my safe, boy?"

Gunn whirled in his squatting position to face his uncle. "I'm taking what is mine. I'm nineteen years old. You never told me about this, but I remember now my father handing it to you. My father's note says it's mine."

Even in the dim candlelight he saw the veins stand out in his uncle's neck and his face flush with rage. "I'll be damned if it is. I've raised you, paid good money to send you to school, clothed you. That money's mine."

Gunn squatted there a moment staring up into Thaddeus's eyes. "Sir," he said, his voice soft, controlled, "what about the years I've spent working for you, doing all the menial tasks you could heap on me—while you paid me next to nothing? No. I've more than earned what little I got."

"That money's mine. You'll not take it." Thaddeus's voice had thinned to a squeak. He walked quickly toward the door. "I'm calling the police."

All the talk in the world would not change his uncle's mind. From squatting, Gunn dived, grasped Thaddeus around the knees, and knocked him against the wall.

Thaddeus was a big man, tall and brawny. Gunn stood a little over six feet, but was slim, wiry. He had his work cut out for him.

Thaddeus rolled to his knees and lurched to his feet.

He ran at Gunn, swinging as he came. His fist grazed Gunn's cheek.

Gunn faded back out of range of his uncle's forceful charge and thrust with his left. It caught Thaddeus square in the teeth, but like a bull, he came on, swinging.

Gunn jabbed again with his left and opened a cut under his uncle's right eye.

Thaddeus brought a right up from his waist and connected with Gunn's stomach, causing his breath to gush past his slightly parted lips.

Fighting to draw air into his lungs, Gunn dropped his right fist to his side and swung, coming onto the balls of his feet at the moment he connected with Thaddeus's chin. The spring steel of muscles developed on the store's loading dock paid off. His uncle dropped like a sack of oats, groaned, tried to get up, and sank back to the floor.

For a moment Gunn's gaze rested on his uncle. His only thought, his only emotion, was thanks that he'd spent so much time in the gymnasium after the store closed at night. He boxed any who would take him on. That training had paid off tonight. His strength alone would not have been enough.

He tore Thaddeus's nightshirt in strips and securely tied his uncle's hands and feet. The soft cloth wouldn't hold him for long, but it would provide enough time to get away.

When Gunn pulled the last knot tight, Thaddeus stirred, opened his eyes, and stared at him.

"Help!" he yelled.

Gunn dived for the pile of cloth strips, grabbed a handful, stuffed them in his uncle's mouth, and tied them in place. He had no doubt that as soon as Thaddeus escaped his bonds, he'd alert the police and they would be looking all over New York for him.

Reaching inside his shirt, he untied a canvas tube he'd sewn together with heavy cord. When he'd made it, he had had no idea what he'd use it for other than as somewhere to carry his small belongings. Now he was glad he had it.

Carefully he poured the coins into the end of the tube, leaving only three to go into his pocket. Finished with that, he tied the tube securely around his waist, put on his pea jacket, picked up the rest of his belongings, which were only a spare shirt and a couple of pairs of socks, all rolled into a heavy pair of woolen trousers, and turned to his uncle.

"Going to Santa Fe, Uncle Thad. Got a horse waiting for me, so I'll be in New Jersey by the time you call the police." His words were all a lie, but he hoped they'd give him more time. He was boarding a ship.

He checked the knots one last time, pulled them tighter, blew out the candle, and slipped out the store's front door, hoping never to see it again.

Walking close to the buildings, Gunn tried to ward off the drizzle that with time would soak him.

He shivered, inhaled the rain-washed air, and thought that anywhere else it would be sweet and clean. Here in lower Manhattan, only three blocks from the waterfront, the air had a fishy smell, mixed with sewage from the city.

Only a block from the store, the shrill blast of a policeman's whistle sounded behind him. Gunn shrank closer to the buildings. It had not taken long for his uncle's bonds to part. Gunn cursed himself for not having prepared better. He should have had a length of rope. He picked up his pace.

This part of town housed the worst element of New York society. He stopped long enough to pull the knife from his boot top and put it in his waistband, close to hand.

Another two blocks and a man in sailor's garb stepped from an alley.

"Hold up there, mate. What's your hurry?"

Gunn didn't slow, but reached for his blade and pointed it toward the man.

"Aw, matey, didn't mean ye no harm," the man said and stepped back into the alley.

Several whistles sounded behind Gunn now. They'd better catch him fast, because from here he could see the tall masts of a frigate spearing the night sky. That was the *Sea Eagle,* the ship he'd signed on to as an ordinary seaman.

His breath came easily. He had not dared run, for fear of drawing attention, but his pace had been fast, what one would expect on a night like this.

He guessed the time at about 3 A.M. Another glance toward the masts showed them to be about two blocks away. Coming on a street corner, he rounded it to head directly toward the waterfront—and bumped squarely into a bluecoat.

The policeman grabbed his shoulders. "Say, lad, what's the hurry?"

"Just trying to get to my ship, sir. This rain is a mite cold."

The officer smiled and patted him on the shoulder. "That it is, sail—"

The sharp blast of a whistle cut into the officer's words. Gunn didn't stop to think. He twisted toward the cop, swinging as he turned. His fist connected with the officer's jaw, causing him to stumble back.

Gunn didn't wait for another punch. He did an about-face and ran, not toward the ship, but parallel to its anchorage. He didn't want to lead the police to his means of escape. He passed an alley, slid to a stop, and came back. Looking into its dark maw, he thought he saw a stack of crates at the end. A few steps brought him to them.

Another whistle, and shouting voices told him they were closing in. Frantically, he dug into the stack of crates, crawled into the hole he'd made, and pulled garbage and boxes over him. He lay still, hardly daring to breathe.

Footsteps sloshed down the darkness toward him. He heard a foot hit something, a stumble, a curse. "You see him come in here?"

"Naw. I thought he ran right on by. We better look while we're here, though. Be careful. The lad has a punch like one o' them prizefighters."

"Yeah. Damn this stinking weather anyway. Bad enough being cold. This rain's been pissing down my back so I'll never get warm again."

"He said he was going to his ship?"

"Yeah, but he lied. He wasn't a sailor. Didn't have the dress or look of one. Hell, he even ran *away* from the dock area when we got after 'im."

Gunn heard them splash their way to the end of the alley. "He must've gone on. Hell, he's a mile from here by now."

Believe him—believe him, Gunn thought, the stench of rotting garbage suffocating him.

"Yeah, think you're right," the other commented. "I'd sure as hell like to bend my nightstick across his friggin' skull, teach him to hit an officer of the law."

"You betcha . . ." Their voices faded beyond Gunn's hearing.

He didn't stir. He still heard the distant shrill of whistles. They sounded as though they were drawing away from the waterfront. Maybe the words he'd left with his uncle, and the route he'd taken after slugging the cop, had decoyed them.

With any luck, they'd block off the ferries leaving the city and cease looking for him elsewhere.

He was surprised that he'd not felt great panic. Oh sure, he thought, he was scared, but he'd still done what he had to do. He'd seemed to accept the danger, react to it, and look to his next action. He must have gotten that from his mother. He remembered her only vaguely.

She'd been a slim, pretty woman. The first seven years of Gunn's life had been spent with the Indians, until his mother died. Soon after his mother's death, his father had become sick from the same malady, lung fever, and brought him east to his brother.

Gunn cocked his ear to listen for further sound. He'd not heard a whistle for a few minutes.

Carefully, he shoved the boxes from on top of him, stood, and slipped from the alley.

He walked as he thought any late-returning sailor would. Hoping not to draw attention, he paced when he could at a second's notice dodge into a doorway or alley.

He headed toward the waterfront while brushing at his clothes.

When he was only a block from the alley, the dimly lit front of a pub showed through the drizzle. They frequently stayed open all night here close to the water. Sailors were notorious drinkers.

Gunn had never had a drink of anything stronger than milk in his life, but thought if he went in the pub he could mix with those in there, and when a couple of them left, he'd walk with them to the waterfront.

At the bar, he ordered an ale. The sailor next to him glanced around after a while, sipped his drink, and said, "Hi, mate. What ship you off of?"

"*Sea Eagle*."

The sailor squinted at him and nodded. "She's my ship too—or was. I'm headin' home. Ain't been there for four years. You just sign on?"

Gunn nodded. "Yeah. Never been to sea before."

The sailor looked at the small bundle Gunn carried. "You already stow your gear aboard?"

"No," Gunn said. "This is all I have."

The sailor studied him a moment, then said, "You can't go to sea with no more'n that. You'll freeze to death."

Gunn shrugged. "Don't have much choice—no stores open this time of night, and they told me the ship would sail on the tide this morning."

The sailor said, "You're right about that." He scanned Gunn from foot to head. "Stand up. Let's see how tall you are."

Puzzled, Gunn stood. The sailor stood and looked on a level into Gunn's eyes, grinned, and said, "Damned if we're not about the same size. You got any money?"

Wary of admitting that he had more than a few dollars, Gunn shrugged. "Not much—but some."

"Tell you what," the sailor said, "my seabag, hammock, clews, oilskins—the works—are right here at my feet. I got no need for 'em anytime soon. Figure the whole batch o' gear's worth maybe twenty-five dollars. Let you have it for twenty, save me toting it."

Gunn thought a moment. The sailor was telling the truth about him being ill prepared. He reached in his pocket, thumbed two of the double eagles to the side, and withdrew one.

"You called it, sailor. Twenty dollars is all I've got." He shrugged. "But I'm going right aboard, so I'll need the money a lot less than I need your gear." He stuck out his hand. "You just sold your seabag."

"You're lucky I didn't pack any dirty clothes for Ma to wash. Everything you bought is clean and mended."

They shook hands. Gunn handed the sailor the coin, and allowed his friend to buy another ale to seal the agreement. He felt guilty for the lie, but knew it would be stupid to show any money. In this area a man could get rolled for the price of a drink.

The sailor grinned. "You sure picked a good ship for your first cruise. She's a seagoin' sonuvabitch, don't stop for nothin' 'cept about once a year to get her bottom scraped. Ain't much on liberty, but she's a feeder, a good ship. I s'pose she can outrun damn near anything afloat, and you might have to."

"Why?"

The sailor looked at Gunn as if he'd lost his mind. "Why, for Christ's sake, don't you know nothin'? We're at war. Naw, I don't know what side we're on, but the North and South are fightin'. We carry goods to whichever side'll buy 'em. And them contraband ships don't give a crap which side you're on—they take what they can get and sell it to the highest bidder."

Gunn thought for a long few seconds, then asked, "Doesn't the government do anything about trading with the enemy?"

"If we got caught, it'd go rough on us, but so far we ain't got caught."

Christ almighty, Gunn thought. I'm shipping out on a smuggler.

He was trapped, neatly trapped. He couldn't attempt crossing the city again. The ship was his only means of escape. The sailor pocketed the change from the two ales and left.

Two sailors down the bar a few feet from Gunn drank the last of their ale and told a couple of others in their bunch they were going back to the ship.

"If you're going to the *Eagle,* I'd like to tag along," Gunn said to the tall one.

"Sure. Come on. Don't think we'll get much sleep before we get under way, but yeah, come on."

As soon as they walked onto the quay, Gunn saw a couple of policemen checking all sailors before letting them aboard.

"Wonder what's going on?" the tall sailor to Gunn's left said.

"Don't know. I guarantee you one thing, though, the skipper ain't gonna let those bastards aboard to check nobody," the short, stocky one grunted.

Gunn went still inside. He hadn't come this far to let a couple of cops stop him.

Still a hundred yards or more from the gangway, he looked at his new shipmates. "They're looking for me, I expect. Some landlubber gave me some trouble, and I kicked hell out of him. Don't think I killed him, but they been after me since supper." He looked from one to the other of them. "You mean it when you say the skipper won't let them aboard?"

They nodded at once. "Cap'n Thorsen don't let nobody on his ship lest he wants 'em there."

"Will you help me get aboard? It might get you in a bunch of trouble."

The tall, lean sailor on Gunn's left grinned and held out his hand. "Meet Sean *Trouble* O'Malley."

The other sailor, short, stocky, and redheaded, smiled widely. "Hell now, don't that beat all? My middle name's Trouble too. Timothy *Trouble* Sullivan."

Gunn returned their grins with a head shake. "Okay, let's walk to the gangway three abreast. I'll be in the middle. When we get close, you two turn away as though to walk around those police. I believe they'll head for you, and when they do, I'm going to run like hell right up the middle."

"Jeez! Where you been all night? I ain't had this much fun since grandma caught 'er tit in the ringer," O'Malley said.

Approaching the gangway, O'Malley and Sullivan moved, one to the right and one to the left, opening about four feet between them and Gunn. As he had predicted, the officers split to try to contain them.

"Here, you men stay where you are," one of the officers yelled.

His words triggered them to spread farther. Each officer went with the one on his side.

Gunn didn't wait. He sprang forward. His newly acquired seabag bumped precariously on his right shoulder as he clutched the rail with his left hand, pulling himself up the steep gangway.

With Gunn's first step, both officers saw that they had been suckered. They yelled and started toward him.

Only a few feet to the top. It seemed a mile. He grasped his seabag with both hands and threw it with all his strength toward the quarterdeck.

Gunn felt one of the officers' hands grab at his clothing. He planted his left foot and kicked backward with his right. His foot connected with something soft, and at the same time he heard a grunt. With both hands free, he pulled at the railings as hard as his strength allowed.

Rough hands grabbed him under his arms and dragged him aboard. He rolled to his side and saw that he lay on the ship's decking. The quarterdeck watch stood at the head of the gangway blocking the policeman's passage.

"You ain't comin' aboard this vessel," the sentry bellowed.

"Th-th-the hell we're not," one of the police officers stammered.

O'Malley and Sullivan squeezed around the two and stood shoulder to shoulder with the watch.

"He says you're not, and he's said it all," O'Malley said. "If you want to try and come by us, you got four to fight."

Gunn noticed that he had been included. He rolled to his feet and stood with them.

The police looked at them and then at each other, shrugged, and said simultaneously, "What the hell." They retraced their steps down the gangway.

The quarterdeck watch said to Gunn, "What's your name?"

"Rafe Gunn, sir."

The sentry stepped to the side and picked up a tablet from a bitt. He scanned it a moment, took a stub of pencil from his pocket, licked its point, and made a check mark alongside Gunn's name.

"O'Malley there can show you where to swing your hammock. You swing it after working hours and take it down and stow it every day before the morning watch." He cocked an eyebrow at Gunn. "You been to sea before?"

"No, sir."

"I'll show 'im around, Boats," O'Malley cut in. "'Tween Sullivan here an' me, we'll get 'im squared away."

The ship's boatswain nodded. "Good. I'll be on watch until we single up for getting under way." He grinned at the backs of the departing policemen. "Don't think I want to know what that ruckus was all about. I would probably get nothing but a bunch o' crap outta you men anyway."

"Aw, c'mon, Boats, you know we'd tell you the truth." Sullivan's grin alone said he knew the boatswain would not believe a word of *any* story they told.

"Just stow your gear for now. You won't see it again until tonight anyway," Boats said. "Your first day at sea will be behind you by then. *Or* you might even be wearing it."

"What did he mean by that?" Gunn asked when they were headed toward crew's quarters.

"Aw, he thinks you'll be seasick. Don't worry about it. Most of us have been at one time or another," O'Malley said to comfort him.

On the way to the sleeping compartment, O'Malley and Sullivan talked incessantly, telling Gunn things to do and not to do. They said, don't ever stand in the bight of a coiled line, don't stand inside the swing of a cargo net, don't do this, do that, and above all, *never* volunteer for *anything*. There were as many do's as don'ts. Christ, Gunn thought, I'll never remember all those things.

He began to get the idea that a life at sea was going to be rough, a lot rougher than working on the loading dock. He shrugged mentally. He could stand anything for a short while. New Orleans would take only a couple of weeks' good sailing, and he counted on jumping ship as soon as they anchored there. He wanted to go to the Dakota Territory. As soon as he got anywhere to put his feet on dry land, any land not part of New York, he was leaving.

CHAPTER
TWO

GUNN STOWED HIS gear where O'Malley showed him and had started topside when he felt the deck roll slightly.

"We're under way," O'Malley said.

"Shouldn't we be doing something?" Gunn asked.

Sullivan glanced at him and grinned at O'Malley. "Listen to the man, O'Malley, me lad. He's anxious to get to work." He again gave Gunn his attention. "Me boy, ye'll have all the work you can handle before this day is out. Ye'll drag your arse below at the end of the day so tired you'll think ye don't have the strength to swing your hammock. But, you'll find the strength and tomorrow's work will be easier, and the next day even better."

O'Malley pulled on Gunn's sleeve. "Come, we'll stand by for orders to make sail. Stay close to me and I'll show you what to do. Boats'll want you to follow me for a while and do as I do. You'll learn faster that way."

As soon as the bow pointed seaward, true to O'Malley's word, orders were passed to make sail. Gunn again felt a tug at his sleeve as O'Malley said, "Follow me, lad."

Gunn's friends, no older than he, were veteran seamen. With every order that came down from the bridge, they knew exactly what their role was in carrying it out.

He followed the two of them forward of amidships to the base of the tallest mast. O'Malley stopped and pointed to the top of it. "This is known as the mainmast. Our job is to make sail on that uppermost yardarm. We'll be running before the wind. If the wind gets too strong, we'll reef sail." He squinted at Gunn. "You know—reefing is to shorten sail so it'll not have as much surface to the wind. That will take some of the strain off the mast and ship. The tops'ls are always our job."

Gunn stared at the top of the mast majestically spearing the sky. His chest tightened. The thought of being up there with nothing to hold him brought a gasp that he hoped the others didn't hear.

Without further ado, O'Malley started up the rigging. "You go ahead of me, lad," Sullivan ordered.

Gunn watched the way O'Malley handled the climb and aped him as much as inexperience allowed. His stomach turned over and felt like it had jumped to his mouth. He climbed as fast as his arms would pull him, but knew that he slowed Sullivan in his climb. He swallowed, and swallowed again, damned if he'd show anyone how nervous he was.

O'Malley stopped and slipped out on the starboard yardarm. Gunn followed suit.

"The sail secured to this yardarm is our responsibility," O'Malley said and moved over for Gunn to make room for Sullivan. "Until you get used to moving about up here, be very sure you have a good grip on a line so's not to fall. Make certain of that if you don't do anything else. That's a good idea whether you're used to it or not."

Gunn felt queasy. He thought he might get sick. He sucked hard at the fresh air and felt better. He told himself that seasickness came from the mind. Don't think about it, Gunn. Think of something else, think of what O'Malley and Sullivan are showing you.

Up here, the ship seemed to roll and pitch more. Thinking of mathematics lessons learned in school, he knew the ship's hull acted as a fulcrum and the masts as levers. The mast tops *did* move a lot more—and they weren't helping his sick feeling at all.

The bow quartered into troughs and slammed and cut into the swells coming off their port bow. With each swell, the ship shuddered and rolled hard starboard. Gunn looked down. There was nothing but blue water below. The ship's deck cocked off to port. They had told him, port left, starboard right. Gunn didn't give a damn what they called it, he called it scary. He gripped the lifeline so tight his forearms hurt.

"Look aft, Gunn," Sullivan called above the wind. "'Tis a sight no sailor likes to see until he's broke."

Gripping the yardarm so tight his legs hurt all the way into his groin, Gunn did as directed and saw Long Island dropping behind off the port quarter. He felt as though his stomach had a chunk of lead in it. Whether he *wanted* to go to sea was not the question now—he *was* at sea.

He remembered the streets of New York and said a silent prayer that he would measure up to the kind of guts and manhood he must have here.

They made sail and returned to the main deck. Gunn found that setting sail only started his first day at sea. Lines had to be made up, new lines spliced, decks holystoned and clamped down. "Clamp down," he found, meant swabbing the deck with clear water. When he finished with one task, another waited.

After the workday, which Gunn had thought would never end, all hands scrubbed their clothing and took a saltwater bath. Fresh water was used for cooking and drinking only.

O'Malley looked over from his bucket of soapy water. "Gunn, me lad, the ladies ashore tell me there's a saying that sailors have the cleanest bodies and filthiest minds of all humanity."

Gunn remembered the sea stories told by the deckhands at work. Slinging suds from his hands, he nodded. "Now I know where they get the saying."

He swung his hammock, and crawled into it that first night thinking he would never be able to roll out of it in the morning. Sullivan had been right, sailors *worked*.

Stretched out, he felt the canvas tube of double eagles and realized that if he fell overboard with them around his middle, he would go straight to the bottom. He had to find someplace to stash his valuables. Besides, they made him feel like he was sleeping on sharp stones. He pondered that problem but didn't resolve it before sleep came.

Eight bells sounded the start of the workday. Gunn groaned and heard the rest of the crew cursing, with some trying to catch one more minute of sleep. "Christ, four o'clock in the morning," Gunn muttered.

Before he got his eyes opened good, the master-at-arms

came into the compartment banging on the bulkhead and shouting, "Roll outta your sacks—turn to."

"Ah, hell," Gunn growled and turned out of his hammock. He rolled it and lashed it with a lanyard to hold it secure in storage.

His eyes felt as if they were seated in sockets of fire. He was certain he hadn't slept an hour. Every time he moved, that damned hammock had threatened to toss him to the deck. He had fought it all night. His muscles had staked out their own bit of hell to torture him. He choked off a groan, hoping today would be better.

Leadenly, he followed O'Malley and Sullivan to the chow line. They ate in the same compartment in which they slept.

After eating his bowl of gruel, he was working on his second cup of tea when O'Malley said, "I know yesterday was hard, lad, but by the time we get to Glasgow, you'll be climbing that rig—"

"Glasgow? What do you mean, Glasgow?" Gunn's words tumbled over each other.

"Glasgow, Scotland," Sullivan cut in. "Ain't ye never heard of it?"

"Hell yes, I've heard of it. I thought we were going to New Orleans. Who changed the goddamned plans?"

O'Malley shook his head. "Plans? There never was any plans to go to New Orleans. Where'd you get that idea?"

Gunn sat there, stunned. Where *had* he gotten that idea? Maybe the sailor who sold him his seabag had told him. Maybe he just figured that all ships went to New Orleans. No, *that* idea was *too* stupid. He looked over the rim of his cup at the two of them and shook his head. "I don't know where I got the idea, men. Just damned foolishness, I suppose."

He thought a moment and asked, "What are we going to do in Glasgow?"

Sullivan raised his eyebrows. "Who knows. The skipper goes where he can get cargo that'll bring the best price in the North, South, anywhere. Don't count on getting ashore, though, when we load or off-load in America. We'll probably slide into an inlet somewhere, and men will come aboard and take charge of whatever we're hauling. They'll pay the skipper and leave in the dark of night. We never get ashore during those times, but we *will* get ashore in Glasgow." He pursed his lips and whistled. "Wait'll you grab an armful of one of them Scot lassies. They give a roll in the hay ye ain't likely to forget."

Gunn just stared at them. He had never been with a woman. After a while, little above a whisper, he said, "Jesus Christ." The words were more of a prayer than anything else. He had no idea how long he would be on this ship—he might never see the Dakota Territory.

This day proved easier—but not much. At least O'Malley had been right about *that*. Gunn believed every day had a bright side, and today was no different. He had less fear of climbing the rigging, and that queasy feeling in his stomach was gone.

By the end of the first week, Gunn admitted to himself that he liked the sea. The feel of the deck heaving under his feet, the wind whistling in the rigging, the snapping of the sails, the rough friendliness of his shipmates, the quick efficiency with which everyone did their jobs—he liked it, but he hadn't changed his mind one whit about going to the Dakota Territory.

"Great life, eh, lad?" Sullivan smiled at him. "In a couple of days ye'll know the rough side of this life, though."

Gunn looked at him. "You mean it gets rougher than this?"

"Aye, lad, it does. This is like a sail on a lake. We'll be comin' into foul weather soon. The quartermaster said to me during chow that the barometer is falling—fast, 'tis already low enough to bring on a fine bit of a blow. Then, lad, ye're gonna discover what work at sea is really like."

They sat next to a stanchion, backs braced against it to roll with the ship. Well, Gunn thought, it looked like he would find out what he was made of. He had heard that a storm at sea was like no other experience.

"Cap'n called you up to see 'im yet?" O'Malley asked.

Gunn shook his head. "Why? I do my work."

"True, lad, but the skipper likes to know who's sailing with him. He'll get you in his cabin and ask you enough questions to fill a book. When he gets through, he'll even know how often you go to the head." O'Malley swiped his watch cap off and scratched his scalp.

"Y'know what, Gunn? Ye're going to find Captain Thorsen hard as iron—but fair. A man needs punishing, the skipper gives him what he deserves—no more, no less. And he's honest too. He ain't never cheated a man outta one red cent owed to 'im."

The idea took form in Gunn's head that maybe, just maybe, he could trust the captain to hold his inheritance.

Sullivan continued where O'Malley left off. "There's another reason the skipper wants to know his men. If he finds a troublemaker, he'll put 'im ashore in the next port." He stopped and glanced at Gunn with a sly look. "Know that yardarm we spend so much time on?"

At Gunn's nod, he continued, "The skipper uses it for other things."

"What things?" Gunn asked.

"One thing the cap'n hates bad as wharf rats is a thief. I've sailed with 'im a few years now, and I've seen two men hang from up there." Sullivan leaned back and looked at Gunn. "That's the kind of man he is, and we like him for it."

Gunn nodded. "Way it should be."

"Doesn't surprise you, lad?"

Gunn shook his head. "If I caught someone stealing from me, or anybody else, I'd throw him over the side."

Sullivan and O'Malley looked closely at him, then grinned. "Good, lad," O'Malley said. "We've saved the skipper the trouble of hanging a man a couple of times already. We just drag 'im out of his hammock on a dark night and toss 'im over the side. By the time he's missed, Davy Jones has 'im comfortably stashed in his locker."

Gunn felt better about carrying his money around, but the amount he had on him would have tempted many an honest man. He had to get rid of it for another reason too. It weighed close to six pounds, and hauling that extra weight when climbing the rigging might be the little that could cause him to lose his hold and fall.

That night he thought long about what he should do. Finally he decided that his best bet was to ask the captain to keep it for him. He would show him the note left by his father. That should prove how he came to have the money. Trusting the captain was risky, but since coming aboard, he had looked for somewhere safe to stash his money and had found no place that satisfied him.

There were a couple of men aboard that had a look about them Gunn didn't trust. They had not done anything to arouse his suspicions, he just didn't trust them—the Portuguese and the Bostonian.

Thinking of them, he wondered if he could throw them over the side—and decided he could. It was a horrible way to die, but shipboard was like a crate of apples—one bad one and the whole batch would rot.

The next morning a fine spray blew across the deck ahead of a freshening wind. The sky was brassy, and though there wasn't a cloud, a film shadowed the sun.

"She's acomin' lad," Sullivan said, walking up behind Gunn. "The quartermaster don't miss very often. Even without him, that sky tells me we're in for it."

Gunn's heartbeat quickened. Surprise flooded him—he looked forward to the storm. His fear, if that's what it was, was that he wouldn't measure up. There were better sailors, but only due to their experience. He looked up the mast and saw the canvas stretched taut. He might not know how to do everything yet, but he determined to do whatever his mind and body would allow.

"We'll be reefing sail in the next hour or two," O'Malley said from behind Sullivan. "You had better stand down here and watch. No point in getting hurt."

Gunn stared at the angry sea a moment. Wind whipped the tops off the dark, heaving, rolling mass of water, and sent fine spume ahead of it.

Gunn stared at O'Malley a long moment. "You go, I go."

Sullivan punched O'Malley in the ribs. "Told ye last night it would do ye no good to make that offer." He shot Gunn a sly grin. "S'pose we'll just have to mollycoddle you while we're aloft."

Gunn felt blood rush to his face. "Timothy Sullivan, I'll tell you one damned thing, you'll not mollycoddle *me*. Tell me what to do. Tell me and show me once. I'll handle it."

Sullivan slapped him on the back, and at the same time threw his other arm over O'Malley's shoulder. He laughed. "That's another thing I told O'Malley last night, lad. I said to him, 'Sean O'Malley, me lad, when we go aloft, Gunn's going to be right there with us.' And so ye are. The best advice I can give ye, though, is *be careful*. A fall and the deck'll break ye to bits. If we're in a hard list, ye're gonna fall in the water. With a heavy sea and this wind, we can't come about to look for ye."

The words were hardly out of Sullivan's mouth when the boatswain yelled orders to reef sail. All hands ran for their stations. O'Malley grabbed a line first, pulling himself upward, followed closely by Gunn, and then Sullivan.

A solid, moving wall pounded Gunn, trying to tear him loose from the lines. He clutched tightly, loosening his hold only enough to slide farther up and pull again. Before he reached the yardarm his shoulders felt as if they would rip from his body. His thigh muscles cramped from the agony of clamping them to the lines.

When he reached the spar, the noise shrieked into and past his hearing. Sound filled his head. The wind tore, clawed, pulled, and hammered, trying to rip him from his perch. Nature—berserk, insane—seemed bent on destroying everything. The dull, explosive roar of the ship pounded into each trough as it dropped from the crest of a swell. A tug on his arm and Gunn saw that O'Malley was trying to get him to lean his head to listen.

"Fold sails . . . shorten . . . lash to yard." O'Malley yelled. Gunn heard only parts of sentences, but enough to understand. O'Malley motioned that he and Sullivan would pull in the canvas and for Gunn to help fold. Gunn nodded his understanding. Then the most frightening part of the operation— they stepped off the yard onto the foot lines, the only thing between them and a broken, lifeless body on deck, or a fruitless swim for survival.

The sail shortened, Gunn watched a moment to ensure he knew how to fold and secure the canvas to the yard. Seeing how they did the job, he helped. He soon folded and lashed with moves as deft as theirs.

His legs, tense against slipping from the lines, were now long extensions of torture holding him to the only safety available. Knotted, cramping pain engulfed his body. They struggled and wrestled with the heavy canvas for what seemed forever. When Gunn thought he could not endure another moment, Sullivan slapped him on the arm, nodded, and motioned below.

On deck, O'Malley told him the next move would be to furl sail if the wind velocity increased much more.

"You mean we're going to climb back up there and take it *all* in?" Gunn couldn't believe it. He didn't know if his body would answer the call.

O'Malley shook his head and cupped his hand over Gunn's ear. "The next time, we bring the yard to us, finish furling it, and lash the whole thing to the deck."

Gunn sighed. "'Bout ready to quit this job and go ashore," he mumbled, though he knew no one could hear him.

O'Malley cupped his hand to Gunn's ear again and yelled. "Go get a cup of tea. It'll be cold, but better'n nothing. Sullivan and I'll handle things here." Gunn shook his head and motioned for O'Malley to go, which he promptly did.

Just as O'Malley's head disappeared below the hatch coaming, orders to take in all sail came from the bridge. Gunn looked at Sullivan, shrugged, and headed for the mainmast.

By nightfall, the sky was a leaden, lowering mass which changed the blue of the sea to gray-black. The sullen canopy over them had become a gigantic upturned bucket dumping tons of water. Rain, in ever-increasing torrents, pounded face and body like barbs of steel. Winds that drove it horizontally threatened one minute to capsize the ship, the next to stand it on its stern, and then its bow. Gunn realized for the first time how fragile a ship, or anything, was in the face of such a destructive force.

Every man had a manila line tied around his waist, with the other end secured to the ship's structure. All sail had been furled hours ago. Now the crew worked feverishly to rig a sea anchor. They used canvas and spars, tied an eight-inch hawser, as large around as a man's forearm, to the spars, and coiled the heavy line around the capstan. The sea anchor, thrown over the side, would trail on the surface and stabilize the ship, keeping the bow into the wind.

Gunn fought to keep his footing. He had already been swept from his feet more times that he could count. Tons of crashing water swept over the bow and along the deck each time the ship burrowed into the monstrous waves pushed ahead of the wind. The line around his waist almost cut him in two every time it snapped him up short. Long ago he would have been swept overboard had it not been for the lifesaving length of manila.

Again he tried to brace his feet against any object on the deck while he slowly fed the giant hawser over the side. Every available man worked at getting the huge line with the sea anchor over the side. A team of about ten men worked on one side of the capstan and slowly let out the line coiled about it.

The sea grabbed the anchor and snapped the ship like a bullwhip. The bow came into the wind and held steady. Gunn sighed and flexed his tired muscles.

The boatswain motioned for those on the sea-side of the capstan to secure the hawser to a couple of bitts.

That rest didn't last long, Gunn thought, and he inched his way to the end of the hawser. When they had taken several turns about a double bitt, those on the capstan released their grip. They all looked at one another and grinned tiredly.

The middle of the second day, a strange quiet settled about the ship. "We're in the eye," Sullivan informed Gunn. "Let's go topside. There will be much to do, lad. We'll check and tighten the lashings on all gear. When this storm comes back, ye'll likely find that it's as bad, or worse, than what we've already been through."

On the weather deck, Gunn looked at the sky and saw the wan glow of the sun trying to break through. "It looks like the sun's going to shine."

"That it does, lad, and it may shine for a while, but we still have the other side of this blow to get through."

While checking the lashings, they found two broken manila lines, the bitter ends tied to a bitt. Those lines answered their questions as to why Pete Johnson and Lyle Adams hadn't swung their hammocks the last couple of nights.

They rode the storm-tossed sea for another two days before the wind abated and the clouds broke. The seas were still monstrous. Gunn would have bet they sailed over one and under two of the huge swells. That night the captain sent for him.

Gunn had not seen the skipper up close until now. He stood at least an inch taller than Gunn and must have been fifty pounds heavier. Not fat, Gunn thought.

"Come in, lad." Captain Thorsen stepped aside for Gunn to enter. "Had your ration of grog today?"

"No sir, Captain. I don't drink."

Thorsen's head snapped around at Gunn's words. "What? You don't drink? What the hell kind of sailor are you?"

"If it takes drinking to be a sailor, I may never be one, sir. I don't like the taste of it, and from the way it makes some people act, I think I can do without it."

The captain stared at him a moment. "No, lad, the reports I get on you are that you are already a pretty good seaman. You learn quickly." He stuck out his hand. "Glad to have you aboard. Now, sit down. We'll talk."

Gunn soon leaned that the talk was to be more like an inquisition. He answered all the questions directly, looking the captain straight in the eye.

Finally the skipper leaned back, his hands clasped on his desk. "You read and cipher, eh?"

"Yes, sir. I've had ten years of schooling, and as you said, I learn fast. I also like to read." Gunn smiled. "I like to read when books are available, that is."

Thorsen nodded with a sharp jerk of his head. "Good. I want you up here every night after secure. I'll teach you celestial navigation." Gunn understood this as an order.

"Yes, sir. There's one thing I'd like to ask of you, Captain."

"Ask."

Gunn told him about his inheritance, showed him the note his father had left, and asked if he would take care of his money.

The captain agreed. Gunn pulled the canvas tube from around his waist and handed it to Thorsen. The captain hefted it a couple of times and looked at Gunn, his eyebrows raised. "Feels like a goodly sum in here, lad. How much is it?"

Gunn shook his head. "Captain, I don't know. I've never had the privacy anywhere to dump it out and count it."

Thorsen pulled the threads from the end of the tube and upended it on his desk. "We'll take care of that right now. You'll want to know how much I owe you plus your wages."

The captain counted the coins twice. "You have three thousand, one hundred and twenty dollars here, lad. More than most men accumulate in a lifetime. I'll take good care of it."

He stuffed the coins back in the tube and deposited it in an oiled and polished teakwood chest at the foot of his bunk. Gunn thought the oil enhanced the natural grain of the wood, made it look warm. Thorsen informed him that the chest served as his safe and added, "All right, lad, tomorrow night we'll start making a navigator of you."

Gunn accepted this as his dismissal. "Thank you, Captain."

He went back to his quarters with a feeling of relief, but edgy all the same. He hoped he had made the right decision. And he didn't feel good that he'd been less than honest with his skipper. He still didn't intend to stay aboard longer than it took to get to an American port.

CHAPTER
THREE

GUNN STOOD ON the quarterdeck alongside Captain Thorsen and watched the thin, gray, cloudlike line on the horizon draw nearer—America, the landfall he'd waited four years to see. But even now fifty miles of swamp, moccasins, and gators lay between where they would anchor and New Orleans. The skipper was taking them into Barataria, Jean Lafitte's old headquarters.

The captain still avoided U.S. ports, though the war had ended the year before. He and his crew were wanted men, and he was going into Barataria to have the *Sea Eagle* changed so none would recognize her. After scraping, painting, outfitting, and a new name, he would come into American ports as a respectable merchantman.

"Gunn," Thorsen placed his hand on Gunn's shoulder, "I don't mind painting the *Eagle* black. Fact is I like black, but I hate like hell to change her name. *Eagle*'s a good name and has served me well."

Gunn, now Thorsen's second mate, stared at him a moment. "Skipper, you remember I told you a few years ago I'm an Oglala Sioux?" The captain nodded, and Gunn continued, "How would you like to keep the name *Eagle* without saying it?"

"What the hell are you talking about? How would it be the *Eagle* if it didn't say it?"

"Captain, my Indian name is Black Eagle. The ship's going to be black, so why not call her *Black Eagle* in the Sioux tongue."

"Now, that makes a lot of sense. Who the hell knows how to

24

say it in Indian?" Thorsen shook his head as though wondering if his second mate had lost his mind.

"I do. *Wambli Sapa*—Black Eagle." Gunn looked at Thorsen hopefully. "It's a good name, Captain."

"Why should I name her after you? You won't even go back to sea with me," Thorsen said.

Gunn squinted toward the dark line of landfall. He felt like a traitor, but his dream still nagged at him. He wanted to go to the Dakota Territory. There was something there for him; he had no idea what, but it pulled him in that direction.

"Captain, I've explained all that." He shook his head. "I might go back to sea someday, but first I have to see what lies ahead for me here."

"Go, son. I guess I just had to make one more try. Go with my blessings. You've been one of the best men who ever sailed with me. I hate to lose you." He gazed into Gunn's eyes. "Maybe someday you'll get homesick for the sea and will sail with me on the *Wambli Sapa*." His voice broke as he said the last two words.

Gunn's throat tightened. He and the Captain had grown close during the years, but had never had reason to express their feelings. They wouldn't do so now. The very fact that the skipper would name his ship after him said it all.

Afraid that he might expose his emotions, he asked Thorsen's permission to go below.

While on the *Eagle*, Gunn had grown, hardened, but still looked deceptively slim. And, in Captain Thorsen's words, he'd become the best damned sailor and navigator on the high seas. However he looked at it, nothing he had done or become compared with what the captain had done for him. He had counseled, taught, and disciplined Gunn as a father would. And now that he'd named his ship for him, Gunn knew how much the captain thought of him. His throat swelled. He could hardly swallow.

He had been around the world twice, and visited every major port—except those he'd hungered for in America. He had almost all of his wages plus the money his father had left him. He had deposited over six thousand dollars in the House of Rothschilds in London, and had about eighteen hundred dollars in a money belt around his waist.

At the bottom of the ladder, Gunn rubbed his fingers across his bulging money belt, thankful he'd had the good sense to deposit most of his small fortune.

He hadn't stinted on having a good time, which included an occasional drink, and women when they were available, none of whom he'd ever grown close to. His clothes were fashionable, bought from the best tailors in London and Paris. These things he'd paid for with poker winnings. At first he had lost a little, but once he figured the game and its odds, he won consistently.

Gunn walked from the ladder to the one which went to the officers' quarters. In just a few hours he would leave the sea. Captain Thorsen had paid the crew off and would take on a new one after the *Sea Eagle* changed identity.

Time dragged. The ship glided silently between islands, but it seemed the main land mass was still as distant as when Gunn first spotted it. A few more hours will make little difference, he thought. He had to find transportation to New Orleans when they dropped the hook.

He left Officers Country after checking his gear once more. He had checked it at least every hour since awakening before dawn. Gunn walked forward to the crew's quarters and poured a cup of coffee. They had brought the coffee beans aboard in Port of Spain, Trinidad. He backed up to a bulkhead and slid down it to sit on deck beside O'Malley.

"Ready to hit the beach?" O'Malley asked.

Gunn sipped his coffee before answering. "O'Malley, I've been ready for five years."

"What're ye gonna do now?"

Gunn thought a moment. "I'm heading west. That's where I belong. I didn't think it would take this long to get there, though." He twisted to look at O'Malley. "Where're you goin'?"

"I might visit my folks in upstate New York, but in the end, I'll find another ship. If I had your book learnin' I might get to be an officer, have my own ship someday. I'll study. Maybe I can do it. I'm a sailor, Gunn. I like the sea. I thought you did too."

Gunn stared at the far bulkhead, then nodded. "Yeah, I like it. I've learned a lot, seen a lot, but now I'm going to see my mother's people—if I can find them, and then maybe hunt for gold." He shrugged. "I'm not real sure what I want. The only thing I do know is that I'm not going to live in any stinking, crowded city.

"I want to be out where there's room to breathe." He brought his coffee mug to his lips, tested it, and found it still too hot to drink. "I'll see what I can do to make some money, but money's not that important to me. I want land, and I want it where I can sit and look across miles. Maybe cattle will be part of it." He jerked his head impatiently. "Hell, I don't know, but I'll know when I find it. Maybe I want my own woman. I haven't thought much about that."

O'Malley slanted him an appraising look. "A woman won't be hard for *you* to find."

"It'll have to be the *right* woman, O'Malley. Besides, I'm half-Indian. You remember I told you that? A woman might not take to the idea of marrying an Indian."

Gunn felt O'Malley studying him. "Yeah, I remember. You don't look like no Indian. Green-eyed, dark red hair—hell, you look Irish to me. Even that dark skin would fit an Irishman. Anyhow, ain't no woman gonna be skittish about marrying a man like you. Besides, you don't have to tell her."

Gunn shook his head. "I don't play the game that way. She'll take me as I am, or not at all. If being Indian makes a difference, to hell with 'er."

Gunn swallowed the last of his coffee, surprised that he'd drunk it all. "I won't know until I find her, will I? Come on, let's go topside and see how far out we are." He looked over his shoulder and said, "I'm a Scot, not Irish."

He and O'Malley stood shoulder to shoulder on the bow watching the shore draw nearer. Finally the top men furled sails when Gunn thought he couldn't wait a minute longer. He remembered the first time *he* had furled sail. He listened to the anchor chain run out before he went below, shouldered his heavy sea chest, and headed for the boat to take him ashore.

An hour later he and O'Malley stood in the middle of Barataria. Gunn eased the heavy wooden chest off his shoulder and placed it on the ground. Made of highly polished teak, it was almost identical to the captain's. "From where I stand,

O'Malley, this isn't much of a town. Maybe six, seven hundred people at the most."

O'Malley turned his head from side to side, obviously scanning the metropolis. "Bet we could get our throat cut for the chance we had a dollar on us."

"I won't take *that* bet. We better see how quick we can find somebody to take us to New Orleans. I heard the only way to leave here is by pirogue."

"Pirogue? What's that?"

Gunn thought a moment, then said, "It's a hollowed-out log, sort of like a canoe."

"You mean we gotta ride a damned canoe to N'Orleans?"

"If we wantta get there."

It was late afternoon before they found a man who said he'd take them for two dollars each, but he wouldn't leave until morning. "Ain't goin' row tru dem gators in de black dahk," he said in a thick Cajun accent.

Gunn looked at O'Malley. "Looks like we'll spend the night here." He glanced around and saw nothing that looked like a hotel. "We'd better ask around, see what's available." He was jumpy at the idea. His money belt seemed to take on added weight. For that much money half the people here would kill.

"Better stay together until we get out of this place," he suggested.

O'Malley looked at him solemnly. "Gunn, you could cuss me, beat me, piss on me, anything. But I'll tell you one thing for sure, these people gonna think I'm a dandy, that I like boys 'stead o' girls, for how close I stick to you. Don't even think about leavin' me."

If O'Malley hadn't said it, Gunn thought he would have. This place was spooky. All that gray moss streaming off huge cyprus trees. Palmetto palms filling in the voids. Black slimy water surrounding everything. Many of the people were directly descended from pirates. Hell, he was going to stick to O'Malley like white on rice.

The proprietor of a pub rented them a back room and handed Gunn a key. "Lock the door before you go to bed. Ain' gone be responsible for nothin' happens to you."

The pub stood on pilings high off the ground. If they fell out of it, a sprained back was the least they'd get. Probably build them like this in case of high tides, or hurricanes, Gunn thought.

It had been in the back of his mind to have a beer and drop a hint that they didn't have much money. He looked at the man who rented him the room. "Many ships come in here? My shipmate here and I need a job." He smiled as though chagrined. "We left all our pay down in Trinidad. Strong rum and hot women were too much for us to turn down." He handed the man a double eagle. "That's all we have between us. Take a couple beers and the room out of that."

The proprietor scooped up the coin. "Room fifty cents apiece, beer's a nickle." He shook his head. "Ain' many ships come in here. You have betta chance in N'Orleans." He reached under the counter and took out a small wooden box, raked around through some coins, and handed Gunn his change.

They finished their beers, picked up their gear, and went through the back door into the room Gunn had rented.

Neither Gunn nor O'Malley undressed. They removed their shoes, the only concession they made to going to bed. Even though he had spoken loud enough for all in the saloon to hear, Gunn wanted to be ready in case eighteen dollars and ninety cents tempted the *genteel* patrons of the old pirate in the next room. The townfolk might be honest, but Gunn wasn't willing to gamble on it.

They lay on a pallet, back to back. Myriads of mosquitoes sang and buzzed around Gunn's ears, tempting him to pull his blanket over his head, but he feared it would shut out sound. He didn't want that handicap. His hand closed on the handle of his father's knife as he slipped it from its sheath. While holding it close to his side, he decided to buy a pistol in New Orleans. He wanted one now so bad he could almost feel it in his hand.

Sleep eluded him. Every small noise caused him to tense and grip his knife tighter. The sounds from the bar did little to cover the skittering sounds of mice, or limbs brushing the roof, or wind whining about the shack. The smells of rancid backwater, fishy and smothering, caused him to breathe shallowly.

Had it not been for the money strapped to his waist, he thought, he would have felt differently. He didn't like the fear that caused him to jerk at every sound.

Finally, despite vowing not to sleep, his eyes got heavy and he dozed.

Gunn's eyes snapped open. He didn't know what had awakened him. He lay still, his hearing seeking sound that shouldn't be in this room. His eyes, by now used to the dark, searched but saw nothing to disturb him. But he trusted his senses. *Something* had awakened him.

He nudged O'Malley and heard him groan. At the same time he heard the whisper of cloth. When the proprietor rented him this room, he had told Gunn that he and O'Malley would be its only occupants. That was all well and good, but right now there was someone else in here with them.

Whoever it was had to have climbed the pilings and entered through the window because Gunn had locked the door and stood the room's only chair against it.

Gripping his knife, he rolled away from O'Malley, pulling the blanket with him. Coming to his feet, Gunn twirled his left arm to wrap the blanket about it. In the dim light from the window, a shadowy figured moved toward him. A dull gleam of metal showed in the intruder's hand. A harder look and Gunn identified a knife. Apparently thinking there would not be a fight, his assailant's left arm looked bare, devoid of any shield.

Gunn moved on the balls of his bare feet, silently but swiftly, to try and put the intruder between him and the room's one window.

"What the hell's goin' on?" O'Malley grunted.

Gunn didn't answer. Any doubt in the intruder's mind as to Gunn's whereabouts gave him a slight edge. He moved again and had the silhouette of the man, knife in hand, about three feet in front of him. Gunn glided another bit to his right and launched himself at the intruder.

He thrust his slim blade and felt it take hold as he drove it hilt-deep. Gunn moved to the man's side, slicing as he pulled his knife free.

His attacker groaned and tried to spin toward him, but Gunn moved in a circle to keep the knife hand of the other man to the side away from him.

A match flared, lighting the room. Before it could die, O'Malley touched it to the lantern wick. Now Gunn saw his adversary—a square-built man, powerful, with a red stain spreading above his belt.

Gunn continued circling. He knew knife fighting. He'd learned it at sea, the hard way, and had the scars to prove it. The intruder gave him another opening. He darted in and sliced. He connected with the left arm, on the same side where his blade had hit the man's stomach.

The intruder lunged toward Gunn and swiped at his gut. He didn't miss. Gunn felt the cold steel burn downward across his ribs and hit his money belt. He moved away and then toward the man, who had still not uttered a sound, except for the groan when Gunn sank his blade into him the first time.

They circled silently, each striving for an opening. The man came at Gunn again, straight on. Gunn gave ground, parried a blow with his blanket-wrapped arm, but felt the other's knife bite into his left wrist. He swung his right. His knife sliced down the length of his assailant's knife arm. The thief dropped his knife and reached for a pistol in his waistband.

If he got that pistol in action, it was all over. Gunn moved into his man quickly and jabbed straight out with his knife, feeling it hit bone and slide off, sinking into the chest cavity. With his other hand, Gunn grasped for the hand that reached for the gun. It was unnecessary. Both arms of his attacker hung limply at his sides. Gunn wriggled the knife from side to side and up and down, to cut every organ it would reach, before he pulled it from the man's chest and let him drop.

Lying on his side, blood drooling from the corner of his mouth, the man sighed and blood froth bubbled from between his lips. He twitched, folded his legs up tight against his body, straightened, and lay still. He died as silently as he had fought.

Gunn bent, slipped the revolver from the man's waistband, and stuck it in his own. All of this had happened in tomblike silence—in less than a minute.

Over his shoulder, Gunn said, "O'Malley, let's get out of here. When these people find this man, there'll be hell to pay."

O'Malley picked up his seabag and started toward the door.

"No. Out the window. First help me rip our blankets. I'll use them to lower our gear to the ground. You go first, hang by your hands and drop. I'll lower the gear to you and follow."

Gunn bent over the dead man again and went through his

pockets. He found what he'd hoped for—a handful of cartridges—but nothing else except a sack of Durham. He left it. His assailant could smoke it in Hell. After stuffing the cartridges in his pocket, he picked up the man's knife and followed O'Malley.

On the ground, Gunn's eyes flicked around the area, searching for anyone who might sound an alarm. There were no people about. Probably asleep or in the pub, he thought, for it was late. He grabbed O'Malley's shoulder. "Get to the shore."

"Let's steal one o' them boats and get out of here." O'Malley's voice sounded reedy, scared.

Gunn stared at him for a moment, and let it stretch into an even longer silence. "You know how to get from here to New Orleans?"

"No."

"Well, that's something you need to think about. If we go into that swamp, we might never get out. If we stay here and these people find that body, we won't stand a chance. I'm for gambling on the swamp."

O'Malley stared goggle-eyed at him. "You *killed* that man up there?"

"Hell yes. He would have killed us."

"You ever kill a man before, besides those you hung on the ship?"

"No." Gunn shook his head.

At the water's edge, there were several pirogues pulled onto the beach. The only thing Gunn knew was that New Orleans was somewhere to the north, and to get there he needed one of these boats.

O'Malley glanced from the boats to the swamp. "You s'pose we could fight our way outta here? There's still some of the crew hanging around. That blackwater swamp looks scary."

"These people have guns. None in our crew has anything but a knife. We better get out of here—now."

O'Malley shook his head. "Times like this, I wonder why Sullivan and I didn't let those cops get you in New York." He shrugged. "What the hell. We ain't got much choice. Let's go."

They took time to pick one of the sturdier boats and make sure it had paddles and a pole in it. After they had loaded their gear, Gunn used the pole, a long sturdy sapling, to push the boat from shore. It was quieter than paddling. The water was shallow. He thought he would use the pole to push the boat as long as he could reach bottom. He didn't know he had made the right choice.

Frequently Gunn let the boat glide in order to listen. He heard no shouting or other sounds of pursuit. After an hour he looked at O'Malley and grinned. "I think we made it, shipmate, but we better pray we get a sight on the stars every once in a while or we could spend the rest of our lives roaming these swamps in circles. These trees are so thick I haven't seen the sky since we left Barataria."

While pushing the pirogue from shore, Gunn had taken a bearing on a large cyprus to the north. As he approached it, he took another bearing. He had been doing this since leaving and was fairly certain he wasn't getting too far off course, but even one degree would cause a far miss on finding New Orleans. His only consolation was that heading north they had to cross the Mississippi River. He would get his bearings then.

He pondered going to the sheriff, or the U.S. marshal, and telling them what had happened. If he did, he might be arrested; If he didn't tell them, he would be a fugitive. Would anyone back there in Barataria be able to describe him well enough? Gunn shook his head. He didn't know.

Once in New Orleans, he would make up his mind whether to take a riverboat to Saint Louis, or buy a horse and go west into Texas. From there he could go north to the Dakota Territory. It would depend on whether he had to run. He wouldn't be the first to whom the phrase "Gone to Texas" applied. Most of them ran from something.

He let the boat coast for a moment while he peered ahead, trying to spot another distinctive hummock, landmark, or tree on which to bear.

Another four hours, twenty gallons of sweat, and at least a million mosquito bites by Gunn's best guess, and a thin, murky light seeped through the heavy foliage overhead. "Don't believe it ever gets full daylight in here," he said, and getting no response, he looked and saw O'Malley curled up in the bottom of the boat asleep.

His shoulders ached, causing pain to shoot into his back. Pushing a pole had not been one of the things he'd done aboard ship. He could climb masts, hang in the rigging, furl sail—any job a sailing vessel required he could do from sunup to sundown. Pushing a big hollowed-out tree trunk through swamp was not a job he'd ever attempted, or wanted to try again.

He stared at a log floating along with the boat. He looked at the water on the other side to be sure they were moving. He glanced again at the log and shook his head in dismay. He felt no current in here and failed to see what drew the tree trunk along with him. The light grew faintly. Gunn gasped. The "log" was a gator, about twelve feet long. Gunn glanced and saw more of them.

Carefully, very carefully, he placed the pole against the swamp's bottom and pushed. My God, what if they should capsize? Now he understood why the old boatman in Barataria had not agreed to make this trip at night.

With each push, he placed the pole meticulously and wondered what would happen if a gator should attack the boat. He decided to awaken O'Malley.

He leaned to touch him. "Wake up, boy. It's time you did a little work." O'Malley's eyes opened, and Gunn said, "Sit up gently. Don't do anything to rock the boat. We have company."

O'Malley reacted as Gunn had known he would. A sailor gets used to being awakened and doing as told. Anything else could get you killed. "Company? Some o' them people from town?"

"No. Look over the side."

O'Malley's eyes followed Gunn's gaze. "My God," he whispered, his words a prayer.

To swap places so O'Malley could pole proved a ticklish operation, but they got it done, and the boat didn't teeter an inch.

The water deepened. They took the paddles and moved out from under the trees into open water. Gunn, although he liked the idea of being able to paddle, didn't like the lack of cover. They were not thirty minutes into open water before he looked back and saw two boats following—and gaining on them.

He shook his head, thinking the men in those pirogues had grown up using paddles.

"We'll never outrun them, O'Malley. I have this pistol; maybe we can take care of them with it."

"You gonna kill somebody else?"

Gunn, looking aft at the approaching boats, nodded. "If I have to. If they found the man I killed, I may have no choice."

Still staring at the approaching boats, Gunn said, "All right. Keep paddling. Don't hurry. We can't outrun them anyway. I'll see if I can out-talk them."

"You're just like Captain Thorsen, Gunn. You're hard as a whore's heart, but I never heard one o' the men say you wasn't fair."

Gunn watched the boats a moment longer. "O'Malley, if we can, I want to keep both boats on the same side of us. Try to make that happen even if you have to swing broadside to them as they get close."

When he saw that O'Malley understood, Gunn slowly moved his hand up to grasp the handle of the pistol. He had read on the side of the barrel that it was a Colt .44. He didn't know much about firearms, but had heard somewhere that these pistols were preferred by those who carried both rifle and pistol, because they required the same ammunition as a rifle and were more powerful than pistols of smaller caliber. At any rate, he was happy to have anything that would shoot.

The boatmen slowed their pirogues, bows facing the starboard side of Gunn and O'Malley's boat. Two men crouched in each boat. Gunn knew he couldn't get all of them, couldn't have even if he'd known anything about guns—and he had never fired one.

"Where you go wit dat boat?" The man spoke in a patois of French or Cajun dialect.

Gunn wanted to pull the pistol, but each of those in the other boats had a rifle casually lying in the crooks of his arms. Those guns rested there as if the men holding them had used them all their lives.

They didn't change expression, but just stared at him.

"We needed a boat to get to New Orleans and couldn't wait until morning." Gunn thought they hadn't found the man he'd killed or they would have come shooting. "We didn't know who owned the boat or we would have paid him for it."

"Maybe he doan wan to sell."

Gunn stared at them a moment, wondering whether he could reason with them. "Let's look at it from my side. I didn't know whether you would sell or not, and I've got to get to New Orleans. I didn't take a chance. I took the boat. I'll pay you for it now. Which one of you owns this boat?"

"Iss my boat," a slightly built man, the one closest to Gunn, said.

"What's it worth?"

"Is worth twenty dollah, but I don't wan no twenty dollah. I wan my boat."

Gunn studied the man before he made his final offer. If he didn't accept, Gunn didn't know what to do next. He was sure that in a shoot-out he'd lose, and O'Malley would get hurt, or killed. He sucked in a deep breath. He had to try.

"Look, I'll give you twenty dollars now and give you the boat back when we get to New Orleans. I'll pull it up on the levee when we get there, and you'll have your boat *and* twenty dollars." The chilling thought hit him then that these men, if not honest, could take his twenty dollars, his money belt, dump him in the swamp, and nobody would be the wiser.

The thin man looked at his companions. "Sounds like I tak heez offer. I get heez money an keep de boat all same." He turned his attention back to Gunn. "You give money now and we follah you close all way to levee."

Gunn reached in his pocket and pulled a double eagle from it. "I got what's left of one more of these to eat on or I'd give it to you too."

"No. We honest mans. I mak you de deal an dats it. Trow me de money."

Gunn tossed the coin and the man deftly caught it. "You go. We follow."

Gunn sighed, realizing only then that sweat poured from him, and it wasn't from the heat.

Despite what the man had said, one of the boats took the lead, and Gunn felt a degree of satisfaction when he saw they stayed on the same course he had set.

With the other boat in the lead, he and O'Malley both rowed. If it had come to a showdown, he would have been tagged as a thief and a murderer. He was satisfied to pay the man what he'd asked. Now he just wanted to get free of them as quickly as possible.

About four hours later, a clock somewhere in town struck three just as they dug the paddles in and drove the pirogue as far onto the bank as it would coast—only a few feet behind the first pirogue.

"Your oars and pole are in the bottom of the boat." Gunn picked up his sea chest and, followed by O'Malley, climbed to the top of the levee.

He stood there, and watched the man whose boat he'd stolen pick up the oars in his boat and shove off.

When Gunn turned to walk from the levee, he heard the slim man shout across to the others. "Dat dumb sombitch, for twenty dollas he can tak my wife and kids. His money gonna buy me one fine woman for mebbe ten day."

Gunn allowed a slight smile and thought, *That* dumb son of a bitch could have had twice as much if he had asked. He shrugged, satisfied with the deal and with now being in New Orleans.

CHAPTER
FOUR

NEW ORLEANS VIBRATED with sound. People shouted, wagons rumbled, teamsters cracked whips, and the sounds of pianos and clarinets crashed and vibrated in Gunn's ears.

Musty smells of decay emanating from the swamps inter-mingled with the scents of coffee brewing, meat roasting, vegetables boiling, and a myriad of spicy odors gave the city an atmosphere he would remember. He twisted to look back at the Mississippi, over a mile wide here.

Gunn felt he might breathe fast enough and not need to drink water, it was so humid. The cloying, sticky heat stifled any desire to move.

"Let's find a place to eat and have a beer." He draped an arm over O'Malley's shoulder. "This is probably our last night together, old shipmate. Think I'll stay here until I decide where to go and how to get there. Suppose you'll take the first boat to Saint Louis?"

O'Malley pushed his seaman's cap off his forehead. "Yeah, those paddle wheelers run pretty often. I noticed one tied up to the wharf. Soon as we eat, I'll see if I can book passage. If not, maybe they need a deckhand as far as I'm going. Anyway, after we eat, I guess that's it." He shuffled his feet, and Gunn knew O'Malley had the same reluctance to part that he did. To relieve the emotion, Gunn clapped him on the back and said, "C'mon, let's eat."

One bite of the spicy Cajun food, and Gunn thought he'd swallowed the lining of his throat. His tonsils burned out with the same bite. Grabbing his beer, he drank as long as he could hold his breath.

O'Malley smiled at him across the table. "Little warm?

Black pepper, red pepper, any other kind o' damn pepper just make it better to these Cajuns. And wait'll you sample one o' their women. Whoeee, man, you ain't never known what pur-dee *enjoyable* heat is. I think before I set out for the riverboat, I'm gonna relieve some of that pressure I built up at sea. If I don't, I'll bust my boiler."

Gunn finally got his breath. "You sack in with one of these women, be sure you keep a hand on your money or you won't go anywhere. You'll have to find a job. Somehow I can't see you toting cotton bales. Besides, after you catch every known disease, you might not have a boiler to bust."

O'Malley spooned another mouthful of gumbo, forked up some jambalaya, and frowned. "On second thought, my boiler ain't gonna bust if I wait until Saint Louis."

"Smart." Gunn nodded. "Real smart. Hoped you'd say that. And even there, I think before you go prowling around, you should put your money in a bank, and leave it there until you're ready to leave."

Gunn downed the rest of his beer while O'Malley sopped the last of his gumbo onto a chuck of French bread. They pushed back from the table.

"O'Malley, before you go, I want you to go by the sheriff's office with me."

"What for?"

Gunn studied the ground for a moment, then said, "I don't want to be looking over my shoulder for some law officer the rest of my life. May as well get it settled while I'm here. I'll tell the sheriff you were only a witness. Don't want you involved. If he'll let you write an account of what happened at Barataria and go, fine. If he won't, then go anyway. I'll fight it alone."

"I'll stay with you."

"No, you won't."

They asked only two people before finding where the sheriff's office was located.

The sheriff had not come in, but Deputy Sheriff Le Bouf sat at his desk. The deputy, a ponderous backwater cajun, smelled as bad as he looked—lank black hair hung over his forehead, his dirty shirt stood open at the neck, filthy red suspenders held up trousers missing the two top buttons of the fly, and he must have weighed, Gunn thought, at least two hundred and fifty

pounds—all fat. Gunn thought that the last bath the man had
had was when they cut his umbilical cord.

"What you wan?"

Gun stared at him a moment, thought of walking out, and
changed his mind. "I want to report a killing and an attempted
robbery."

"Wheah?"

"Barataria."

The sheriff slouched farther into his chair. "Doan tell me
what happen down dere. Doan nobody pay me no mind in dat
town." He spoke in the same dialect as the boatmen who'd
chased Gun and O'Malley.

Gunn didn't want to tell the lazy bastard anything, but
thought he had best be on record as having reported it. "I'm
going to tell you about it anyway. No, better than that, I'm
going to write it down and leave it with you. My shipmate here
will witness it."

Gunn wrote down everything that had happened. He didn't
mention how much money he had, but called it a considerable
sum. This man was the law, but Gunn was leery of letting him
know how much he had on him. He signed it. O'Malley read
it, signed it, and handed it to the sheriff.

Le Bouf sat there like a giant toad and read it aloud. When
he came to the words that mentioned Gunn had money, his
attitude changed.

"I tink I bettah hold you till I get somebody up heah from
dere. *You* mighta stolen dat money youseahf. You haf too turn
dat money over to me till case clear up."

Gunn went still inside. That fat bastard had shown no
interest until money was mentioned. Now, suddenly, he became the epitome of law and order.

Gunn stared at Le Bouf a moment. "No, Deputy, you're not
going to hold me. Nor are you going to get my money. You
must think I'm some sort of damned fool."

A flick of his hand retrieved the paper he'd written. "No one
from there had reported a crime. I have my report back."

The deputy grabbed for the paper, but Gunn waved it away
from him. "As far as you're concerned, you don't know about
this incident. I'm going to walk out of here with my money. If

you're smart, you won't reach for that gun you're thinking about."

"I start to arrest you an' you doan let me, you break law again. I t'ink you get in more trouble all time."

Gunn stared at the deputy a moment, then said, "You go to hell, Deputy. You want me bad enough, you better send plenty of men to do the job." He backed toward the door. "I'll be in town for a while. If you come after me, I'll tell you now, I won't have the money on me. Don't waste your time."

When they were on the sidewalk, O'Malley exploded. "Jesus Christ, Gunn, we're not at sea now. You don't have the authority to do things like that."

"You're right, but I do have the good sense to do it. That son of a bitch was already taking my money to the bank." Gunn looked down the street to the waterfront. "Let's get you on that side-wheeler, then I'm going to see if there isn't a U.S. marshal here. I'll turn myself over to him."

O'Malley stopped, his jaw thrust out like a stubborn mule. "I ain't goin' nowhere. I'm stayin' till I know you ain't in more trouble than you can get out of."

"Don't worry about me. I can take care of myself. C'mon, let's get you aboard that boat."

O'Malley shook his head. "Ain't goin'."

Gunn looked at O'Malley, then toward the river. He nodded. "All right, you stay, but only until I can find the U.S. marshal. After we talk with him, you're getting on that damned boat if I have to haul you aboard."

"I'll go when I'm sure you ain't goin' to jail."

Gunn shouldered his sea chest, walked up Canal to Bourbon Street, turned and went down it about four blocks to a hotel, and signed for a room. O'Malley grumbled every step of the way.

As soon as they were in their room, O'Malley pulled off his shoes and flopped on the bed. "It's too late to try to find the marshal. This time of day he could be in any of a hundred saloons or whorehouses. You do whatever you're gonna do. I'm gonna get some sleep. Ain't had but a wink since we left the ship."

"All right. We'll see him first thing in the morning. Then you're getting on that boat." Gunn thought for a moment of going to bed himself but decided against it. He wanted to see a little of the town.

After a bath and shave, Gunn dressed in his finest suit. He'd had it tailored in London, and when he walked out on the street, he knew he looked as well as any. He glanced at his watch again to confirm whether it was too late to try to find the marshal, and saw that it was. It was also too late to buy the clothing and firearms he wanted, so he decided to walk about the town.

He had made his way down Canal Street for the third time when he saw three men he'd seen twice before during his walk. He slowed, they slowed. He picked up his pace, they picked up theirs.

He turned at the corner of Bourbon Street and hit a fast jog. Looking over his shoulder, he saw that they followed but kept the same distance from him they had before. Gunn ran to the next corner, rounded it, and turned on the speed. He came to the next corner and turned away from the direction of his hotel. No point in leading them to where he would sleep. He ran to the next alley, turned the corner, and pressed his back against the wall. Gunn pulled the .44 from his waistband, and waited.

Fast, jogging footsteps approached and pounded past the mouth of the alley. Before Gunn could congratulate himself on evading them, the footsteps stopped and came back. The three pulled up short, warily peering into the dark maw of the alley. Gunn pulled the hammer of his .44 back. At the sound, the Cajuns' eyes focused on him—then the pistol he held.

"You seem interested in me." He waved the pistol muzzle to cover them. "Now, tell me what you want."

The first one around the corner looked at Gunn in the fading evening light. He was tall, thin, unshaven, and dirty. "We doan wan nothin'" His eyes—black, flat, and deadly as a snake's—stared unblinking into Gunn's. "We wuzn't following you." To Gunn's surprise, the man showed no fear.

"You're a damned liar," Gunn said flatly. "Looking down this gun barrel, seems to me you might do better than that. Now, I'm gonna ask you again—why are you following me?"

"Ain't followin' you."

"All right. Have it your way," Gunn said, "but if you

continue, I won't be so congenial." His voice hardened, "Now, get."

They left, shambling along as if they had all night to get where they were going. Gunn waited a moment, then, knowing they would be back, he followed them.

As soon as they turned the corner, Gunn raced ahead and peered around it.

Halfway down the block they split. Gunn watched while one of them ran to an alley and turned in. That alley would intersect the one he'd hidden in before. The other two headed back toward him.

Gunn nodded. They would try to take him from in front and behind. He hugged the side of the building and waited.

The two turned the corner, and this time their faces did show emotion—and fear.

Gunn grinned. "Surprise, you bastards. You must think I'm dumb as hell." Still holding the .44 in his hand, he waved them ahead of him. "We'll greet your friend when he comes down the back side of that alley."

He prodded them ahead and pushed them into the alley in front of him. Soon a shadowy form turned toward them.

"Quiet, or I'll lay this gun barrel across your skull," Gunn whispered.

The third man approached, ducking from one pile of boxes to another until he stood within arms's reach of his friends.

From behind them, Gunn spoke quietly. "No sudden moves and I'll let your friends live." While talking, he raised his pistol and brought it down on the head of one of the three. It sounded as if he'd slapped a side of beef. Before that one fell to the ground, Gunn dropped the other one he'd marched back to the alley.

The man left facing him was the one who'd done all the talking when he'd met them before.

The skinny bastard reached to the back of his belt.

"You pull a knife and I'll blow your damned head off," Gunn said.

The man's hands dropped to his sides.

"You gonna tell me why you're following me? If you want money, you'll not find any by tomorrow night. I intend to buy goods to ship north—I'll be broke."

"Ain't gonna rob you—but I tell you why we follow when I kill you."

Gunn studied the skinny man a moment. He had to admit a grudging respect for the man, who showed no fear; he seemed to think Gunn had wronged them in some way. Gunn knew he wouldn't get any more information until the man was ready to tell him. He motioned to the two lying on the ground and said, "Take care of your friends. Don't try to follow me again tonight. I've had all of you I can take in one day."

He backed out of the alley and took an erratic course back to his hotel, watching his backtrail all the way.

He wondered who had put them on him. He turned it in his mind every way he could think and decided the deputy must be responsible. The four men in the boats who had followed him from Barataria didn't seem the type.

The next morning he and O'Malley ate a leisurely breakfast and walked out to see the town by daylight. Gunn didn't mention the three men.

They stopped first at the U.S. marshal's office. While shaking Marshal Ford's hand, Gunn decided that he liked and trusted the square-built, solid man. He looked and acted the way Gunn thought a lawman should.

Gunn told his story simply and to the point. He showed Ford the written report he had prepared the day before, with O'Malley's signature, and O'Malley verified that the signature was his.

"If *you* want to hold me, Marshal, fine. I didn't trust the deputy. Perhaps I did wrong in not submitting to his arrest, but if you're going to turn me over to him, I'll be honest with you. I'm going to run."

Gunn stared grimly into the marshal's eyes. Ford broke the gaze and looked at Gunn from head to foot. He shook his head and laughed. "You're the first man who has ever looked me in the eye and said he would run." Standing behind his desk, he motioned to a couple of chairs. "Sit down. Let's talk."

Ford subjected Gunn to the same kind of prying interrogation that Captain Thorsen had many years ago. When he had finished, he knew as much about Gunn as Gunn himself knew. He even knew Gunn was a mixed-blood Sioux.

"Son, I'm not going to hold you. You've told me essentially

where you're going. Give me your word you'll come if I send for you, and you can go any damned where you wish." He stuck out his hand and, while Gunn shook it, said, "You better do something with that money. This is a bad town in which to have anything of value on your person."

"Like I told you, Marshal, I'm going to start buying goods with it today."

Gunn watched while Ford filed his report. "You, my captain, and O'Malley here are the only ones who know the amount of money I'm carrying, Marshal."

Gunn stepped out on the street and heard the marshal mutter, "Don't bet on it."

"You willing to get on that boat now?"

O'Malley nodded. "Yep. I trust that marshal. He's the kind of man I'd like to sail with."

"All right. Let's get your gear and get you aboard." O'Malley didn't argue this time.

Saying good-bye to O'Malley was almost as hard for Gunn as parting from Captain Thorsen had been. He and O'Malley had said good-bye to Sullivan in London. But oddly, when O'Malley walked over the gangway, Gunn felt a sense of freedom. Now he need not worry about anyone but himself. His gaze turned from the paddle wheeler to look down the street. He had some goods to buy.

He bought a new Henry .44 rifle, a couple of boxes of shells, a gunbelt and holster for the Colt he had acquired in Barataria, and, on a hunch, a Colt third-model .41 derringer. He loaded it and slipped it into his vest pocket, opposite his watch. He smiled grimly. Here he had an arsenal and didn't know how to use any of it, or how to care for it. He'd have to find someone to teach him.

He now stood looking at clothing. The work clothes he had worn at sea would not serve well for the plains or in the mountains. He pondered waiting until Saint Louis, or San Antonio if he went that way, but decided to buy what he needed here.

The clerk who sold him the rifle, a bearded man who looked as though he would be more at home herding cows, told Gunn he had just come from Dodge City, and that prices north or west of here were three and four times as high—for anything.

The clerk's advice also planted the idea in Gunn's mind of the kind of goods to buy. They would have to be goods hard to come by on the frontier, things that would ensure a healthy profit when he got where he was going.

The sun, a fiery red ball, slipped below the horizon, taking with it some of the intolerable heat. Gunn deposited the results of his buying tour in his room, stripped, and bathed, as much for the cooling effect as to take the day's accumulation of sweat away. He then went out on the town.

He was again hungry. The thought of the Cajun food he had had with O'Malley, prompted by the aroma that invaded his nostrils as he stepped out of his hotel, made his saliva glands flow with anticipation. That pepper food burned all the way through a man, but it sure did taste good.

Gunn followed a sign that directed him through a walkway between buildings and into a patio restaurant. It was like walking into a different world.

In the center of the garden area a fountain rippled, chuckled, and whispered as it spouted from the head and penis of a cupid to a basin below. Tables scattered about the area all seemed to claim their own seclusion. Even with the early hour, couples ate, drank, or talked in hushed tones, with their heads close together.

Amused, and yet somehow lonely, Gunn thought most here were lovers, and he wished for someone of his own. The waiter showed him to a table where he could see, but the strategically placed potted plants—ferns, palms, and bougainvillea—gave him a feeling of privacy.

During his travels Gunn had learned to speak French and Spanish. He was fluent in both languages and could read and write them as well.

"You will be joined by your lady, m'sieur?" the waiter asked in French.

"No, I'm alone, a stranger here," Gunn answered in French.

"Tch, tch." The waiter stood back and looked at Gunn. "It is bad to be alone in this town made for love. You wish me to send company to you?"

"No." Gunn smiled. "Perhaps tomorrow. I'll be here a few days."

Gunn ordered a drink, and while waiting, he watched the

people. He faced the entrance and saw all who used the passage. A handsome, distinguished white-haired man came in, looked around, and followed the maître d' to the table adjacent to Gunn's. On closer inspection Gunn saw that the man had a smooth, ageless, olive complexion. He was not as old as Gunn had first thought. Gunn's drink came, and he told the waiter he'd like a typically Cajun meal, and that the waiter should choose for him. He hadn't really wanted a drink, but it was something to do while waiting for dinner.

The waiter brought the white-haired gentleman a drink. He sipped it and nodded his approval.

Sitting there, Gunn found it hard to avoid the other man's eyes. Finally their gazes locked, and the man smiled, nodded, and lifted his glass as though in a toast. Gunn smiled in return and lifted his glass. They sat there silently until the waiter looked in on them to see how they fared.

The white-haired man motioned the waiter closer and said something that caused him to walk to Gunn's table.

"The M'sieur d'Anville invites you to join him at his table. He is fearful you are lonely here in his town."

The invitation irritated Gunn a little. He enjoyed sitting there watching. His first inclination was to refuse, but he thought, what the hell. If he was to be here a week or so, he might as well get to know some of the people. Too, he thought to urge d'Anville to tell him the news—what was happening here in the States. He stood.

"Thank you, m'sieur." He held out his hand. "I'm Rafe Gunn."

Shaking Gunn's hand, his new acquaintance said, "Paul d'Anville. You're a stranger here?"

Gunn laughed. "Is it that obvious? Yes, I just landed here today."

"Sit down—have dinner with me."

Prompted by Gunn's questions, d'Anville talked of the huge migration west, Indians, Texas, the problems Confederates were having with carpetbaggers, occupation troops, and mostly lack of money in the postwar South.

The waiter had delayed serving dinner, and d'Anville and Gunn were having their second drink when d'Anville glanced toward the entrance and stood. Gunn looked in that direction and saw a tall, willowy girl, perhaps fourteen or fifteen years old, approaching their table. Black-haired, green-eyed, flawless complexion—she was a pretty child, and would be a strikingly beautiful woman someday, Gunn thought, and that day was not far off.

"Gunn, my daughter, Eula. Honey, this is M'sieur Rafe Gunn."

She exuded the confidence and poise that most truly beautiful women seemed to have. Gunn was certain she considered herself grown. Her eyes looked directly into his, and she smiled, nodded, and held her hand such that he could shake it—or kiss it—whichever suited him. He shook it.

Oddly, the conversation never went through the formal, stilted, getting acquainted stage. They talked as old friends.

"What are you going to do now that you've left the sea, Gunn?" Paul asked.

Gunn didn't know how to answer his question. He spread his hands palms up. "I haven't the slightest idea. I want to go west, and I intend to take a couple of wagon loads of goods with me to sell wherever there's a need for them. If I get past the Indians, I should make a healthy profit. I may look for gold after that."

Paul wrinkled his brow and smiled. "Yeah, you and ten million others. You will find, I believe, that you'll get rich quicker selling your goods than you will mining."

Gunn felt Eula's eyes on him, studying him. "Somehow, Papa, I don't think Rafe will be satisfied to be a salesman. I don't believe money drives him. I think it's the living, the adventure."

Gunn felt surprise at her perceptiveness. He looked at her and smiled. "Mam'selle, you may be right. I think there is a lot happening out there, and I want to be part of it."

She touched his forearm. "M'sieur, if you'll call me Eula, I'd like to call you Rafe."

Gunn agreed, smiling.

"How long are you staying in New Orleans, Gunn?" Paul asked.

"I don't know, a week, maybe two at the most," he answered, looking at Eula, and thought he saw disappointment touch her face.

Dinner served, they ate in a comfortable silence, broken occasionally by a question and answer.

After dinner they parted with the promise to meet again the next night.

Gunn had walked about a block when he saw one of his three antagonists of the night before. He reached under his coat, pulled the .44, cocked it, and pointed it in the direction of the man, who ran like a scalded cat as soon as Gunn cocked the pistol. Gunn knew now that sooner or later he would have to kill one, or all three, of them. He didn't want it to happen in Le Bouf's parish. He wondered why they were after him. Had the deputy sicced them on him?

The third night the d'Anvilles invited him for dinner in their home. Paul explained that they stayed there when not at their plantation. "Just tell your driver to take you to Magnolia Hills. He'll know how to get there."

When the driver stopped the carriage before the gate, Gunn stared in awe. He had expected to see grounds and buildings in a state of decay, considering that the slaves who had maintained these places were now free. The sweeping lawn had been recently manicured. A two-story white mansion with six columns across the front sat majestically at the end of the long circular drive. Gunn saw no sign of deterioration in anything his eyes beheld.

When he pulled the bell rope, a negro servant, dressed in a white dinner jacket, ushered him into a large foyer, with stairs on each side curving to the second floor. While he studied his surroundings, Paul and Eula appeared from a side room.

Smiling, Paul asked, "Surprised?"

"More than you would believe. I thought planters were having a hard go of it these days, labor shortage and all," Gunn said.

"Most are," Eula answered, "but Papa freed our slaves years ago, and has paid them wages ever since. Many of them stayed with us when the war ended." She laughed. "As a matter of fact, without them we would have trouble with the occupation troops, but our people run them off." She laughed again. "When I say 'run them off,' I mean just that. I saw Mama Jory take a broom to some of them, and they haven't been back since."

After dinner, with still about an hour of daylight, Eula suggested that they go down to the river and shoot. "We have a rifle, and a pistol you can use."

Gunn looked from one to the other of them. "I must tell you, I have never in my life fired a gun. I intended to find someone to teach me before I left. As a matter of fact, I bought a rifle and derringer while shopping the other day."

"You've never fired any kind of gun?" Eula asked. "We in the South do two things from birth—ride and shoot."

Gunn admitted that he knew nothing about either.

"All right, we'll teach you," d'Anville volunteered. "If I'm busy, Eula is just as fine a shot and rider as I, and I don't believe she will mind taking on the job."

"Of course not. I'll be happy to teach you, Rafe."

A week and several boxes of ammunition later, Eula told him that he was as good with a rifle or handgun as any she'd seen. "You can already outshoot Papa or me." She looked intently at Gunn. "Are you sure you've never ridden a horse before? If you haven't, you must be part Comanche. They're the best riders anywhere, and you're that good."

"Eula, compared to a rolling, pitching ship, and hanging in the shrouds during a hurricane, riding a horse is child's play." He looked solemnly at her a moment before continuing, and then shook his head. "No, I'm not Comanche, but I *am* half-Sioux." After his announcement, he cocked his head an stared at her, wondering what her reaction would be.

Unabashed, her gaze raked him from head to toe. "You serve them proud, Rafe. I don't see where any Sioux could be ashamed to call you 'brother.' "

"I was more concerned with *your* reaction. You don't seem at all disturbed, or ashamed that you have been associating with a savage for over a week."

She stared directly into his eyes. "Rafe Gunn, savage you might be at times, but gentleman you have always been with me." She held out her hand for him to shake. "I'm proud to call you friend, and so is Papa."

Gunn held her hand longer than necessary, trying to remember that she was just a child. She didn't try to withdraw it. Finally he released his hold, and she dropped her hand to her side.

He thought she had wanted him to kiss her, but he dismissed that thought as a foolish one. Perhaps by the time he'd seen what he wanted to see, and done the things he wanted to do, he'd return and see if she had grown into the woman he thought she would. Despite her age, if he kissed a girl like her, he would consider it a commitment, and he wasn't ready for that. Dammit, he thought, it wasn't uncommon for a girl her age to marry.

Gunn spent two more carefree, glorious weeks in New Orleans. He and Eula rode and shot everyday, and Paul joined them when business allowed. But all during his stay he was aware that the three men who had followed him that first night were close by.

When not with Eula, he bought boxes of new Henry rifles and ammunition. He bought cases of Cuban cigars, Hudson's Bay blankets, sacks of coffee beans, and tins, called airtights, of fruits and vegetables. And on a hunch he bought several bales of Levi's. He had his purchases carefully crated and loaded on the side-wheeler he had booked passage on to Saint Louis. The captain of the boat gave him a bill of lading for the goods he shipped, and admonished him to keep the papers as safe as he would cash. He said that anyone who produced the bills of lading could claim the goods.

From Saint Louis he planned to take one of the shallow-water stern-wheelers up the Missouri to Fort Benton.

Gunn, living in his stateroom the last two days before getting under way, had changed into Levi's, boots, and a black wide-brimmed, flat-crowned hat, and he had buckled on a gunbelt. When he walked across the gangway to bid Eula and her father good-bye, he looked like a man born of the West.

"You'll come back to visit, Gunn?" Paul asked.

Gunn nodded. "I don't know when, but I'll be back."

Eula, her eyes swimming in tears, said, "Wambli Sapa, you had better come back." Gunn had told her and Paul everything he knew of his Indian heritage, but it still surprised him that she addressed him by his Sioux name.

"Princess, I promise. Will you accept an Indian name from me? It was my mother's."

She smiled through her tears and nodded. "I don't know of anything that would please me more, my huge friend."

"Then I name you Wee-Chop-Key-Cah Oh-Loh-Ahn, Singing Stars. It's spelled W-i-c-o-k-i-c-a Oloan." He shook Paul's hand and turned to bow to Eula, but suddenly she was in his arms. He stood rigid. His first thought was that she was only fifteen years old. Without his willing it, his arms went around her. She pulled his head down and pressed her lips to his. It was not the kind of kiss he expected from a child, or a friend, nor did he return it as one. Her firm woman's body pressed to his set his blood racing. Heat flooded his loins and clouded his brain. This wouldn't do.

Gunn grasped her shoulders and pushed her away. A glance over her shoulder at Paul showed him smiling amusedly.

"I think I'll come back a lot sooner than I expected."

Eula smiled through her tears. "Why do you think I brazenly kissed you like a hussy, Rafe? Sometimes a forceful frontal attack works wonders."

He nodded, turned toward the gangway, and said over his shoulder, "It worked this time. I'll be back. Gonna give you time to grow up first."

CHAPTER
FIVE

STANDING AT THE rail with other passengers, Gunn saw the three men who had followed him talking with a man, whom Gunn pegged as a gambler by his flashy clothes. The four climbed the gangway and boarded the vessel. Gunn had thought that when he departed New Orleans, he would be through with them.

What did they want with him? It couldn't be money. As close as they'd shadowed him, they had to be aware that he'd spent most of it.

The boat whistle blew, and the paddles churned the muddy waters. Gunn felt a throb of exhilaration. Now he was really on his way west. He turned his attention back to Eula and Paul.

They waved until they grew small in the distance, then the steamboat rounded a bend.

Gunn went to his cabin to take a nap. The throbbing of the engines and the wheels churning the water outboard of his cabin changed his mind.

These big, luxurious side-wheelers were designed especially for the Mississippi, Gunn had been told. They could turn 360 degrees without moving off their spot simply by reversing one of the paddle wheels. This maneuverability had saved many of them from being gored and sunk by large, partially submerged trees that could rip the bottom from a boat, called sawyers.

He went out on the main deck and watched the trees on the riverbank move slowly to the rear. Bored, he wandered into the dining room, only to find the room almost empty. Five men sat at a table playing poker.

"Room for one more?"

A man sitting across the table looked up, nodded, and said,

53

"Pull up a chair. Another hand might change the run of cards."

They explained the rules: table stakes, five-hundred-dollar takeout, and the joker worked with aces, straights, and flushes. Gunn sat in.

He won a few, lost a few, and studied the players. There were two men he took to be cattlemen because of their conversation—grass, drought, and Indians. One was a drummer. He seemed to know everything about the latest weapons. And the last two were gamblers—crooked, and not very good. One of them, the flashily dressed one, was the man Gunn had seen talking to the three Cajuns on the dock. The other gambler was dressed in black, including his shirt, and wore a white string tie.

For a while, Gunn folded his hand when it came either of the gamblers' turn to deal. Then, the thought of being on this vessel a week or more and not able to play one third of the hands because of the crooked deals irked him. Anger crept under his collar until he felt choked.

Gunn dragged a medium pot, antied, and watched the gambler across the table stack the deck for a bottom deal. The cards came off the deck the way he'd known they would.

He slipped his finger in his vest pocket, pulled out his watch and looked at the time, returned his watch, and reached into the pocket across from it. He cupped the derringer in his hand and held it covered on the table in front of him.

With his left hand he picked up his cards and flicked them open. He had three tens, a five, and a seven. The hand he held would be second best, regardless of how good it turned out—but he decided to play it.

The cattleman next to the flashily dressed dealer opened, the drummer called, Gunn raised, the other cattleman folded, the gambler dressed in black raised. Gunn called and drew two cards when it came his turn.

Flashy, the dealer, folded, so Gunn knew who would get the bottom deal. He dropped his eyelids to mask his eyes and watched Flashy flip his partner three cards—two off the bottom. Gunn had noticed that they were both just as bad at dealing seconds as bottoms.

Gunn flicked his cards again. He had his fourth ten. When the bet came to him, he pushed his pile into the center of the table. "Let's don't waste time. There's a thousand there—bet it all."

A slight, cold gleam glinted in Flashy's eyes, and a shadow of a smile creased his lips.

Blacky pushed a thousand dollars into the pile and picked up another thousand to raise.

"I'm in. You said table stakes when I sat down," Gunn said, while wishing he had another couple of thousand on the table.

"Yes, but there are two other gentlemen still playing. I raise a thousand."

As soon as the gambler's money was in the pot, Gunn rolled his right hand over to expose the derringer. "All of you, keep your hands on the table." He looked at Blacky and then at Flashy. "Now, you, you crooked sons of bitches, let's look at the cards." Gunn turned his hand faceup. "Four tens. You other gentlemen, I'll lay you ten to one odds I'm second best."

Blacky's oily smile didn't fool Gunn. One or the other of them would pull a gun, but not before they played out their charade.

"Don't either of you pull a gun. You'll die before you have a chance to be sorry you did. This little gun is double-barreled."

Flashy's eyes narrowed, his jaw knotted.

"I'm afraid you have me beat," Blacky said, his voice tight and reedy.

"No," Gunn said softly. "Show your cards."

"I've already admitted you have me beat, sir. What more can I do?"

"You can show us your cards. Do it—now."

Blacky's left hand reached for the cards as his right dipped under his coat. The derringer, although not an accurate weapon, could not miss at this range. Gunn fired at Blacky's head. The little .44 exploded in a cloud of black smoke.

As soon as it had fired, Gunn shoved it toward Flashy's face. He had reached under *his* coat. His hand froze. It all happened so fast that Blacky was still falling from his chair. The .44 slug had torn through his nose and blown the back of his skull away. Brains and a flap of bone hung off the side of his head. His chair tumbled backward and he slumped to the floor.

Gunn again flicked a glance at Flashy, who sat, his hands flat on the table, his face the color of biscuit dough, his eyes wide, terrified.

Gunn calmly looked at the other players. "Turn Blacky's cards over."

One of the cattlemen reached across the now empty chair and flipped the hand over—four queens.

"Now look at that deck. You'll find crimped or waxed aces, and they are probably marked, but I won't bet on that."

The boat's captain arrived and glanced at the men around the table, then at the corpse stretched out on the floor, one leg hanging over a rung of the chair. "Who did it?"

"I did," Gunn admitted.

"What caused it?"

"Cold deck, seconds, bottoms, you name it, and they were not very good at it."

The captain nodded jerkily. "Told 'em when they came aboard I didn't want them gambling on my boat. Told 'em I'd tie 'em to the paddle wheels and drive this boat fifty miles before I cut 'em loose." He shrugged. "I would rather have done it my way, but reckon I'll have to be satisfied with the one left. They paid passage to Vicksburg, so I'll haul 'em that far and get rid of them, but first we'll tie this one to a wheel. Carry on with your game." He turned sharply and walked briskly toward the wheelhouse.

Passengers tried to crowd into the room. One, a pretty girl holding to an older woman's arm, stared at the corpse, retched, and ran to the rail at the side of the boat. Others shuddered and turned away; some crowded closer to satisfy their ghoulish curiosity.

Gunn felt no sorrow that he'd killed a man. If he had caught him doing the same thing aboard the *Eagle*, he'd have hanged him.

A couple of deckhands came in and dragged the body from the room while two others grabbed Flashy, who still sat frozen in his chair. They took him by his arms to drag him to the side of the boat.

They never made it. He jerked free, ran for the side, and jumped over. His only mistake was that he jumped forward of the big paddle wheel. It canceled the captain's plan.

Gunn smiled at the remaining players. "Gentlemen, I believe

that now we can play a little friendly poker." He called over his shoulder to the bartender, "Bring us a fresh deck. These are slightly used."

He pushed the pot into a pile. "Take out the money you put in this pot." They did as he told them. "Now, I'll take mine and we'll split what's left."

"But some of that money belonged to those gamblers," one of the ranchers said.

"You know any way to deliver it to them?" Gunn said. "Let's play poker."

When the game broke for dinner, Gunn had won about three hundred dollars.

After dinner he walked out on deck, lighted a cigar, and watched the paddles dip into the water.

He had seen oceangoing, steam-propelled vessels—they used screws. A heavy sea would wreck paddle wheels in short order, and screws on riverboats would cause loss of maneuverability.

Tiring of watching the water, Gunn wondered if the captain would let him watch him navigate.

When he reached the wheelhouse, Gunn explained that he had been second mate on a frigate and that he would like to see how the captain navigated the river. He got more than he asked for.

The captain explained that river navigation was mostly from memory, and information traded back and forth among the other masters of these vessels. He told Gunn about the hazards of ever-shifting sandbars, snags, changing river channels, storms, and incompetent, or drunk, help. Never moving his gaze from the sluggish, muddy flow of the river, he asked, "You got a notion to take up work on the river?"

"No, Captain." Gunn laughed. "I'm going as far as the Missouri will take me, and then on to the gold fields."

"Missouri, eh? Well, I'll tell you, son, the Big Muddy is a horse of a different color. It ain't like this river. Even the riverboats up yonder are different. Dang near everything on them boats is above the waterline. They don't draw water, though, they draw mud. Hear tell when the water's low, the captain posts passengers and crew on the bow an' has 'em spit.

That way they jest slide them damn boats along slick as a whistle."

Gunn looked at the captain a moment. "I'll tell you something, Captain, even if I have to get out and push, I'm going up that stream as far as I can go."

The captain thumbed his cap back off his forehead and continued as though Gunn hadn't said a word. "Injuns—now, they got Injuns dang near the whole way up it. Sioux, Blackfeet, Crow, Brule, they got 'em all. An' if they ain't out to steal everything you got, they'll take your hair." He shifted his tobacco cud from one side of his jaw to the other and shot a stream across the cabin to a spittoon, hitting it dead center.

The captain spun the wheel wildly. Looking ahead, Gunn saw a giant tree directly in their path. The captain leaned his mouth next to a brass mouthpiece and bellowed. "Starboard engine, reverse." Then he yanked the bell rope.

Gunn didn't count the times the clapper hit the bell, but he was aware that the bell also sent commands. The boat vibrated as though coming apart.

Instantly the bow came about and they were going at right angles to their previous direction. More wild jerking of the bell, and the engines turned them upstream again. The huge tree passed harmlessly to port. The captain chewed his cud a couple of times then again rang the spittoon.

Gunn raised one eyebrow and grinned. "You have that sort of problem often?"

"More dang times than I like to think about, son. Them snags'll tear the wheels apart, rip the bottom out of a boat, and cause a riverboat captain or pilot to turn white-haired by the time he's thirty. Don't blame you fer goin' to the gold fields."

"Yeah, but somehow, Captain, I don't think you'd trade what you're doin' for the pot of gold at the end of the rainbow."

The captain grinned sheepishly and didn't answer.

"Thanks for letting me watch, Skipper. I'd better get below now."

"Anytime, son. Come stand with me when we make a night run. I'll get your blood to pumpin' real good then."

"Thanks, Captain. I'll do that. I'd rather be here with you than in my bunk."

Gunn went back to the dining room, ordered a drink, and

found a table. Every passenger aboard must be in here, he thought. All the tables were full except two. He sat alone.

These Mississippi boats were floating palaces. They had comfortable staterooms, saloons, dining and dancing facilities, and most who had cabins on his deck were obviously affluent. He had only to look about to see that all were well dressed and conducted themselves as ladies and gentlemen.

Gunn had noticed that those on the deck below, mostly men, were not the kind you'd find in the drawing rooms of better homes. They were cowboys, miners, lumberjacks—all good hardworking people. But there were also those who fed on other's misfortune, and those who would take from those who could ill afford it. They were the fortune hunters, gamblers, gunmen, prostitutes, thieves, and bandits. Gunn had read them like a book—causing his heart to beat faster and a thrill to run up his spine.

This was what the country today was all about, he thought. It was a time of growth, courage and cowardice, failure and success, and strength and weakness. Those that survived would build the West.

Progress was slow. Bucking the river's current meant keeping a good head of steam, and that meant high pressure. Pressure that had many times blown boats apart and scattered them over miles of treacherous waters.

In his cabin Gunn wondered what had happened to the three Cajuns. He had not seen them since boarding. That they were somewhere on the lower decks he had no doubt. He wished they were where he could watch them. Now he needed to use caution at all times—and he made certain his door was barred whenever he was in his room. He decided to go below and see if he could find them.

As an excuse, he checked the boxes he'd had brought aboard. While threading his way among the passengers of the lower deck, he looked for the three who had become his shadow. He saw no sign of them, but they were there somewhere. He'd not seen them leave the boat. He went back to the cabin deck.

Several times during the night the boat edged alongside special docks built for plantations that bordered the river. Gunn pointedly watched for the three to disembark while cargo was loaded or off-loaded at these stops. He saw none of them.

Soon after five bells, about 2:30 A.M., he watched as the boat drew away from another dock. Hell, he thought, I'm losing sleep while they are getting all they want. Can't put up with this for long. Come daylight I'm going below again and search until I find them. He didn't know what he would do if he did find them, but, he decided, he'd play the cards the way they fell.

In his cabin he fell into a restless sleep. He wakened to a rainy dawn, looked at his watch, and saw that it was 6 A.M.

After sponging off in the white porcelain bowl furnished to each stateroom, he dressed and went to the dining room. Several passengers were there ahead of him. He nodded to a number whom he remembered from the evening before and seated himself at a table with three army officers—all young second lieutenants, fresh out of West Point.

They were quick to tell him they were going to join Colonel Carrington at Fort Phil Kearney, and that Carrington's mission was to build a string of forts along the Bozeman Trail to make it safe for white men to travel to the gold fields at Bannack and Virginia City. The Sioux and Cheyenne were killing too many whites.

Gunn wondered if it occurred to them that the white man was destroying the Indians' best hunting grounds. That thought caused him to wonder whether he could fit into either society.

After breakfast he went to his room and hid his money belt in the false bottom of his sea chest. His money safe, he headed for the second-class passenger deck.

Gunn moved carefully around men sleeping on deck, some playing cards, others just jawing with one another. He searched the face of each before passing on.

After looking at every man and woman, he worked his way back among the crates, barrels, and bales, moving some and squeezing between others. Almost at the end of the stacked supplies, Gunn decided the three had gotten off the boat somewhere.

He turned the corner of the last stack and came face-to-face with one of those he hunted. The man had a knife in his hand.

Gunn had just pulled his own thin blade when out of the

corner of his eye he saw a shadow swoop down on him. He
ducked almost flat to the deck. The shadow fell behind him. He
had no time to reach for the derringer. His left hand swiped
toward his right side for his .44. The thong held it securely in
the holster.

He straightened and pressed his back flat against a bale of
clothing, waving his knife slowly in front of him. The one who
had been in front of him, a stocky man, darted in and thrust at
Gunn's gut. He missed. Gunn swung his knife and felt it make
contact. Pivoting with his swing, he jabbed the point of his
knife at the slim man, who had landed behind him. Slim
stepped back, graceful as a dancer, just as the knife pricked his
chest. He grinned at Gunn, seeming to enjoy the fight.

"Ah! A bare scratch, mon."

Gunn only grunted. Where was the third man? These two
were enough to worry about, but the third man could come at
him from above or either side.

He had had only a moment to make up his mind how to fight
these two when he noticed sunlight at the end of the row of
bales. Keeping his back flat against the bales, Gunn slid along
them toward Stumpy, while trying to keep an eye on Slim.
Gunn stepped toward Stumpy, thrusting, slicing, moving him
back toward the area in the sun. Stumpy gave ground faster
than Gunn had dared hope he would and broke into the sunlight
just as Gunn twisted, ducked, and jabbed at Slim.

His knife made solid contact this time. The smile slipped
from Slim's face, his lips reshaping themselves into an O as the
knife slipped into his gut. Gunn had him spitted right below his
belt. He pulled his blade free and swung on Stumpy in time to
feel the burn of his assailant's blade as it slipped over his
shoulder and sliced down his back.

Gunn moved out into the clear space beyond the stack of
supplies. He had about ten feet between him and the boat's
stern. Stumpy backed against the lifeline, still moving his knife
slowly, the blade cobra-like, ready to strike.

Gunn closed on him, wanting to end this as quickly as
possible. Stumpy stared him straight in the eyes, then for just
a flicker of a moment he shifted to look above Gunn's head.
Gunn threw himself to the side, swung his knife instinctively,
and reached for his derringer. Now he knew where the third

man was. He had missed landing on Gunn's back only because of Gunn's quick move to the side.

Gunn swung the derringer to get a shot at Stumpy backed against the lifeline, and saw him disappear over the side. The one who had jumped from the bale had vanished. Gunn thought he'd gone back into the mound of boxes and barrels.

He was standing there trying to get his breath when he became aware of the burning down his back, and at the same time felt the slow flow down his spine to his belt. He bled, perhaps a lot. He glanced at the stack of cargo and knew he'd be a damned fool to follow the third one into his hiding place.

Threading his way back to the ladder to go to his cabin, he wondered if he'd killed Slim. If he hadn't, he wouldn't be worried about him for a while. He'd seen others with their guts sliced open. It took the fight out of them real sudden. And the one who had jumped over the side wouldn't be a worry until he could catch another boat. Gunn didn't doubt that that was what the man would do. This left only one for him to worry about for the present.

When he stepped onto the cabin deck, he still had the derringer in one hand and his knife in the other. He had turned to go to his cabin when a deep, but feminine, voice said, "Put them damned weapons away an' come with me. I'll fix that scratch you got down yore back."

Gunn turned, his eyes trained at about the five-and-a-half-foot level. He made a quick adjustment. The woman he faced stood just an inch or so less than six feet. She was rawboned, wide-shouldered, and the dress she wore, although it hung on her like a flour sack, couldn't hide the fact that she was one well-built female. Anyway, clothes didn't make the person.

"Were you speaking to me, ma'am?"

"Hell yes, I'm talking to you. Ain't nobody else walkin' round heah wagging a damned peashooter around in his left hand and holdin' a pigsticker still drippin' blood in the other." She took him by the elbow and steered him to the cabin next to his own. "Git in there 'fore you fall on yore face. You're losin blood faster'n that puny body o' yourn can make it."

She opened the door and pushed him into what was obviously her own stateroom. She guided him toward the bunk.

"Lie down. On yore stomach."

Gunn stumbled to her bed, and feeling fuzzy-brained, he didn't fight the idea of lying down.

He felt her tear his shirt down the back and peel it off his arms.

"Ma'am, it isn't proper for me to be in here in your room like this. I-I think I better go to my own room."

"You try to git off that there bunk and I'll kick your arse up around your neck. You probably done figured out I ain't no lady, an' I don't give spit for what's proper, so just stay there till I git you patched up."

The woman brought the white washbowl and water pitcher to the bedside and placed it on the deck. She then tore the face towel, only slightly thicker than mosquito netting, to shreds and sponged the blood off his back.

"Gotta see how bad you got yourself carved up. Cain't do that till I git the blood away from the slice." She wiped at the cut a moment more, grunted, and said, "Gonna have to take a few tucks in that there cut to keep it closed. Lucky I got a needle an' thread with me."

"You ever do this before, ma'am?"

"Many a time. In that country you're agoin' to, men are always gittin' cut, shot, tromped on, throwed, you name it, and I done fixed 'em all at one time or other. Don't you worry your head none, I'll git you sewed up in a jiffy."

"What's your name, ma'am?"

"Folks up where I come from call me Jake. Name's Jane Carson, but after I growed to man-size that there Jane name just sort o' got lost somewhere. Don't bother to tell me yourn. Ever'body on this boat knows about you. Soon's you killed that slick gambler, ever'body talked about it."

"He wasn't very slick, Jake, or he'd still be around. Matter of fact, he was a pure beginner as far as knowing cards."

"You a gambler, Rafe?"

"If you mean do I gamble for a living, no. I just do it for fun. Mostly to see if I can outsmart the others in the game."

Jake went to her trunk, removed a bottle of something Gunn took to be whiskey, and pulled the cork from it. As soon as its fumes burned the inside of his nose, he knew it wasn't whiskey. Unconsciously he grasped a handful of blanket. Jake poured a goodly part of the bottle's contents on his back.

Gunn knotted the blanket in his hand, pushed it into his mouth, and bit down on it. The burn went up and down his back, knotting its muscles, cooking them. He felt as if his hair stood straight out from his head. Finally the burning eased, and with it, Gunn's strength abandoned him. His muscles felt no stronger than a baby's. He pulled the blanket from his mouth.

"W-what in the name of hell was that you put on my back?"

"Horse liniment. Keep that gash in your back from festerin'. I use it on mules, horses—an' men dumb enough to git themselves hurt. Works every time."

Gunn watched her thread a needle with white thread and reach for his back. He renewed his grip on the blanket and crammed a handful back into his mouth.

Jake finished tending Gunn's wound and slapped him on the rump. "Git up. You gonna be frisky as a new calf right soon."

Gunn swung his legs over the edge of the bed. "If I lived through that, I can sure as hell live long enough for it to heal."

Gunn studied her a long moment. "Thanks, ma'am. I couldn't have done a very good job of tending it myself." He frowned, still looking at her. "Why haven't I seen you around the deck, or in the dining room? We've been under way several days now."

She flushed and toyed with her skirt. "Aw now, Rafe, I don't rightly reckon I'd fit in with most of them people what eats there. I been roughing it so long I fergot any manners I ever had—if I ever had any. I take my eats in my room here."

Never removing his gaze from hers, Gunn picked up her rough, work-hardened hand, held it between his a moment, and said, "Miss Jake, I'd be very proud to have you sit at my table for the rest of this trip."

"Aw, now. You don't owe me nothing for fixin' your back."

"Jake, I'm not trying to repay you. You're a lady I want to know better. Honor me with your presence until one of us leaves this boat."

Jake smiled at him through misty eyes. Gunn would have bet they were the first tears her eyes had felt in a long time. "Rafe, if you really mean that, ah reckon I'd be right happy to eat with you."

CHAPTER
SIX

JAKE CLOSED THE door behind Gunn, went to her bed, stripped the bloodstained blanket from it, pulled the sheet up tight, tucked it under the mattress, and fluffed the pillow. Have to sponge that there blood off'n that blanket soon's I get some more water, she thought.

She cleaned up the mess she'd made tending Gunn's back. Then, satisfied with her effort, she sat on the edge of the bed and tentatively placed her hand on the pillow he had used. She drew back as though the spot burned.

Dang dumb woman, she thought. That there man ain't for you. He's got manners. He's what most would call a gentleman, a danged dangerous gentleman, but one anyhow.

Looking down, she noticed a smear of blood on her dress and thought she might as well wash it out before it set up and wouldn't come out. She stood, pulled the coarse, tentlike garment over her head and saw that blood had stained her pantaloons. "Reckon I gotta warsh the whole danged kit and caboodle," she said.

She took off all her clothes and stood there a moment, glancing down and looking carefully at her body. "Now, them woman parts is right handsome even if I do say so m'self. Ain't many females what looks better."

Jake lifted her ample breasts, inspected them, slid her hands down her body, over her hips, and brought them in over her flat stomach. She continued studying herself. Her legs, large in the thighs, befitted her height. They were long, straight, and tapered into slim, shapely calves.

She again sat on the bed. Any man ought to want me, she thought, and then smiled ruefully. Yeah, but them as do, I don't

65

want. They's a lot of *them* around. Ain't had a man since Jim took off and got his self killed by the Blackfeet. Reckon I'll just wait for the right one. Now, Rafe, he ain't the right one to keep forever. He ain't gonna stop long enough to get tied down to no female.

Jim was a good husband even if he didn't keep clean enough for my likin'. Seems he always smelled like a buffalo. Her thoughts shifted from her husband to Rafe.

That Rafe, now, he's so clean he smells good. It shore would be nice to have him tend my woman needs, even if it wasn't for keeps. She smiled, hugged her arms across her breast, and murmured under her breath. "Yes, sir, Mr. Rafe, I'm gonna eat my victuals with you."

She stood, washed her soiled clothing, and then tended to *her* needs. She scrubbed her body until it tingled, washed her hair, dried it, and brushed until it sparkled like a brook catching sun rays. My hair ain't so bad either, she thought, giving it a few extra strokes with the brush. Ain't many women got naturally corn-silk-colored hair.

She looked disgustedly at her dress. Ain't a helluva lot to do with you, she thought. Maybe when she got to Saint Louis, she could get something more womanly. She laughed. Boy, them folks in Fort Benton would swallow their cud if I showed up lookin' like a shore nuff woman.

Jake spent another hour pulling in her spare dress and sewing it to better fit her body. She had just finished and slipped it over her head when she heard a tap on the door. She answered the knock.

The door opened toward Gunn, and when he could see Jake, he blinked, hardly believing his eyes. She looked softer. She had done something with her hair, and her dress fit better. "My God, Jake, what've you done to yourself? You, well, you look more womanly, more feminine."

"Thank you, Rafe. Danged near scrubbed my hide off. When I got through, there I was, the same durned woman I always been."

Gunn wanted to tell her that what he had first noticed about her was that she, along with the faint scent of rose water, smelled clean. Most women he'd met around the world didn't bother to bathe; instead they splashed on large amounts of perfume to cover their body smell. It didn't work.

"Jake, so far I haven't found a blamed thing wrong with the woman you've always been. C'mon, let's see what they have for dinner."

Over dinner Gunn found out that Jake's husband was dead, that she had worked at his side hunting buffalo and had shipped the hides and pickled tongues downriver. They'd made a good living from the hunting until the Blackfeet put an end to it.

She now worked in Fort Benton's first and only hotel—cooking pies, cakes, whatever the old fiery-tempered German who owned the place, Jacob W. Schmidt, said to cook. He had built the hotel of lumber hauled by bull train from Helena. "Far as I know," she said, "Mr. Schmidt never named his hotel.

"Rafe, I bet there ain't a woman west of the Mississippi what makes better bear sign than me."

Gunn frowned. "Bear sign? I haven't heard the term before. What's bear sign?"

"*Doughnuts,* you danged tenderfoot. I see right now I'm gonna have to learn you a few things about this here land."

Gunn studied her a moment, hoping she meant what she said. "Ma'am, I surely do need to learn, but it'd take an awful lot of your time."

"Don't know of nothin' I'd like more. On the way up—" She stopped and squinted at him. "You *are* goin' to Fort Benton, ain't you?"

Gunn nodded. "Yep."

"Good. Now, like I was gonna say, on the way up I'll show you the different Injuns, the ones to watch out for, where these boat captains git wood, how much they have to pay for it, aw hell," she took a deep breath, "I'll show you everything I know."

Gunn grinned. "Sounds like we're gonna sort of be partners, for a while."

His addition of the "for a while" didn't go unnoticed by Jake. She grasped his shoulder and faced him directly, her eyes locked with his. "Rafe, you don't need to worry 'bout me bein' no clinging vine. I'll teach you, and when you get ready to look at the other side o' them mountains, just pull stakes. I'll count myself lucky to have known you."

Gunn stared her in the eyes for a long moment, covered her big, capable hand with his, and nodded. "Jake, I know others have probably told you this, and I want to add my vote to theirs. You're one hell of a woman. I'd like to believe there are more like you."

"Aw, pshaw now, you gonna make me feel like a young schoolgirl. I ain't very young, an' I danged sure ain't never been in no school. Fact is, the only schoolin' I ever got was readin' old papers and magazines by campfire. Don't even recollect who learned me to read."

Gunn and Jake talked all through dinner. By the time they'd finished, Gunn felt they'd known each other for years.

He walked her to her stateroom and mentioned that he was going to have a drink and play a few hands of poker. "We'll be getting into Saint Louis tomorrow, so I'm not going to play long." He hesitated. "Jake, if anything disturbs you during the night, knock on the bulkhead. I'll come right over."

"You do the same, Rafe. I can handle a gun good as most." He hid his smile. A buffalo-hunting, Indian-knowing woman didn't have to tell *him* she knew how to shoot.

He played only a few hands, won twenty-three dollars, cashed in, and went to his stateroom. His back had stiffened, and it throbbed the length of the cut.

When he got in his bunk, the only way he could lie comfortably was on his stomach.

Before going to sleep, Jake sat heavily in his thoughts. She'd lived a rough life and been dealt some lousy hands, but he hadn't heard her complain once.

Gunn guessed her to be about thirty-five years old. She no longer had the bloom of youth, but she was a damned handsome woman. He wasn't surprised that his thoughts about her included man-woman feelings. His thoughts placed guilt squarely on his shoulders.

He shouldn't be thinking of her that way. She'd lost her husband, and was probably vulnerable because of it. She had spent all of her adult life with one man, and Gunn felt sure she was lonely. He couldn't take advantage of either her loneliness *or* her vulnerability. That didn't stop him from thinking, though. He frowned into the dark and went to sleep.

Although late March had been sweltering in New Orleans,

the farther up river he traveled, Gunn found, the more the weather cooled perceptibly. It was early April when he stepped off the boat in Saint Louis, and he needed a coat.

Before leaving the boat, he'd asked the captain to personally make certain his goods, along with his and Jake's luggage, got on the *Luella*, commanded by a young captain, Grant Marsh.

"Just in case something happens to detain me here, tell Captain Marsh to deliver my goods to the Matthew Carroll and George Steell Warehouse," Gunn told Jake. "I'll keep the bill of lading with me." He was thankful Jake had been able to advise him about where to send his goods. She'd assured him Carroll and Steell were good businessmen and honest as a man could ask.

He saw Jake ahead of him. She walked fast, fast enough that Gunn could tell she hurried for some reason and apparently didn't want company. He lagged behind, and searched the face of every person he passed, looking for the Cajuns. The path he walked took some of his attention—it was rocky, with occasional piles of horse droppings. He had just shined his boots.

He stopped in a saloon, wanting a beer. He had done all of his buying before leaving New Orleans, so all he really wanted was to get off the boat.

He drank his beer and asked the bartender where he might find the *Luella*.

"Damned if I know. All I can tell you is start walking down the riverfront. There are about thirty or forty boats tied up along there. If she's in Saint Louis, you'll find her."

When he'd dressed to come ashore, Gunn had put on the same clothing he'd worn when leaving New Orleans. He had his .44 belted around his waist, and to keep it from hanging up in the holster, if he needed it, or banging against his leg, he had tied the bottom of the holster to his leg with a leather thong. He'd noticed several who wore their guns like that. He *didn't* know that most who wore their guns tied down were gunfighters.

He finished his beer and walked along the river, looking at the name of each boat he passed, but also studying the face of every man he approached.

The Cajuns were nowhere to be seen, but Gunn had the

feeling that they knew exactly where *he* was. He didn't like the cold, hard knot between his shoulder blades.

Damn their sneaky souls, he thought. What the hell do they want with me? He'd never seen them before New Orleans. It was more than wanting to rob him, and that deputy couldn't hold a grudge like this for backing him down. He shrugged mentally, thinking he'd deal the deputy out of the play. This was between him and the Cajuns.

He'd been counting the boats as he walked. The seventeenth one had the name *Luella* proudly painted on the side of the wheelhouse, and also on a shingle hanging from the passenger deck. Gunn walked aboard.

He checked his and Jake's cabin, had Jake's changed so it would be next to his, looked in his room, and found it lacked a lot compared to the comfort of his previous room. Oh well, what the hell, he'd had quarters a lot worse than these. At least he wouldn't have to sleep in a hammock. His gear hadn't arrived, so he walked about the deck, and finally climbed to the wheelhouse.

He found Grant Marsh a likable, serious man. He was well built, clear-eyed, and about thirty-four years old. Marsh would stand out in any crowd. He was quick to tell Gunn that this was his first command.

Gunn smiled. "Captain, we all have to start somewhere. You ever been up the Missouri before?"

Marsh shook his head. "Not to the upper reaches. But if one of these boats'll make it, I'll take 'er. I've been mate on riverboats awhile. Had me a good friend who sailed with me, man by the name of Sam Clements. He quit the river and started writing stories." He shrugged. "Reckon every man does what he has to. Cain't figure him doing that, though, as much money that's to be made runnin' these boast."

Marsh studied the wharf, apparently checking to see that his cargo was moving as fast as he wanted. He turned back to Gunn. "Talking about the river; there are occasions when it'll curl your hair, and others when you get bored as hell seeming to have nothing but clear sailing." He grinned. "The few times I've been bored, I knew I'd pay for it later, in spades."

"You taking much freight upriver this trip?"

"No," Marsh said, shaking his head. "I'm hauling 113 tons,

light by today's standards, but I'll make up for it when I get to Fort Benton. I want it light this time, want to study the river a little, learn where the traps are. There are a lot of odd jobs I'll be able to find when I get to Benton. Boats run aground. Some sink. I might even do some salvage work, and I'll damned sure be able to shuttle back and forth from Benton with loads from grounded boats. Never fear, I'll earn my twelve hundred dollars a month."

Gunn pursed his lips and whistled silently. "Twelve hundred a month. Man, that's good money. I didn't make near that when I sailed the seas."

Marsh cast Gunn a smile that said, "Wait and see. This is like nothing you've ever seen before." Again that cold shiver of excitement ran up Gunn's spine. "When you getting under way, Captain?"

"As soon as they finish loading my freight and all the passengers are aboard. If it's too late, I'll wait till the morning. Don't like steaming at night—too risky."

After Gunn had told Marsh that his supplies would make up a considerable amount of the tonnage, he went back to the passenger deck and stood at the lifeline watching the crew load the boat, and watching the passengers trickle aboard. He wished Jake would come aboard. He didn't want her to miss the sailing.

He was about to turn away when he saw one of the Cajuns standing on the wharf staring at him. Their eyes met, and the Cajun dodged behind a stack of crates.

Gunn's first impulse was to bound down the gangway and try to find the man. He checked the idea and pulled up a chair and sat by the rail. He would sit right here until Marsh pulled away from the wharf, and make sure whether the Cajun came aboard. He'd wait here if it took all night.

There were a couple of things that might prevent his enemy from boarding. He might wait until the one who'd jumped over the stern caught up with him, and Gunn had no doubt but that he *would* catch up.

Gunn sat there until the middle of the afternoon. Each passenger that boarded got his full attention. No Cajuns, and no Jake. Most passengers must be aboard, he thought, noticing at the same time that there were only a few barrels left on the wharf.

He wondered if the captain would get under way this late in the day and had his answer as soon as the question came to mind. Marsh walked to his side and peered at the dock. "One passenger and two or three hundred pounds of supplies and we can get under way. I'll make whatever distance I can and tie up at a wharf to spend the night. There's a docking I know of at the mouth of the Muddy."

As soon as the captain made this statement, Gunn saw Jake, almost running, mount the bottom of the gangway. He sighed, and wondered at his concern. She had her arms full of packages.

She looked his way and came puffing over. "Almost missed 'er. Danged woman had me so tied up an' me astewin' to get gone. Figured y'all might leave without me."

"Here, let me take some of those packages. I'll show you where your cabin is."

Gunn relieved Jake of most of her packages and steered her toward her room. "I took the liberty of changing your cabin to the one next to mine."

"Heck, that ain't no liberty, glad you did. Make it easier for me to change the bandages on your back. You see any o' those varmints what cut you?"

Gun nodded. "Yep. I saw one of them. He didn't come aboard, and if he doesn't soon, he'll miss the boat."

At that moment, the whistle blew and Gunn saw the distance between the boat and the shore widen. He smiled at Jake. "He just missed catching *this* boat."

"Don't mean nuthin'. I reckon there'll be at least a boat a day come into Benton. They ain't gonna have no trouble gettin' to Benton almost soon's we do."

"At least I can relax for a couple of months and not have to watch my back all the way upriver,"

Jake grinned. "That don't mean a damn thing. You gonna have plenty to worry 'bout if you're a worryin' man. We got Indians, snags, sandbars. Hell, Rafe, we could sit here and stew every minute and nary a second of that stewin' would be wasted."

"Jake, I think you've figured out by now that I'm *not* a

worrying man. Now that we're under way, think I'll go to my cabin and take a nap."

"'Fore we eat, c'mon over an' take a drink with me. I brung a half dozen bottles aboard."

"Damn, somehow I should have known you'd take a drink with a man, but just never thought of it. Okay, I'll rap on the bulkhead when I wake up, so you can get presentable."

"Reckon that would take a lot o' doin. No, you just knock, and if I knock back, come on over."

Gunn slept soundly for the first time since leaving New Orleans. It was Jake's knock that roused him. He stood, washed his face, combed his hair, knocked on the bulkhead, and went over.

His surprise this time far outdistanced the time he'd seen her after she'd done her hair. Her dress, fitted at the bodice and waist, was of a fine woolen in dove gray, with black piping on the jacket lapels. Her hair shone as before, and she seemed to glow, standing there expectantly, awaiting his reaction.

"Woman, you've got to quit doing this to me. Why, you're downright beautiful."

"Now, Rafe, I might believe a smidgen o' that hogwash, but don't overdo it." She stood there, an amazon, wanting his approval, but not really daring to hope for too much. Gunn saw all of these emotions flit across her face. He reached for her hands and folded them in his.

"Aw, Jake, I wouldn't say anything like that if it weren't true. You are the most striking woman I believe I've ever seen, and what makes it so wonderful, yours shines from the inside."

Obviously flustered, Jake turned away, turned back, and almost tripping, went to the commode, took a couple of glasses from the shelf above, uncorked a bottle of rye, and splashed a liberal amount into each. She handed Gunn his.

He lifted it before putting it to his lips. "A toast to the woman who's going to set every tongue in the whole Montana Territory to wagging. Where in the world did you find such stylish clothes in one day?"

"Finding 'em warn't no problem, but gettin' any to fit my man-size frame turned out to be worse'n gitting caught in a buffalo stampede. *That's* what took all the time and almost made me miss the boat. I had 'em made."

She chuckled. "Whooee, you should've seen that there seamstress woman when she said I could get 'em in a week. I shoved my purse pistol in 'er face and said she better get busy or she wouldn't *see* next week."

"Aw, hell, Jake, you didn't do that, did you?"

"I shore enough did, and when she finished this one, I had her cut me out two more dresses from patterns she'd ordered from a Lady Goddey's catalogue. I'll sew them cutout dresses together myself."

Gunn used the only chair, and Jake sat on the edge of her bunk. They sipped their whiskey in silence, comfortable in the thought they both knew she had changed her appearance for him.

After a while, Jake stood and refilled their glasses. When she handed him his, she looked him straight in the eyes. "Rafe, I had to have the false bravery that comes in that there bottle to say what I'm gonna say." She nodded. "Yeah, you know I done this for you, but I need you to get it 'tween your ears that I ain't out to tie no apron stings around you. Reckon I just seen a man what I wanted to look good for. Lordy, I ain't so dumb as to b'lieve I could capture a man like you."

Gunn sighed. "Jake, quit putting yourself down. There's not a damned thing about you most men wouldn't kill for. Yep, I've a lot of things I have to do, but that doesn't mean you don't get *all* my attention when I look at you."

The whiskey caused them to talk more than they would have at another time.

"Let's have one more drink and go to dinner." Jake's words were just a little slurred.

"Nope, let's go to dinner, then after we get something that'll stick to our ribs, we'll sit here and get falling-down drunk." Gunn looked at her and smiled. "I don't think you want that, though. I'll bet you've already put down more whiskey at one time than you ever did before."

Jake lowered her eyes. "You're right. I like a belt once in a while, but I ain't no drinkin' woman. Reckon I just wanted to talk and didn't have no good excuse to do it."

"You don't need an excuse, Jake. We'll talk anytime you want. Now, c'mon, let's see what they've fixed for us."

Dinner on the *Luella* wasn't anything fancy, but it sat right there with the best meals Gunn had ever eaten. It was a stew of some kind, full of big chunks of meat, with vegetables and whole onions. With it were the crispest, fluffiest biscuits Gunn had ever eaten. They were crisp on the outside and fluffy on the inside. He buttered his sixth biscuit, poured honey over it, and made short work of eating it.

Finally he pushed his chair back, sighed, and looked longingly at the big pot in the middle of the table. "If I had one spare inch, I'd eat some more," he said. "That's the best beef stew I ever put in my mouth."

"I reckon it would be if it *was* beef stew. Gol-ding it, Rafe, I knowed I was gonna have to teach you a few things, but damn. Don't you even know it when you're eatin' buffalo?"

"Buffalo? Are you sure? I never ate buffalo before."

"You ask me if I'm sure? Why, dang it, I've et it, shot it, wore it, done danged nigh ever'thing with it 'cept sleep with it. Course I'm sure. Reckon you'll believe me when I say Injuns know what they're doin' when they turn up their danged noses at beef. Buffalo's man's meat."

Gunn patted his stomach. "I believe you, Jake. I don't think I ever ate a better meal. Fancier, yeah, but better, no."

They sat and watched the last of the passengers trickle in to dinner, then as if on signal they stood and walked toward the hatch.

"I'm going to take a few turns around the deck and walk some of this dinner off," Gunn said. "Want to come with me?"

"Reckon if you hadn't asked me I'd a followed you around like a whipped pup. Yeah, I want to come."

They walked, not talking, and Gunn felt that conversation wasn't needed. Finally they approached their cabins, stopped, and stood by the rail watching the water flow past. Twilight slowly closed in, softening the harsh reds of the bank and blackening the trees. The sounds were the muted sounds of the engines below and the splish-splash of the paddles dipping into the water.

"Captain Marsh'll be tying up for the night pretty soon. He told me earlier he'd travel at night only when he knew he had deep water free of snags. He has deep water here, but I suppose one can never be sure about snags," Gunn said.

"Tomorrow, you're gonna see a river that ain't got no water,"

Jake responded, "just mud. And if they's been any rain upriver, whole trees'll be comin' down on us. That there captain's gonna earn whatever they pay 'im."

The boat whistle blew and the engines slowed. "This must be where we're tying up. I think I'll turn in." Gunn said it, but part of him wanted to spend more time with Jake—and it wasn't fair. He was only thinking of himself. Damn, he thought, that isn't like me. I should be thinking of her feelings, not my desire.

"Yeah, me too, Rafe." Jake cut into his thoughts. "Remember, knock if you need me."

Gunn wanted to answer that he *needed* her now, but he squelched the impulse.

"You too—and, Jake, if you're in trouble, knock only once. I'll be there quicker'n scat. If you just want to talk, or something, knock twice."

He went in, lighted the lantern, undressed, and lay down. Looking up at the overhead, he frowned. He liked Jake, liked her as much as any woman he'd ever met, but what he felt wasn't the feelings she deserved, not like he felt about Eula. A woman like Jake needed a man she could be a partner with. She probably had a lot of love to give the right man. He wasn't the right man. He knew it and didn't want to do Jake wrong, or let her believe he might be the man she'd been waiting for.

He turned the light out and was a long time in going to sleep.

Something awakened him. He swam out of the fog of a deep slumber wondering what it was. He heard it again. Two knocks.

He answered the knocks, dressed, and tapped on Jake's cabin hatch.

"It's unlocked, Rafe. Come on in."

Her lantern was dark when he opened the door. "Close the door and lock it. I didn't light the lantern. Reckon I was ashamed to let you look at me. I'm a terrible woman, Rafe. I knowed you was just the other side o' this wall from me, and I couldn't stand it. I wanted you here with me."

Gunn felt his way to her bed and sat on its edge. "Jake, don't say anything else. If this had happened when we had our drinks this afternoon, I'd have gone in my cabin and locked the door. I should leave now, but I haven't the willpower. I don't want to take something that tomorrow you'll be sorry for giving. There's no alcohol now, Jake, so be sure about what you're doing. I want to stay your friend."

"Lay here beside me, Rafe. I know what I'm doin'. Ain't never had but one man in my life, never wanted any other until I saw you. I thought about you and the two months we're gonna be on this here boat, together. Decided I didn't want to miss one danged bit of it." She grasped his hand. "Oh, sounds like I ain't even thought 'bout your feelin's. I have, Rafe, sure nuff I have. If you want, go on out that door—or stay, and we'll still be friends in the mornin'."

"Hush, hush, woman." Gunn leaned over, felt for her face in the dark, and with his lips smothered any other words she might say. His arms went around her shoulders and pulled her toward him.

After a long while, he lifted his lips from hers. "Jake, I want you to know something. I *like* you better than any woman, but I don't want to confuse this with love. Hell, I don't even know what love is."

"I ain't askin' for love, Rafe. Somehow, I'm thinkin' that *likin's* better'n love anyhow. Likin' lasts longer. Now just lay here beside me and hold me close."

After a *long* while, Gunn dressed, lighted the lantern, and they had a drink.

He slipped out of her cabin before sunup and went to his bunk, tired but never more relaxed and happy. He knew that what he and Jake had shared, and would share again, was something very special—not love, but a friendship that would respond to whatever need they each might have.

Long after the sun peeped under the cabin hatch, he thought of Jake—and he thought of Eula. He didn't try to compare them, but tried to picture each in a rancher's cabin, living the life she would be forced to live here on the frontier. Neither of them came up short. He smiled at the overhead, thinking that it was ironic—Eula ten years younger than he, and Jake about ten years older. Neither of those comparisons bothered him either.

CHAPTER
SEVEN

A FEW DAYS later Gunn visited Captain Marsh. From the wheelhouse, the river looked vastly different from the Mississippi.

They had talked for the better part of an hour when Marsh looked away from the wheel. "Been plowing our way up to this stretch of mud for five days now. Plowing's a good term." He nodded. "And even then it's not quite right. Most of the old river men describe it as too thick to drink and too *thin* to plow."

Gunn laughed. "Captain, I'm no judge, but I'll certainly agree. I've bothered you enough for now. Think I'll go below."

"Anytime, Mr. Gunn. I enjoy your visits."

A few days later Gunn and Jake stood at the rail of the hurricane deck, talking quietly, changing the subject when something ashore drew their attention.

Gunn pondered what they had come to mean to each other, lovers by night and friends by day. He detected no change in her attitude, yet he knew the bonds of friendship were stronger.

The only difference Gunn noticed was that she had become even prettier. She seemed to glow. He told her so.

"Rafe, you know danged well any woman what's got a man in her bed regular-like is gonna be prettier, softer lookin'. She will be, that is, if she likes the man an' he likes her." She looked straight into his eyes and blushed to the roots of her honey-colored hair. "Reckon I couldn't 've done what we're doin' if you wasn't somethin' special. I knowed it soon's I seen you."

Gunn wanted to put his arms around her and assure her he felt the same, but they stood out there in the open where all could see. Instead he gripped her shoulders, swallowed twice, and said nothing. Somehow that said more than any words.

Changing the subject, Jake held out her arm and with a sweeping motion said, "See them plains? Well, ain't nothin' gonna change about them for a long way yet. Seems like a body can see out yonder forever"

"I like 'em. I've sat in ravines by a smokeless fire many a night listenin' to the wind sing its song, blowin' through thousands of miles of grass. Even with the chance I'd lose my scalp to some Indian, I still liked it."

"How long you been out here, Jake?"

"'Bout twenty year. Come out with my husband, a trapper then, just as the beaver trade went to hell. We just changed what we was lookin' for and stayed on. I come out with Jim when I was just short o' fifteen."

This was the first time Jake had mentioned her husband by name. Gunn thought maybe the pain she'd had bottled up inside her was finally melting.

Leaning against the ladder to the wheelhouse on the hurricane deck, Gunn saw black, boiling clouds to the northwest. Jake had gone to her cabin. He watched the storm come closer and climbed the ladder to talk with Captain Marsh.

"Looks like twister weather," Marsh said, his eyes darting from one shore to the other. "There's a big cottonwood on the bank just around that bend. If we can make it to her before the storm hits, we'll tie up and just let 'er blow; if not, I'll try to lay up close to the bank off our starboard side and keep steam on to hold her there."

Marsh called for more steam. The paddles increased speed, churning the brown water to a froth. There was *no* wind, and then, from a dead calm, a gale buffeted the boat, coming off the port bow.

"Outblow from the storm," Marsh yelled above the wind noise. He coolly corrected his course to offset the wind force. "Gonna be tricky getting to that tree. Might not make it, but we'll give 'er one hell of a try."

Gunn saw within minutes why these upriver boat captains were worth every penny paid them. Marsh's eyes continued to dart from the shore to the river's surface, back to shore, back to the water, and all the while he made course corrections.

After the first hard blow, it set in to rain. Not rain like Gunn remembered at sea, but rain that came in sheets that blanked out the bow and made navigation impossible.

Marsh yelled to slow engines, his eyes now fastened toward the starboard side of his vessel. The riverbank materialized through the wall of water. He again called for less speed on the engines. "This wind'll do our work for us. It'll blow us gently up against the bank and hold us there till it's ready to turn us loose."

Marsh talked, but Gunn knew *he* wasn't being addressed. The captain probably talked himself through most crises. When they rested firmly against the bank, the paddle wheel barely turned. "Let 'er turn just enough to keep us from floating downstream." This time he *was* talking to Gunn.

Gunn had been holding his breath. He let it out slowly. "Man, that took skill."

Marsh grinned and winked.

The storm had lasted less than half an hour. Marsh called for steam and headed out to where only he and the riverboat captains knew the channel to be. Another twenty minutes and they tied up to the cottonwood Marsh had told Gunn about.

"Didn't make the place I wanted to take on wood, but we'll get there early in the morning. I want to tie up now 'cause the water's gonna rise pretty quick with this rain, and it'll bring down all sorts of trash with it. We'll stop in Independence for wood. I'll need ten cords. At four dollars a cord, we use up about eighty dollars' worth of wood a day."

"Looks like you'd use up all the fuel within miles of the river."

Marsh nodded. "Getting to be a problem, but we can burn almost anything, of any size. When we get to Council Bluffs, you'll see stacks of cross-ties. The Union Pacific is starting its line there, and they're gonna have one hell of a time finding timber of the right size to cut after they leave there." He twisted the wheel to miss a snag, brought the boat back on course, and continued.

"We don't have *that* problem. The U.P.'s stocking as many ties as they can, but they'll never be able to haul all they need.

They'll wind up searching creek banks for anything of the right size. There aren't many trees here now, but they'll strip this land of what it does have."

The next day they pulled in to Independence and made short work of loading what they needed. No one had a chance to go ashore.

Marsh told Gunn that if he'd chosen to take his supplies by wagon, he might have off-loaded at Independence, but the smart move would have been to leave the boat at Council Bluffs and take the Mormon Trail west. Boat, or wagon train—either way was fraught with danger.

Gunn told Jake what Marsh had said. She grinned at him. "You reckon we'd 've had the comforts in a danged wagon we got on this here boat?"

"Nope. And you'd be cooking, washing clothes, and driving a bull team, while I rode with rifle in hand to guard against attack."

"Now, don't you get to feelin' so danged comfortable, Rafe Gunn. They's gonna be enough Injuns botherin' this danged boat to keep you busy once we get to the Cheyenne country. Which makes me mindful that we better do some practice shootin' every day. We kin shoot at snags, snakes, whatever comes to hand. You got plenty o' bullets for them weapons I seen you with?"

Gunn nodded. "I brought a case of .44 cartridges aboard."

"Good. You might use all of it 'fore we get to Benton. I brung a batch too."

They decided an hour a day would be good practice time. That afternoon they fired at their first targets.

Gunn watched several bits of flotsam to gage the speed with which the river carried it past them. He picked a chunk about hand sized, drew, and fired. His bullet hit, splintering the wood. He did this four more times with the same results. He opened the cylinder, shucked the cartridges, put the empties in his pocket, and reloaded.

"Damn, Rafe, you don't need no practice." She looked at his tied-down holster. "You a gunfighter?"

Pleased with his accuracy, he grinned at her. "If I told you I never fired a gun of any kind until a couple of months ago, would you believe me?"

"Hell and damnation, no, I ain't gonna believe that hogwash. Reckon I seen some of the best and they ain't as good, or fast, as you."

"Aw, c'mon now, Jake. I've never seen a gunfight, but those who make a living at it have to be better than this."

Jake looked straight at him. "They ain't no better than what I just seen you do. You never missed a time, and the way you got that there gun outta its holster was like a strikin' snake. Then you never seemed to aim—you just up and fired it."

"If I'm really that good, it must be something I was born with. Honest, I never fired a gun until a couple of months ago."

Jake stared at him a moment, seemed to accept what he'd said, turned, sighted on a snake, and cut it in two.

Gunn raised his eyebrows, smiled, and said softly, "Yep, we'd make good partners in more ways than one."

"Yeah, but if you gonna give me a druther, I'll settle in on the *one*."

Gunn's smile spread to a grin. "Now that you talked me into it, we going to your cabin or mine?"

"Damn, Rafe, don't argue 'bout it. We'll take the closest one. C'mon. We'll shoot some more tomorrow. We don't need it as much as I figured anyhow." She took his arm and led him toward the cabins.

The next day they practiced with rifles, using water targets rather than ones ashore, because they could see the splash and estimate better how they were doing. Gunn did just as well with this weapon. Jake, using an old Sharps, amazed Gunn with her distance shooting.

"This here's the same gun I hunted buffalo with. I had to be good or they was times I'd a starved. This here big woman ain't never gonna miss a meal 'cause of poor shootin'."

A week later Jake informed Gunn that they were coming into Indian country. "Oh, hell, we been in it for a while, but from here on in we gonna see them what'll take pure pleasure in pesterin' us. Reckon the way we been shootin', me an' you gonna do some pesterin' of our own. We gonna have troubles more'n Injuns too. You notice the river's gettin' shallower?"

Gunn grimaced. "Jake, how can a body tell the river's getting shallow? Hell, I haven't seen the bottom of this mud flat since we left Saint Louis."

"You have to feel it, Rafe. 'Fore we reach Benton, you'll get the feel of it."

As soon as Jake said it, Gunn felt it. The boat bumped, slowed, and came to a stop, the paddle wheel still churning.

"Told you this danged river was gettin' shallow."

Gunn didn't hear her. He watched crew members run forward. They put the two long bow-mounted spars over the side at about a forty-five-degree angle, with cables attached to the upper ends.

"Now you gonna get to see a boat grasshoppered across a mud bar. Ain't a pretty sight, but it gets the job done."

As soon as the engine turned on, the cables, attached to a capstan, began to walk the poles aft, like crutches. When the poles were robbed of their leverage, the crew brought them in and repeated the action. They had done this four or five times when Gunn heard a racket such as he'd never heard—screams, sharp yipping from Indians strung out along the shore, and cursing from the crew.

"Injuns," Jake yelled, lifted her old Sharps, and fired. Gunn followed her line of sight off the starboard side and saw a redskin fall from his horse. That's shooting, he thought. That Indian was at least four hundred yards from us. His blood raced. He was in his first Indian fight.

Gunn raised his Henry, drew a bead on a warrior riding straight toward the riverbank, and fired. The rider swerved to the side, clinging to his horse's mane. Gunn's gut tightened, and a brassy taste rose in his throat. Arrows, and bullets, rained about him. The acrid stench of gunpowder stung his nostrils.

Not thinking, he wrapped his arm about Jake and pulled her to the deck. "Stay down. Harder to hit you."

In the back of his mind he heard other guns firing from the boat. He picked another rider and fired. The warrior threw his hands up, losing his bow, and fell from his horse.

The crew manning the grasshoppering gear stayed on station, seeming to ignore what went on about them.

The *Luella* slid from the bar and picked up speed. The attackers strung out along the bank. Their horses ran with their bellies almost touching the ground, the Indians controlling them with their knees, using both hands to shoot their arrows.

Gunn knew that shot for shot the Indians were getting off more than the crew and passengers.

He stood. As fast as he could lever shells into the chamber, he aimed and fired.

A hand grabbed him in the back of his belt and yanked him to the deck. "Gol-danged fool. You wanta get your danged thick-skulled head blowed off. Stay down."

He looked at Jake and gave her a tight-lipped grin. "You just want me to save you a few." He raised up, fired, and sank back to Jake's side. He looked at her wide-eyed and innocent. "Now, that's downright selfish, Jake. You wanting to hog all the fun."

She grinned, poked him in the ribs, and fired again.

Gunn looked for another target and saw at least six riderless horses racing with the war party. We've hurt them, he thought. Wonder how many we've lost. He picked a straggler and shot him from his horse.

The raiders pulled their ponies to the side, out of range. When Gunn stood to see how the boat's crew and passengers had fared, he realized they had been under attack from both sides of the river. The war party on the port side had pulled away too.

"C'mon, let's see how bad they hurt us." He reached for Jake and pulled her to her feet.

Three men and one woman had arrows in them. Two men were hit in the chest, the woman had an arrow in her side below her rib cage, and the last man sat on the deck cursing. He had an arrow sticking all the way through his thigh.

Gunn grabbed Jake by the arm. "Take this woman to her cabin and fix 'er up. I'll take care of the men."

He motioned to one of the crew. "Get me a bucket of water. I don't mean this damned muddy river water either." He pointed at another of the crew. "I see another man lying up there by the capstan. Get him back here where I can care for him."

They obeyed Gunn's commands without question.

The two hit in the chest died before Gunn could get the arrows from them. He inspected the arrows and saw that they were tipped with steel heads. They had gone all the way through and protruded from the men's backs. Gunn broke the fletch end off and pulled shaft and all through and out of the bodies. He turned to the man, still cursing, with the arrow in his leg.

"You gonna pull this through my leg?"

Gunn nodded. "Yeah, unless you got a better idea."

The man gave Gunn a hard, straight look. "Send one o' the men for a jug then. Might as well enjoy it a little."

Gunn looked at a slender youngster standing at his side. "Get me a bottle—a full one."

The lad departed just as the crewman arrived dragging the man Gunn had seen lying by the capstan.

One look and Gunn realized it had been wasted effort. The man had taken a bullet through the front of his face—the back of his head was trailing a string of grayish matter through a flap of bone still clinging to his shredded scalp.

The youngster he had sent for the whiskey ran to Gunn's side, panting, and handed him a full jug of rye whiskey. Gunn pulled the cork with his teeth, poured some on where the arrow stuck out the back of the man's leg, and handed the wounded man the remainder.

Tight-jawed, he gave Gunn a white-faced, thin-lipped grin. "Let me take a couple swigs o' this, then do what you gotta."

Gunn squatted by the man's side. "Let me know when you're ready."

Grimly, jaw knotted, the wounded man nodded and turned the bottle up, swallowing until Gunn thought he'd drown in the burning liquid. When he pulled the bottle from his lips, he squeezed his eyes tightly shut, opened his mouth, and exhaled forcefully. He held his eyes closed another moment, and when he opened them, he nodded to Gunn. "Get it done."

Gunn broke the fletch end off, raised the man's leg, grasped the arrow, and pulled with all his strength. The wounded man relaxed, completely. He'd passed out.

Gunn took the bottle from his lax hands, where it rested on his chest, and poured its contents into the holes on both sides of the man's leg, then wrapped it with a bandage he tore from his own shirt.

A couple of crewmen stood there, sweating. "You know where this man usually sleeps?"

They nodded in unison.

"Take him there and make him as comfortable as possible."

When they reached for the man, Gunn yelled at them. "No, goddammit, I don't mean drag him. Get something to put him on and carry 'im."

When he saw them on their way with the wounded man, Gunn looked for Jake, and not seeing her, he climbed to the wheelhouse. Several arrows stuck into its wooden sides. He hurriedly poked his head in to see if Marsh was all right.

Marsh nodded. "Yeah, I'm okay." He winked at Gunn. "You and Miss Jake did a fine job down there, both during and after the fight. You ever fight Indians before?"

Gunn slowly shook his head and wondered if he'd killed some of his own people.

"I'd have never known it the way you settled in and did what you had to. I noticed the way you took charge *after* the little skirmish. Looked like you're used to command."

Gunn shifted his rifle to his left hand. "Captain, I've had my share of it. I was ready for my master's papers when I decided to leave the sea."

Marsh spun the wheel and then spun it the other way before he looked at Gunn. "Figures. I'd have bet money you'd had a sea command or one in the Army."

"Thanks, Captain. Just came up to see if there was anything you might want me to do—short of intruding on the duties of your officers."

"No, but thanks for offering, Mr. Gunn. If I think of anything, I'll remember your offer."

"Please do, sir." Gunn returned to the cabin deck to look for Jake.

He didn't have long to look. Jake stuck her head out the door of one of the cabins. "Rafe, get in here. I need help with this woman."

When he stepped through the door, Gunn saw that Jake had the woman's bodice peeled down to her waist. She lay on her side. He turned his eyes away, not wanting to embarrass her.

"Goddammit, you seen tits afore. Look at her. She's hurtin'. Right now she don't give a damn if the whole crew looks at her. She just wants to stop hurtin'."

Gunn stooped by the bedside. The woman breathed shallowly. He could tell that she did so to keep from moving the arrow. The pain must have been excruciating, but the woman looked him in the eyes and gasped, "Sir, this is no time for modesty. Help Jake remove that Satan's device from my side."

She was young, and pretty, probably in her early twenties—and she had guts.

Gunn looked at her back. A large purplish bruise spread around a place where the flesh pushed out in a sharply protruding lump. "Ma'am, I'm going to cut this flesh where the arrow head is just under the skin. I'm going to have to break off one end in order to extract it. Can you stand the pain?"

Her smile was strained. "Do I have a choice, sir?"

Gunn felt like an idiot. "Of course not, ma'am. That was a dumb question."

Gunn looked at Jake. "Get a bottle of rye."

Jake departed on the double. While she was gone, Gunn looked in the lady's mouth and nodded, satisfied that he saw no blood. The arrow had not punctured a lung.

Jake came back in time to see what he did. "Rafe, she done peed. Ain't no blood in it neither."

Gunn noticed the young woman blush. "Sorry, ma'am, but I have to know things like that."

"I understand, sir, and my name's Molly."

He pulled his bowie knife, struck a match, and ran the flame down the length of the blade, then poured whiskey over it.

Talking to himself, he said, "Shouldn't have to do more than slit the skin. That arrowhead'll pop right through." He placed the razor-sharp blade where he judged the tip of the head to be and sliced, very gently. The arrowhead did what he had guessed it would. Molly sucked in her breath.

"Sorry, Molly."

"No, if anything, I believe it helped the pain a little. Seemed like it relieved pressure somewhere."

"Molly, I'd like you to drink a few swallows of that whiskey Jake brought back. It's going to burn your throat like fire, but it'll help you stand what I have to do next."

She nodded, and Jake held the bottle to her lips. She swallowed, gasped, sucked for air, and drank again.

"That there man is unconscionable about gettin' innocent young girls to drink whiskey, Molly. You shoulda seen the shape he got me in onct." Jake held the bottle to Molly's lips again. "This time you better drink a few more swallows." Jake looked at Gunn and grinned devilishly at him. "Figured I might's well warn her 'bout you."

"Yeah, I'm a horrible, lecherous varmint that preys on defenseless females."

While they talked, Gunn manipulated the arrow such that he could grasp the head. Without warning he broke the tip off.

"Aaaah-aah." Molly moaned and buried her face in the pillow.

"Sorry, honey, I had to do that. Now, stuff a corner of the pillow in your mouth and bite down hard. This is going to hurt worse than the other."

Gunn watched as she did as she'd been told. "Ready?" she nodded. Gunn pulled. The arrow resisted a moment then slid, fletch first, out the nasty hole in Molly's side.

While she still trembled from the pain, Gunn poured the burning whiskey into both sides of her wound. She moaned again, then relaxed into the bedcovers. In a moment, through her pain, she giggled.

Gunn frowned, and at the same time saw Jake also frowning. He looked narrow-lidded at Molly. "What the heck was that giggle about? I wouldn't think you'd feel like *that* right now."

"I just happened to picture the look on my husband's face when I tell him the most handsome man in the Dakota Territory was my guest in my cabin, and me without a stitch on from the waist up."

"Ma'am, when you tell 'im that, let me know beforehand so I can be in the next territory."

"Naw, I think if Molly's as smart as she looks, she'll unload his gun 'fore she tells 'im—he might shoot *her*."

Molly had pulled the blanket up to her chin. Gunn asked, "What does your husband do, Molly?"

"Rafe Gunn, get yore arse outta here. This pore little thing needs some rest. I'll answer all them questions you're itchin' to ask soon's I clean up the mess we done made in her room. I'm gonna get her to sleep, an' then I'll come have a drink with you. Figger we slapped our brand on bein' deservin' of one."

Gunn felt the blood rush to his face. He had been inconsiderate. "Oh. I *am* sorry, ma'am. I should have thought."

Later, while eating, Jake told Gunn that she thought she should sleep in Molly's room in case she got feverish. "So don't go to beatin' your damned knuckles off agin that wall 'tween us. This's one gol-danged night I ain't gonna answer."

Gunn thought that a good idea. "I'll check on the man who got the arrow in his leg, then I'll turn in. Damn, if we get in more Indian fights, I might get some rest once in a while."

"You say anything like that there agin, an' I'll give you all the rest you could ever want."

"Aw, Jake, I was just kidding."

"Yeah, reckon I know that. Besides, I'da probably been the one rappin' on that wall." She looked at Gunn steadily a moment. "You looked at that young woman sorta like she was a dish o' deep pan pie. Try yore luck with her an' I'll cut your gonads out."

Gunn unconsciously clutched his groin. Jake laughed. "Rafe, Molly's husband is a young lieutenant, right out of that sojur school in New York. They got married the night he graduated, had one night together, and he come here to join the First Battalion of the Thirteenth Infantry, Company F. I reckon she told her folks she liked that one night, so out she come."

Jake went back to Molly's room; Gunn checked on the wounded man and went to his cabin. One of his last thoughts before going to sleep was that the women who came west, for whatever reason, were the gutsiest, whang-leather-tough ladies he'd ever met.

CHAPTER
EIGHT

DAYS CHURNED INTO weeks. Most days the *Luella* had to be grasshoppered at least once, and often two or three times. Indians were a constant problem, but there were eighty-three passengers aboard the *Luella*, all with guns, too many for the hostiles to attempt a boarding.

The few passengers or crewman wounded received Gunn and Jake's care. They all mended well. Molly and Jake became almost inseparable.

They were deep into Sioux country now and kept lookouts posted day and night. Fort Rice was behind them. The next stop would be Fort Lincoln.

When they passed Old Fort Pierre, Marsh had told Gunn they were halfway to Fort Benton, 1,334 miles, and that the river was far more treacherous the last half of the journey.

Gunn noticed that the crew stayed about half-drunk. He asked Captain Marsh about it.

Marsh cocked an eyebrow and grinned. "Gunn, I'll tell you why these men drink. They drink when expecting Indians to attack, then they drink because they did attack. If the Indians don't attack, then the men drink from boredom, and if not boredom, they drink because the damned boilers might blow up. If they need an excuse, there are plenty of them around. To tell you the truth, though, I never saw a riverman that needed an excuse."

Gunn shrugged. "Yeah, I s'pose so. The passengers drink for the same reasons, I guess. Is that bar on the lower deck a concession, or run by the boat's owners?"

"A concession. Now, if you want to make a lot of money, and I mean a *lot,* lease you a concession spot on one of these boats. Run the bar for five years and you can retire a wealthy man—if you live that long."

They had passed the wrecks of several boats on the way up, and many of them had been the victims of burst boilers, which had blown them over a mile or so from the river. Gunn shook his head. "No, thanks, Marsh. I'll make mine some other way." Marsh found that funny and laughed until tears came to his eyes.

The next morning, the *Luella* slipped quietly alongside the dock at Fort Lincoln. Jake, Molly, and Gunn went ashore. Marsh had advised them that they would remain there overnight.

"Whooeee. I ain't seen this many folks since we left Saint Louis. They's sojurs, trappers, miners, buffalo hunters, an' them danged reservation Injuns that ain't got guts enough to fight. All o' them pushin' and shovin' for space to move around in," Jake said.

"Sounds like you don't have much respect for the reservation Indians." Gunn looked questioningly at Jake.

"Don't. No sirree, ain't got much use for nobody what won't fight for what's his."

"You look on this land as belonging to the Indians?"

Jake stopped, placed her hands on hips, and glowered at Gunn. "You tellin' me you think it b'longs to the white man?"

Gunn laughed. "Nope. Just wondered how you thought about it." Gunn looked at Molly. "All due respect to you and your husband, Molly, knowing he is Army, but I think the Indians are getting the dirty end of the stick out here."

Molly frowned. "How do you arrive at that conclusion, Rafe?"

"Well, I'll tell you. We've made treaty after treaty with them, and have never honored a single one."

"Oh, but the Indians have always broken them by massacring settlers, or Army units."

"Ma'am, that's what the bleeding-heart press, politicians, and some generals want people to believe." Gunn took Jake and Molly by the arm. "C'mon, lets see the sights. We'll talk about this some other time."

They went first to the sutler's, looked through his goods, and found nothing fit to buy. Gunn found a better brand of rye whiskey than the bar had on the boat, so he bought a half dozen bottles. "Might need to dress some more wounds," he said, grinning at Jake and Molly.

"Yeah, reckon I know you, Rafe Gunn. You figger to get me an' pore li'l ole Molly here drunk an' take advantage of us."

Gunn's grin broke into a laugh. "Lord help the man who tried to take advantage of you, Jake—unless you were truly taken with the idea."

Jake stared narrow-eyed at Gunn as though daring him to say more. He quit while he was ahead.

Gunn saw an old trapper and decided to talk with him, despite the way he smelled. Jake looked at the trapper, sniffed, and said, "Damned if you don't smell like my husband used to. Think I'll take Molly here and travel on. See you on the boat, Rafe."

Gunn squatted by the old man. "Name's Gunn. What are all these Indians doing here? Looks like they'd be with their band."

The trapper slanted him a look, took in his clothing, and then studied his face. "You know anything 'bout Injuns?"

Gunn thought a moment and decided that despite being half-Lakota he really knew next to nothing about his people. "Nope, can't say I do."

The old man continued studying Gunn. Finally he stuck out his hand. "Name's Cat Bavousett, part French, rest mountain cat an' grizzly." He shifted his weight to his left leg. "You takin' that boat yonder up to Benton?"

Gunn nodded.

"Well, I'll tell you, young'un, you gonna see real Indians. These here ones are only the scum of the bands you'll see. These done got themselves to likin' that poison liquor they get sold, or trade pelts for, so's they done forgot this here land b'longs to them. All they want is 'nother drink of whiskey."

Gunn frowned. "That's pitiful. Poor devils, and they don't realize that it's a steep trail they're on. They won't stop until they hit bottom—then it'll be too late."

"You're right on that count, young'un."

"You know where the Oglalas might be ranging now?"

"Now, what you want to know that for?"

Gunn shrugged. "Don't know. I knew an Oglala once. Thought I might like to renew my acquaintance."

Bavousett started shaking his head before Gunn finished his sentence. "Naw. You don't want to go traipsin' around lookin for no Oglala. They'd take your hair 'fore you could 'splain you was friendly.

"To answer your question, though, the Oglalas range just about anywhere they want. They might be up by the South Pass country, or right here close to Fort Lincoln. Ain't no tellin' where they might be. Depends on where the buffalo are."

Gunn felt as if someone had let the air out of his balloon. That was a lot of country the old mountain man had spiked out. Finding his people might be a bigger job than he'd thought.

A thought began forming in his mind. Maybe he could leave Jake in charge of his cargo and find someone to show him the way across the plains.

He talked a few more minutes and walked on, studying the people. Gunn judged that every strata of society was represented. He overheard conversations that spoke of highly educated people, and others that indicated the people had never seen the inside of a schoolhouse. Every material, from buckskins to fine imported woolens, adorned the teeming mass. These were the *real* people of the West.

Heat boiled up around him. The sun-parched earth reflected back as much as the sun sent down. Gunn walked close to the walls of each building to take advantage of the little shade they offered and tripped over the leg of a man sitting leaned against the wall. He would have sworn the man lifted his leg deliberately, but Gunn turned to apologize.

"Watch where the hell you're steppin'." The dirty, unkempt form unfolded from his sitting position. He stood a couple of inches above Gunn.

"Sorry. I didn't see your leg stuck out there," Gunn muttered, anxious to move on and find better shade.

"You saw it all right. Just figured to walk any damned where you wanted."

Gunn stared at the man a moment. He was a bully, no doubt about that, but he had the size and meanness to back it up. "I don't suppose you're going to accept my apology, so how do you want it—knives, guns, or fists?"

The bully stared back, flexed his shoulders, and drew his neck down into them. "Reckon I could take you in any of 'em, but I'll take fists. Shuck your gunbelt."

Gunn stepped out of reach of his antagonist and, never taking his eyes off of the huge, filthy lout, slowly unbuckled his gunbelt. He used the time to study his man, who shed his gun and knife. Gunn looked hopefully for a roll of fat above the man's belt. Only a flat expanse of filthy shirt rewarded him.

He knew then that his only advantage might rest in his boxing skill. He'd fought big men before, and until now had not lost. He wrapped his belt around his knife and the pistol holsters and handed them to a grizzled old corporal looking on.

The bully rushed in swinging as soon as the corporal reached for the holster. Placing his weight on the balls of his feet, Gunn stepped back and to the side, bringing his right fist in hard to the man's gut. He shifted his weight and hooked a left to the side of his opponent's filthy, bearded head as it rushed past. The left hook brought blood from the man's ear.

Bully spun and threw a roundhouse right in Gunn's direction. It caught him on the shoulder. The man could punch. Gunn slipped a left and a right off his forearms and moved in close, pumped a left, a right, and a left to the heart and moved out of range again. He took some punches in the exchange. They hurt.

A crowd had collected, and they all screamed for Gunn to stand and fight. Their yells were a constant din against his ears. He moved in closer for a right to the head, but Bully caught him coming in and stood him back on his heels.

That punch was to Gunn's chest. It was a solid lick. Gunn danced back out of reach, sucked air into his lungs, tightened his muscles to try and rid himself of the pain, and quickly moved in for another right. It caught the filthy giant flush on the chin. Gunn felt the shock of it all the way to his elbow. Bully stood there, his eyes slightly glazed.

Gunn thought he had him then.

He moved in for another punch. It was a mistake. Bully grabbed Gunn's arms and threw him over his hip.

Gunn landed flat of his back. His breath left him in a whoosh of air.

Bully swung his foot. Gunn saw it coming and rolled. He

came to his knees and staggered to his left. That was all that saved him the full weight of Bully's charge. Gunn kicked out his left leg and caught the man on his right kneecap.

Bully fell in a heap about five yards from Gunn and lay clutching his leg. Gunn stepped quickly to his side and swung his right foot with all his strength. His boot toe caught the man in his ribs. Gunn heard them crack. He kicked again and caught the man alongside his head. Gunn backed up to the side of a building close to where the fight had taken place. He leaned against it, sucking air into his lungs, feeling sweat trickle down his face and off the end of his nose.

Without a word he motioned the corporal to bring him his guns and knife.

He buckled them on, tied the holster to his leg, and walked to stand over the man he had beaten. "If you decide you want more, try guns or knives next time. You aren't worth a damn with your hands."

He turned to walk away, and the grizzled old corporal fell in at his side. "You're gonna have more trouble with Muldoon there. People call him Bear. He's a buffalo hunter and has been known to take other hunter's kills. He's mean, young'un. You'll run into him again somewhere. I'll bet on it. I hear he runs a trading post out around the forks of the Powder and Yellowstone rivers. They say he sells watered-down whiskey and rifles to the Injuns."

"Ain't no say about it," Cat Bavousett, who had joined them, said. "I been in his place out yonder, an' I seen 'im take a whole winter's pelts from them Injuns an' give damn near nothin' for 'em—'cept some o' that rotten whiskey."

"Where can I find a drink? We'll talk while I rinse the blood outta my mouth," Gunn cut in.

The corporal stood back and squinted at Gunn. "That all you got to say? You ain't bothered that maybe Bear'll kill you?"

Gunn shrugged. He felt the anger begin to subside, and with that came an infusion of pain. He'd not been aware until now that he'd taken a pretty good beating. "To answer your questions, Corporal, I don't give a damn when or where we meet. I'll kill him next time. I don't even know what that fight was about. Now I'll know the next time I see him."

The corporal pushed Gunn toward the center of the compound. "Get on over there to the horse trough. Wash the blood off'n your face and I'll buy you a drink." He turned to Bavousett. "You too. C'mon."

Gunn ducked his head into the tepid water, scrubbed at his face, and quickly pulled his hands away. He had a cut over his right eye and a split lip. He splashed water on his hair and combed his fingers through it.

Drying his face with his neckerchief, he said, "Let's get that drink."

The corporal escorted them to his barracks, pulled a bottle of rotgut from his knapsack, and handed it to Gunn.

The whiskey was raw. It took Gunn's breath, but he would not hurt the grizzled old man's feelings, so he drank deeply and handed the bottle to Bavousett, who drank and passed it to the corporal. By then Gunn had gotten his breath.

"Much obliged, Corporal. If you'll come with me to the sutler's, I left six bottles of rye for him to keep for me until I went back aboard the *Luella*. I'd like you to have one of them."

"Aw, now, you don't have to do that."

Gunn smiled, and felt that every seam in his face split open when he did. He clapped the old man on the shoulders and said, "Come on. I want you to have it."

Gunn collected his package from the sutler, bought an additional bottle, and handed it to the corporal even though he still protested that Gunn didn't have to do it.

Gunn and Bavousett walked out together.

The thought he'd had earlier about leaving the *Luella* had just about jelled. He turned to Bavousett.

"You going back to the mountains when you leave here?"

"Reckon so. Ain't got nowhere else to go."

"Would you let me ride along?"

"Now, what in the tarnation hell would you want to do that for? You got a good bed on that there boat you're on, an' it'll take you all the way to Benton."

Gunn eyed Bavousett a moment, toyed with the thoughts of telling him about his Indian background, and decided to wait. "Well, old-timer, I reckon I want to see more of the West than some of these towns. I want you to take me along—teach me. I can ride and shoot, but I know nothing about living and making do where it's just me and my gun."

They held to the shade as long as they could, then Bavousett squatted by the side of a building. "Set and let's talk." He took out his pipe and slowly tamped it while eyeing Gunn.

He said, "Gunn, I gotta tell you. Me an' the Sioux—the Lakota 'specially—are pretty good friends—as much friends as they'll allow. But if we get in any trouble, I don't know as I can keep your scalp for you."

"I'll take the chance. You know how to speak Lakota?"

"Yeah. Probably better'n I talk American."

Gunn nodded. "Good. I know some of it, and I want you to teach me so I can talk with them."

"Might not get no chance to do no talkin' if we get that close." He squinted at Gunn. "Where you learn to talk Lakota?"

"I'll tell you about it later. You gonna take me with you? I'll pay you wages." Gunn held his breath waiting for the old man's answers.

Bavousett looked at the ground, scratched little figures in the dirt for so long Gunn wanted to drag an answer from him, and finally slanted a look at Gunn.

"Yeah, I'll take you along, but only 'cause I don't figure you for the tenderfoot you let ever'body b'lieve. We got to buy you an outfit, horse, saddle, bedding—the works. You got any money to speak of?"

"Yeah—some."

"Good. Let's get about it, then."

Gunn depended on Bavousett to pick a good horse for him, and after they bought it, the old man told him the finer points of choosing good horseflesh. They also bought a packhorse.

When they had completed an outfit for Gunn, they bought a few things that Bavousett said he needed. Gunn told him he'd meet him at the fort's gate at daylight, that he had a lot of loose ends to wrap up aboard the *Luella*. He felt the old man's eyes on him as he walked toward the boat.

Back aboard the *Luella*, Gunn went to his room. He had stowed his liquor on the packhorse. He flopped on the bunk, feeling as if his bruises had bruises, and his feet and arms hung like chunks of lead from his beat-up body. He soon fell asleep.

The sun hung low in the west when he awoke. Gunn rolled out of his bunk and splashed water on his face. He had a lot to do if he intended to leave before daylight. He knocked on the bulkhead, hoping Jake was in her cabin. She answered his knock.

When he opened her door, she stared at him a moment and said, "What the hell's fire happened? Looks like you done tangled with a grizzly."

"What it looks like is exactly what it was," Gunn said. "Some filthy bastard wanted a fight, so I gave him what he looked for. A guy called Muldoon—he wouldn't have it any other way."

"Muldoon? A big man, filthy, all mouth?"

"Well, I don't reckon I'd say he was all mouth, but, yeah, that's the one," Gunn said. "Only he backed up most of what his mouth got him into. I tried to apologize, even if I didn't owe him one."

"If it's the trash I'm thinkin' about, you probably ain't seen the last of him. He's a part-time buffalo hunter, but most of the time he runs a trading post over on the Yellowstone River. The Indians leave him alone 'cause he sells 'em rotgut. Next time you see 'im just blow his damned head off. Don't let on that's what you figger on doin'—just do it, or you gonna come out second best."

Jake stood and pushed him to the edge of the bed. "Sit down while I sponge off them cuts."

"Yeah, I already heard about him and the Indians," Gunn said while he held his head so Jake could readily reach his face.

"You win this here fight?"

Gunn nodded.

"Good."

They talked while Jake worked on his cuts. Gunn found himself avoiding his reason for coming to her cabin. He let her baby his face for a while and finally grasped both her wrists.

"Hold up a second, Jake. I have something to tell you. Don't want to say it, but I have to."

Gunn felt her wrists relax in his grip and turned them loose.

She glanced at his hands still in the air, looked from them into his eyes—and turned her back to him. "Damn that buffalo-huntin' Bavousett anyway. He done talked you into headin' out with him—ain't he?"

Although she couldn't see him, Gunn shook his head. "No,

Jake, he didn't talk me into anything. I practically had to beg him to take me."

"Why, Rafe? What the hell's out yonder besides grass, dry water holes, and Injuns like you ain't never seen afore."

Gunn patted the bed beside him. "Come, Jake, sit down. I'll tell you something I should have told you before."

Jake sat stiffly beside him. He didn't know quite where to start, so he started with his mother, father, and him out here on these Dakota Territory plains, their deaths, his being raised by his uncle, and how he had always longed to return to the land of his people—and how he'd finally made his way back.

The longer Gunn talked, the softer Jake felt in his arms. When he finished, Jake leaned into the contour of his body, her arm around his waist. She turned her head so as to look into his eyes.

"Rafe, you know 'your people' will probably blow your arse off before you have a chance to tell them who you are, and what about your goods you figured to sell in Virginia City?"

"I hoped you might take care of that problem for me. Need to see Marsh and tell him these goods are to be managed by you—I'll give you the bill of lading. If I don't show up in Benton in two months, I'd like you to get them to Virginia City before snow flies and set up a store. If I don't show up there in a year, the goods—or money you make from them—belong to you."

Jake stood and pulled the bottle of rye whiskey from her drawer under the washbowl. She filled two water glasses about half-full and handed Gunn one of them. "Knowed I couldn't hold you for long—but I gotta tell you, Rafe Gunn, I wouldn't trade one minute I done had with you for a lifetime with any other man. Let's have a drink and go talk to the captain."

Gunn stared into the amber liquid in his glass and, studying it, knew that if he drank a gallon, it could not wash the lump out of his throat. Jake had taken the news of his leaving just as he'd thought she would. No tears, no asking him to stay, no laying of guilt. He almost changed his mind—but he had come out here to see what this country held for him, and he had to finish what he'd started.

"After we talk with the captain, Rafe, you an' me—we're gonna tear this here bed all to hell 'fore daylight."

CHAPTER
NINE

BAVOUSETT SAT LEANING against the wall. He looked from under his hat brim when Gunn walked up. "Figgered you'd be along about now. Nigh on to first sun. Ready to travel?"

"That's why I'm here," Gunn answered. He sucked in a deep breath of fresh morning air, trying to get the fuzz out of his brain from his night with Jake.

Bavousett had the animals saddled and the packhorse on a lead. They climbed aboard, crossed the river, and had not ridden a mile when the fort dropped from view behind a land swell.

The ocean of grass bent and rippled with the breeze as far as Gunn could see, and the soft whisper of wind through the dry blades sang a song.

"Young'un, you gonna notice I ain't goin' in a straight line. the reason for that is, I done got used to wearin' my hair. Long's we don't stick our danged heads up where they'll show agin the sky, we gonna be harder to see. My druthers is to see other folks 'fore they see me. This way we can sort o' weave our way around the bottoms of these here hills an' keep outta sight."

Gunn nodded.

"'Nother thing—you figger on learnin' to talk Lakota, we ain't gonna talk nothin' but it from here on in. You say somethin' in American, I ain't gonna answer yuh. You don't know how to say it—ask."

They had ridden another hour in silence when Bavousett said, "I'm gonna say this in American so's I know you understand. *I'm in charge.* Ain't no other way we gonna stay alive. When I begin to think you done learned a little—I'll ease

100

up." He cocked his head and slanted Gunn a look out of the corner of his eye. "You get to thinkin' you cain't put up with me—cut out—leave."

Gunn laughed. "Bavousett, I've taken, and given orders. You're in charge. What you want me to do?"

In Lakota, Bavousett said, "Nothin'—for now."

They rode for two days, and the terrain remained unchanged—rolling hills and grass. Gunn's Lakota language was coming back faster than he'd anticipated. Bavousett had complimented him.

The third day Bavousett pointed toward a dark line in the distance. "That there's trees—prob'ly water there too. Don't never pass up the chance to take on water. The animals cain't live without it. But don't never ride up on a water hole less'n you scout it first. Might be some folks done got it staked out an' wouldn't take kindly to sharin'. We gonna get water there, but we gonna be downright careful about it."

They rode most of the afternoon, and the tree line didn't seem to draw closer. Bavousett pulled in close to Gunn. "If they's any Injuns down yonder, I might not get a chance to tell 'em you're friendly before we have to fight—be ready."

Sundown came, and by Gunn's estimate they were still a mile or more from the trees. Bavousett said, "Stay here. Gonna sashay down yonder an' take a look-see. Thought I seen a flicker of light." He dismounted and handed Gunn his horse's reins.

As well adapted as Gunn had become to picking out sounds, the old mountain man just melted into the darkness surrounding him. He deserved his name—"Cat."

Thinking he'd be harder to see, Gunn stepped down from his horse. For what seemed like an eternity he kept his eyes on the area Bavousett had disappeared into. Then from behind him the old man said, "If I'd been a-lookin' to take your hair, you'd be skinheaded now."

Gunn whirled toward him. "Old man, don't scare me like that."

"Gonna have to pay more attention to teachin' you how to move out here—an' how to watch. You gotta learn to see with your eyes, ears, an' nose—an' when those don't work, you gotta trust your feelin's." He took his horse's reins.

"Feelin's can tell you by your hair tingling in the back—or you get a knot 'tween your shoulders. You'll learn, young'un—if'n you live long 'nuff."

"See anything down there?"

Bavousett nodded. "That there Muldoon, the smelly one you had the fight with back at Lincoln, well, him an' five others like 'im are camped down yonder. Couldn't tell what they was talkin' 'bout, but figger they be headin' back to Muldoon's place on the Yellowstone."

"We gonna wait here until they clear out in the morning?"

"Naw. We can circle 'em an' head on out. Know the whereabouts of 'nother water hole west o' here 'bout four hours. We'll camp there."

By the time they had circled Muldoon's camp, Gunn thought that if they had ridden straight to the next water hole, it would have taken only two hours of riding. He tucked that away in his head. He had started analyzing everything Bavousett did and then why he did it that way. He began to understand why the trapper had lived as long as he had.

It took all of the four hours Bavousett had estimated, and after they set up camp, Gunn took the first watch while Bavousett slept. Bavousett explained that he wanted to be the one on watch come daylight.

Gunn heard night animals scurrying about, and one of the horses occasionally blowing, but nothing to disturb him. He had already learned to separate sounds, and to know whether they meant harm.

About three o'clock he touched Bavousett on the shoulder, and when he stood, Gunn lay down and went to sleep.

He would have sworn he hadn't closed his eyes when Bavousett whispered, "Get your rifle an' lay just below the creek bank."

Without a word he took station as Bavousett directed. Then, not too far out, he heard the soft thud and swish of horses' hooves in the dry grass.

"I'll do the talkin'," Bavousett said.

Gunn nodded.

The horses drew close enough for Gunn to see six riders skylined against the still-dark sky.

"What you ridin' so early for, Muldoon? You got no business in our camp, so keep ridin'," Bavousett said.

"You turnin' riders away from a water hole, Bavousett? Ain't had water for nigh on to three days now."

"You're a lyin' bastard, Muldoon. I seen yuh camped back yonder."

Muldoon sank spurs into his horse, yelled, and rode straight at the camp.

Gunn fired and emptied a saddle. Fire lanced at him from one of the raiders' weapons. Bavousett's rifle spoke at the same time, and another man fell. Gunn swung his rifle to fire again, but the remaining four split—two right and two left. They rode down each side of the camp, into the creek bed, and up the opposite bank.

"They ain't through yet—just hold your fire. They gonna try to sneak up on us next time, so watch sharp."

Gunn nodded, knowing that Bavousett couldn't see him.

Hardly daring to breathe, Gunn strained his eyes to pick out shadows that might show him one of the men. The trees stood ghostly in the dark, and Gunn gaged from them how a man would differ from his surroundings. Finally, less than ten feet in front of him, he saw a shape slithering toward him. He pointed his rifle and squeezed the trigger. All he got was a sharp metallic click. Misfire. Bavousett's rifle roared almost in Gunn's ear.

Gunn's hand swept for the back of his belt, pulling his bowie knife. He launched himself over the bank and closed with the man he'd drawn a bead on. He swung his blade and felt it bite into flesh.

Gunn pulled his knife free and spun to look for another of their attackers. He should have made sure he'd finished the man. He felt a blow across the backs of his legs. He twisted in time to have the man land straddling him. A knife plunged toward his chest. Gunn swung his bowie up and caught the descending blade against the hand guard of his own knife.

He rolled, trying to throw the stinking hulk from him. Now they both lay on their sides facing each other. With his left hand, Gunn grabbed the knife hand of the man and twisted—at the same time trying to get room to swing his own blade.

Straining to keep the knife from his throat, he pushed against the dank earth with his own knife hand. He finally flipped to his knees. He swung his bowie. It found its mark. The man grunted, dropped his knife, and clawed at his gut, trying to grasp Gunn's knife handle to pull the blade from his bowels. Gunn saved him the trouble—he jerked his knife free and pushed it twice more into the man before letting him fall.

Gunn spun, balanced on his toes, to face another adversary—there was none. Bavousett stood over a body, a dripping string of hair in his hand. "Other two run," Bavousett said. He motioned toward the man Gunn had just pulled his knife from. "Take his hair."

Gunn's stomach tightened and turned over. He opened his mouth to argue, then closed it, his jaw muscles tight. If Bavousett said take the man's hair, he must have a reason.

Gunn walked to the stinking, sour-smelling hulk and kneeled at his head. He twisted his hand in the greasy hair and placed his bowie against the back of the skull. Before pulling the blade around, Gunn looked into the sightless eyes staring at him— then he pulled his knife around, reached to the back of the man's head, dug his fingers through the slit to the slick skull, and snapped the scalp free.

"Looks like you done that afore," Bavousett said.

Gunn swallowed, trying to clear his throat of the bitter bile that threatened to come up and embarrass him. "First one," he muttered.

"Next one'll be easier," Bavousett said and pointed to the man Gunn had just scalped. "You done good work with that'un, but I seen ya stick 'im and turn your back—lookin' fer somethin' else to fight." Bavousett tied the scalp he'd taken to his saddle horn and turned back to Gunn. "Tell ya somethin', boy, even if there's ten men you're tryin' to fight, be damned sure the one ya turn yore back on ain't in no position to do ye further harm." Then, in his first show of caring, Bavousett patted Gunn's shoulder, and said, "Good work, boy."

"We gonna bury these two?" Gunn asked.

"Cain't take time, son. We gonna water the horses, fill our

canteens, bile a pot o' coffee—then put distance 'tween us an' this here place."

While the coffee boiled, Gunn held his watch close to the low-glowing coals, and saw that it was four-thirty. He sighed, staring ahead at a fourteen- or fifteen-hour day.

Noon pushed up on them before Bavousett glanced at Gunn and said, "Reckon you're a-wonderin' why I had you take that scalp back yonder." Without waiting for Gunn to reply, he continued. "We come up on a band o' Oglala, reckon it's gonna be a lot easier fer them to believe we're friendly if they see white man scalps hangin' from our saddles. Need all the help we can get."

"Thought you said they were friendly toward you."

"Did—but with them folks it don't hurt to reestablish yore intentions ever time you meet 'em." Bavousett cast a questioning glance at Gunn. "When you gonna tell me the reason you wanted me to bring you out here, teach you, an' maybe make you acquainted with the Sioux?"

Gunn stared a long few moments at the old man, nodded, and said, "All right. Reckon I can tell you. Bavousett, I look like a full-blooded white man. I'm not. My father was Scot; my mother, Singing Stars, was Oglala. Don't know where I fit in and I've got to find out. If I don't live with them, learn their ways, I don't know that I could ever make any kind of judgment where I belong."

Bavousett stared ahead. For the longest time he didn't say anything, then he slanted a glance across his shoulder at Gunn. "Been studyin' what you told me, son. It's a hard question you done put to yoreself. You might find you can fit into either of them. The Indian is a lot more tolerant than the white man. If he knows you're his friend, he won't judge you by the color of yore skin—the white man, now, he's cut from a different bolt o' cloth. Long's he knows you're part-Injun, no matter yore skin is white as them little clouds up yonder, he's gonna figure you for all Injun—ain't never gonna trust you."

In the weeks ahead Gunn found that he'd opened the door for a lot of conversation between them. The old mountain man might ride a full day, sometimes two, then he'd pose another problem, or a solution to one they'd discussed a few days before.

Bavousett had almost no education, but Gunn soon realized that he'd never come in contact with a sharper mind—and the only time he had ever seen Bavousett make a snap judgment was in a fight.

Every day Gunn learned more about the land, the grasses, the streams he rode across. Bavousett taught him about the Oglalas.

Although they traveled mostly in a westerly direction, Gunn noticed that they slanted to the south when the terrain permitted. Three weeks and two days after leaving Fort Lincoln, Bavousett stopped, dismounted, and studied some pony tracks—the first they'd seen since running Muldoon. "Injuns," he grunted. "Figured we'd be seein' some purty soon."

A chill crawled up Gunn's spine. "We gonna follow them?"

"They're travelin' the same direction we are. Looks like they ain't in no hurry, so figger we'll catch 'em by sundown tomorrow."

He was finally going to meet his people. A mixture of fear for what he was going to discover and an almost unbridled urge to hurry tightened his throat. His feelings must have shown, because Bavousett said, "Don't git too happy 'bout that, young'un. We might have a fight on our hands, an' you damn well better be ready to fight—but don't kill 'less'n you have to."

"I'll fight," Gunn said. Then he thought that at least he would get a chance to meet his real people—not the whiskey-soaked kind he'd seen in Lincoln.

Bavousett picked up the pace a little, and kept a close eye on the trail. He didn't alter their course at all from the one the Indians took.

Sweat streaming down his face and between his shoulders, Gunn spit what he figured was half dust.

Bavousett glanced at the sun and said out of the corner of his mouth, "'Bout three o'clock. Reckoned we'd be comin' up on 'em 'bout now. Don't look around, don't do nothin' unusual. That there war party is all around us. They gonna ride down on us yellin' like monsters from hell—*don't make a move for a weapon*."

The knot between Gunn's shoulders deepened. He had felt it

for some time now, but thought it was tiredness. Now he knew better. He muttered, "Hope you know what you're doin'."

"If I don't, we gonna be deader'n hell in a few minutes. It don't make no difference if we don't take a few o' them with us."

They had not ridden another ten feet when Bavousett's prediction came true. Gunn took his cue from the old trapper. He crossed his hands on the saddle horn and stared at the screaming demons, trying to lock gazes with each as they came close.

They rode in. Each warrior touched Gunn and Bavousett on the shoulder with his coup stick—all but one. He sat his pony to the side of the melee. Abruptly, he held his lance high and yelled, "Enough."

Out of the side of his mouth, Bavousett said, "That's Curly; some call 'im Crazy Horse. He'll be a great war chief someday."

Gunn heard, but he stared unblinking at Curly.

"Mountain Cat, I know you. You are a warrior to be honored as a friend—or enemy. But I do not know this pale one sitting his horse next to you. He does not show fear. He makes no move for his weapons. I think he wishes to test Crazy Horse."

Crazy Horse's band bunched close to Gunn and Bavousett. Their odor, wild and smoky, sat strong in Gunn's nostrils.

Gunn didn't have long to wait for Crazy Horse's explanation of "test." The lithe, long-muscled Indian reached for his knife and jerked it from its sheath. Gunn made no effort to explain that he was a brother. He reached for his bowie knife.

Crazy Horse slid off the side of his pony, and Gunn did the same. They circled each other. Gunn felt the Indian's eyes stabbing into his own. He wanted to yell that he was also of Lakota blood, but feared it would be taken as a sign of weakness. He circled, weaving his knife out in front of him, looking for an opening.

Bavousett had said, don't kill. To hell with that; he would kill if he had to.

His dark skin a blur of motion, Crazy Horse rushed, slicing across and back. Gunn stepped back and sucked in his gut. The Indian's blade missed by scant fractions of an inch. Gunn's knife stabbed straight out and up. He missed, and charged past the young warrior while throwing his arm up and forcing his opponent's knife arm over his shoulder.

Gunn twisted and spun on the balls of his feet, hoping for his foe to have an unguarded side. Sweat ran into his eyes. He blinked, trying to see better. The Lakota had been as fast on his feet. He stood facing Gunn, his knife weaving like a serpent.

Again they circled, searching for an opening. The Indian pushed off on his right foot and came at Gunn again. Gunn jumped back and swung his knife. It brought blood down the length of Curly's arm—only a scratch. Gunn rushed, trying to get in another swipe before the Indian could get set again. A searing streak shot down his own arm. He backed off, his gaze never breaking from the flat, emotionless stare of the leader.

Then some silent signal triggered them, and they ran at each other, knives held low for a stabbing motion. Crazy Horse thrust. Gunn caught the blade against his own, twisted and threw the Indian's knife from his hand. The warrior then made the only sound since the fight started. He said a word in Lakota that Gunn had not heard. It must have been a curse.

Crazy Horse dived for his weapon. Gunn got there first and kicked the knife farther away.

The warrior slid to a stop, straightened, and stared at Gunn. No fear, no anger showed in his eyes, but the flat, emotionless glaze was gone. Respect had replaced it.

The fight could end here by counting coup on Crazy Horse—or killing him. Gunn didn't want it either way.

He straightened and tossed his own knife toward Crazy Horse's. He held his arms slightly extended from his side, hands open in an invitation to continue the fight hand to hand.

A slight smile touched the corners of Crazy Horse's lips. He nodded slightly—and came at Gunn again. Gunn outweighed Curly by a good fifty pounds. He felt like a bully.

He grabbed the Indian's arm and threw him over his hip. Crazy Horse landed on his back, scrambled to his feet, and rushed. Gunn threw him again.

Wary now, the thin, almost delicate-looking warrior stood, walked on the balls of his feet toward Gunn, ducked abruptly, and dived at Gunn's feet.

The tackle drove Gunn backward. He landed on his rump, rolled, and came to his knees before the Indian landed on him.

Squirming in the grass, they hit, bit, grabbed for any hold they could get on each other. They grunted, sweated, slipped against each other's sweat—and strained for advantage.

The young warrior was slim—but his muscles were like wire. Gunn couldn't believe such strength existed in one this much smaller than him.

Trying for a hold on the other was impossible due to the blood and sweat that coated their bodies.

Gunn tried a trick. He relaxed momentarily, then abruptly rolled to his knees when Crazy Horse hurled his body into the space Gunn had occupied only a moment before. Gunn fell on top of the exhausted Lakota—and pinned him tightly to the earth.

"Crazy Horse, I am Lakota. My mother was Singing Stars, an Oglala. I am your friend," Gunn pushed the words past short, jerky gasps.

Crazy Horse relaxed under Gunn. Crawling free of him, Gunn knelt on his knees.

Crazy Horse rolled over and faced him. "No," he said, and took Gunn's wounded arm in his hands and pressed Gunn's wound to his own, mixing their blood. "Not only friend—now brother. When the sun is down, and we sit by our fire, we will smoke the sacred pipe binding us together."

Blood-chilling yells went up around them. The two weary warriors stood and picked up their knives.

CHAPTER
TEN

THE WARRIORS CROWDED close to Crazy Horse and Gunn. If Gunn had not seen their smiles, he would have sworn they meant to cripple him with the pounding he took on his back. They apparently didn't care who had won the fight—both had fought well.

"Why are you out here in the land of the Lakota with Mountain Cat, brother?" Crazy Horse asked.

"I asked him to take me to my people," Gunn answered, then smiled. "He warned me you might not accept me as an Oglala. He said you might kill me before I could tell you."

"You have found us. What do you wish of us?" While talking, Crazy Horse gestured for his men to mount. Gunn climbed back on his horse and fell in beside his blood brother. Bavousett drew his horse to Gunn's other side.

Gunn studied his horse's ears while wondering how to answer Crazy Horse's question, then decided to tell him the truth. "I have not lived as an Oglala since I was a small boy. I do not know my people, and I must know them to fill the empty place in my heart. I would live as one of you, learn your ways, and—if you are willing—again become an Oglala. My Oglala name is Wambli Sapa—now I would like to earn it."

A slight smile touched Crazy Horse's lips. "It is not whether *we* are willing," Crazy Horse said. "It is whether *you* are willing. Here, in our land, is cold, often hunger. Now there are many buffalo, but the white man kills them for only the hide and tongue. Soon there will be only a few, and Lakota stomachs will be empty."

"I have seen what the white man is doing to our brothers with whiskey and bad promises," Gunn replied. "And I can believe that the killing of the buffalo to cause hunger might be a cruel but well-planned maneuver."

They rode until the sun hung low in the west before coming to a small stream. Crazy Horse motioned to make camp.

Gunn noticed how efficiently Curly's band went about setting up camp. They all seemed to know what to do, from collecting firewood to starting the fire. A warrior Gunn had not seen before rode in and dropped a deer carcass by the fire. Others set about skinning and gutting it. Occasionally a few words passed between the warriors. When finally a haunch of venison hung over the fire, Curly sat by Gunn and Bavousett.

"Mountain Cat, will you ride far with us?"

"Well, Curly, I done been givin' that a bit of thought. Figgered to stay with Black Eagle here awhile. He might need a body to take care o' him—rock 'im to sleep and such. He ain't much, but I done took a likin' to 'im."

Crazy Horse and Bavousett concentrated on poking at a coal at the side of the fire, waiting for Gunn to take the bait. Instead he nodded. "Yep, Curly, I've gotten used to this smelly old goat tucking me—"

"Why, gosh dang ye. I done splashed water on me ever' time you did. If I smell, so do ye."

Gunn laughed, right along with Curly, who said, "Mountain Cat, Black Eagle shoots his arrows from a tight string."

Bavousett stared at Gunn a moment, then a smile wrinkled his face. "Gosh dang it, boy, reckon I'm gonna be a mite careful 'bout proddin' ye. You got a tongue sharp as a bowie knife." He looked at Crazy Horse. "You ain't told me where you be headin'."

"Wherever the Crow are," Crazy Horse answered. "It is said at every Lakota fire that the Crow have too many horses. I have with me some young warriors who have too few. We think the dog's dung Crows should share."

"Yeah, an' I figger ye're gonna ask 'em real nice to share a few pieces of hair with you too."

Crazy Horse looked at Bavousett across his shoulder and nodded. "They may even have a few young women who want to live among The People."

"You shore are makin' it hard fer me to decide to ride on, Curly."

Crazy Horse tested the air, stood, and went to the fire. He carved off a hunk of venison and again sat. That seemed to be the signal for the others to help themselves.

The mouth-watering aroma wafting from the sizzling meat had about driven Gunn to forget his manners. When the members of the band headed for the fire, Gunn and Bavousett were right there with them. They had not finished eating when two more warriors rode into camp and silently went to the fire to help themselves.

Gunn shot a questioning look at Bavousett.

The old mountain man finished chewing before answering. He swallowed, nodded, and said, "Scouts. They done made sure they ain't nobody gonna per-vent us from gittin' a night's sleep."

As soon as the sun bedded down, the small band of men put the fire out and turned in.

The next morning their course slanted west-southwest. Bavousett grinned at Gunn. "You wantta git to know your people—well, you're 'bout to. We be headin' straight for Crow country. If my reckon is right, we gonna camp on Fallon Crick tonight." He pushed his hat to the back of his head and squinted into the distance. "Ain't heered of no Crow this far east—but they's always a chance."

True to Bavousett's prediction they camped on Fallon Creek. They had a fire also, which told Gunn that Crazy Horse was not worried about any hostiles—yet. In this camp Gunn carved himself out a set of chores. He helped with the wood. He brought water from the creek and made coffee even though Bavousett told him most Indians didn't like coffee. They drank it, though, when they found out he had sugar to go in it. Gunn couldn't believe the amount of sugar they used.

"Figger they like a little coffee in their sugar?"

Gunn shrugged. "When it's gone, it's gone."

Crazy Horse called his warriors around him. He included Gunn and Bavousett. "We will try to avoid meeting our enemy between here and their big camp. It is better that we are not expected. They are many and we are few." He toyed with a twig, then tossed it toward the fire. "If we encounter a small band, none of them are to get away to warn the others." He made a sharp chopping motion with his right hand. "I have spoken."

They broke into bunches of two or three, and all talked of the impending raid. Gunn tried and eventually succeeded in getting Crazy Horse alone. "Curly, you know I've never been on a raid before. Why do you trust me to do the right thing?"

Crazy Horse studied him a long moment. "Wambli Sapa, I have fought you. You are a brave warrior. There are many things you don't know yet. I will teach you. On this raid I will not have you doing anything that could jeopardize our success." He twitched his lips toward Gunn's saddle. Gunn had learned that this was the way the Lakota pointed. "You have scalp hanging from your saddle horn, a white man's scalp. When we get back to our main camp, I want to hear about that fight."

Satisfied that he wouldn't be given a job that he might do poorly, Gunn went to his blankets and turned in.

He lay awake, thinking of the distance—not in miles, but in beliefs, tradition, training—that this life was from the way he had been reared. Bavousett had taught him a lot. That he had much more to learn he knew. He had practiced sneaking up on the Mountain Cat and had gotten very good at it—but the few times he had failed would have cost him his life if Bavousett had been an enemy. He had to get better. He had learned to stalk game—always from downwind. Making clothing from hides came easy—all sailors knew how to sew.

He lay there studying the sky. It seemed to hang within reach of his hands, yet was infinitely larger than anything he had seen since coming ashore. The sky at sea was like this. Abruptly it came to him that he unconsciously tested the air every so often for subtle scents that might be foreign. He did it now, deliberately, picking out the smell of horses, the delicate scent of crushed grass where he lay, and an even fainter scent of some faraway pines. And there was the ever-present pungent odor of smoke.

He went to sleep thinking that he had come far since arriving in New Orleans. This brought his thoughts to Eula. She was there when he went to sleep, and she crept into his dreams.

The next day they crossed the Powder River and camped on the Tongue between the Pumkin and the Yellowstone. They had no fire that night. Jerky served for their supper. The usual banter between the warriors was muted to almost a whisper. Gunn's blood pumped faster. He seemed more alive—and the senses he'd thought were finely honed took on a larger dimension; even his sight sharpened. So this is how it is, he thought, knowing he was ready for whatever came.

The scouts were late in returning, and when they slipped into camp, Gunn heard them and caught a faint whiff of their odor. Even as early as last night, he thought, he wouldn't have detected them. He watched as they went to Crazy Horse and squatted at his side.

Whatever they said, Crazy Horse must have thought it could wait until morning, because he waved them to their blankets and turned on his side to sleep.

The next morning, Crazy Horse motioned them for a talk. "Gray Wolf and Sitting Beaver have found the hated Crows encamped on the Greasy Grass," he said. "They have with them women and children. We will take horses first. Black Eagle will stay with our horses, and we will bring our new possessions to him. When he has all the horses, he will yell and wake their camp. They will chase him."

He pointed to eight warriors. "Leave your horses with Wambli Sapa. Stay behind and keep them from catching him. The rest of us will keep our horses and wait outside their camp until they chase Black Eagle, then we will go in and take the women we want. Kill those who are not worthy to be our slaves."

Crazy Horse looked at a tall warrior standing on the outskirts of the ring. "Two Buffalo, you will take the women who are having their moon period. There should not be old ones among them. Their tepee will be separate from the others."

That morning they crossed the Rosebud, watered their horses, and rode on. An hour before sunset Crazy Horse called a halt. "We wait here until dark."

Gunn knew they must be close to the Greasy Grass River. Bavousett had told him that that was the Indian name for the Little Bighorn.

The warriors slid off their horses and sat in the short grass. Some sharpened their knives, some took the opportunity to walk off to the side to relieve themselves, a few went to sleep.

Crazy Horse sent three men to keep watch. This time they went afoot. Gunn studied all of them and could not detect nervous actions from any.

He rubbed the back of his neck to relieve the tightness—but could do nothing about the crawly feeling in the pit of his stomach.

Night slipped in on them with changing colors, from rose, to orange, to purple—and then the purple faded to a deep velvety black. Crazy Horse held them until, by Gunn's estimate, about ten o'clock. They mounted and rode slowly, quietly, with only the swish of the grass to tell of their coming. Finally Crazy Horse motioned a halt.

Without words each warrior assigned to protect Gunn's rear led his horse to Gunn, gave him the halter, turned, and joined up with Crazy Horse.

When the night swallowed them, Gunn had never felt so alone. The scurrying of night creatures seemed loud. Many of the night sounds had quieted, and Gunn knew his presence was the cause of it.

He stood close to his horse and rubbed its neck, needing the feel of being with something alive. Crazy Horse had not given him the task of minding the horses to keep him from danger. He thought about that and realized his job might be the most dangerous of all—a few of the Crow were sure to reach him.

Bavousett had explained that the horses would stay pretty closely bunched, and for Gunn to get them started back toward the Rosebud—then look to his back. They could round up the horses the next day.

Time stood still. It seemed to Gunn that the war party had been gone forever. He began to imagine that things had gone wrong, that the Crow had been lying in wait for the Lakota. He shook his head. If anything had gone wrong, all hell would have broken loose—there would have been noise, a lot of it, shots, shouts, screams. As soon as he realized that he was just borrowing trouble, the horses came—there must have been fifty of them, and they made very little noise, a lot less than Gunn thought they would have—and behind them were Crazy Horse's band. They turned the horses over to him.

Gunn got the cavvy headed northeast, turned his face to the heavens, and cut loose with a scream so savage that he wondered if it came from his throat. He stayed behind them, yelling every so often to be sure they stayed on the run—then he turned back.

In mid-turn his horse bowled over a warrior. At the same time, another Indian jumped a-straddle his pony's rump. Gunn threw himself backward into the Crow and twisted to grab him around the waist.

They fell. Gunn grabbed for his knife. He hit the ground, rolled, and came to his feet. The Crow closed with him— wrapped his arms around Gunn's shoulders. His musky smoke smell strong in Gunn's nostrils, Gunn tried to break the Indian's hold. They strained, grunted—each trying to get in a position to use his knife. Gunn twisted free and swung his blade. He felt it bite into flesh—but the warrior still came at him. Gunn feinted to the left, jumped right, and swung again. This time he made a good cut. His assailant's head hung loosely to the side, held to his shoulders by only one ropy muscle. Pounding feet came at him from another direction.

Gunn dropped to his stomach and caught his enemy's feet. The Crow crashed to the ground. Gunn came to his knees and dived on top of him. His knife hit the warrior in his chest before Gunn's body did.

Gunn rolled to his knees, looking for another to fight. A shadowy figure on horseback came out of the darkness. Gunn's right hand swept toward his holster.

"It is me, your brother. Do not fire." Crazy Horse's voice cut through the night.

Gunn thumbed the thong back over the hammer of his Colt. "Curly, you better thank Wakan Tanka that the thong held my pistol in its holster."

Gunn turned his attention from Crazy Horse to the two men he had killed, with great care he ran his knife around their heads, and with each he snapped the hair loose from the gleaming white skull. These were his first Crow Scalps, and he wanted every strand of them.

When he held the last one in his hands he turned toward Crazy Horse. "Good raid?"

"Yes." Crazy Horse said. "My warriors are bringing the women, about as many as the fingers of both hands, and twice that many scalps. How many horses came to you?"

Gunn said, "All the fingers of both hands on five men is about how many horses I figure we got tonight."

"*That* I thank Wakan Tanka for. And *we* didn't lose a warrior."

When the members of the band gathered about Crazy Horse with the spoils of the raid, he told them they would rest, and in the morning gather the horse herd. Then, he said, they would go back as far as the Rosebud before making camp. Gunn gaged the time as about five o'clock. He was surprised at the lack of jubilation over their success—but then, he thought, it had been a long day.

Most of the warriors sat or lay in the grass, and Gunn followed suit. He wanted to nod off, catch a short nap, but every joint in his body ached. When the Crow warrior ripped him off his horse, the fall had jarred his hips and shoulders so that they now seemed to be each a separate point of hell. He squelched a groan and forced his thoughts into the night's events. He wondered what he would have to do to become a Lakota warrior—maybe he was one now. He had met the enemy—and won. He had two pieces of hair to prove it. The way he felt now, he thought, he was not going to push it.

He thought of Jake and wished he could reach out and touch her. But he went to sleep thinking of Eula.

CHAPTER
ELEVEN

EULA STOOD AT the river's edge and watched another side-wheeler churn its way out of sight. Her shoulders slumped, and she angrily brushed a tear from her cheek.

Rafe Gunn, she thought, you're my man—the land, another woman, nothing is going to take you from me. She jerked her arm up and fired four shots as fast as she could trigger them at an old snag drifting by.

"Whoa now, young'un. I think you killed whatever you fired at," her father said. He walked up, put his arm around her shoulders, and handed her a glass of iced tea. His look soft, showing all the love a father could have for a daughter. "You're thinking of Rafe. Honey, he's gone. He's searching that world he has never known. He may have even left the boat somewhere upriver. I'm sure when he gets where he can write, he will."

"Papa, you're going to tell me I'm only fifteen, almost sixteen—and that I'll have many beaus court me, and . . . and I'll soon forget Rafe. I *know* I'm young, but, Papa, I went through the war. I've seen men die—I've even helped nurse them, young though I was. I grew up pretty fast during those years, Papa.

"I'm going to give Rafe one year to come for me. If he doesn't come by then, I'm going to find him."

Paul studied her face a long moment. "Eula, I promise you that if that time comes, I'll go with you. We'll find him somewhere. You'll be almost seventeen then. If you still feel the same, we'll find him—but first I insist that you have some communication with him. Write him care of Fort Benton, that's where he said he was going. See how he thinks. You know, honey, he may not feel the same way you do. To him you may still be a child."

Eula felt her lips tremble as another tear threatened to shame her. "Papa, you saw how I kissed him goody-bye. He won't forget that kiss—or of the feel of me in his arms. I made certain of that, and I know how he responded. He doesn't think of me as a child—and the longer we're apart, the more of a woman I'll become in his thoughts. He may not write for a long time—but I'll wait."

Paul squeezed her shoulders. "A man doesn't stand a chance when a woman sets her cap for him."

"You can bet your next cane crop on that, Papa."

She put her revolver back in her purse and turned toward the house. "C'mon. I'm hungry as a field hand. Let's see what Mama Jory planned for us."

Days ran into weeks, and weeks into months. Eula still had no letters from Rafe, yet every day, regardless of the weather, she walked to the river's edge and watched the swirling brown waters inexorably make their way to the gulf. Her belief that Rafe would someday write had not waned. She made excuses: he had found a gold mine and was busy working it, or he was hurt—or he had gone to his people and didn't intend to return to the white man's world.

If he has done that, she thought, I'll live that life with him. Nothing her father said diminished her resolve.

Eula walked slowly to the house from her daily ritual. A cold rain tried to creep past the protection of her coat. She shivered and lengthened her stride. On the veranda she removed her hat and shook water from it before going inside. Mama Jory stood there with a blanket to wrap around her.

"Lordy, child, you gonna catch yo death of the miseries. That man you been mooning over for so long, if he ever shows up heah, I gonna bust his haid for treatin' you like this." She peeled Eula's coat off and wrapped the blanket tightly about her.

"Mama Jory, Rafe isn't to blame. I've been writing him at least twice a month since he left, and I don't even know whether he has gotten any of my letters—but I'm going to keep writing. They'll catch up with him some day."

Mama Jory stared at Eula a moment, shook her head, and

went toward the kitchen, which stood separate from the house. Paul's voice, from behind Eula, said, "If Rafe could see the woman you've become, he'd crawl on his hands and knees to reach you." He handed her a hot buttered rum, saying, "Drink this. It'll knock the chill out of your bones." He put his arms around her shoulders and guided her to the parlor. "Here, sit in front of the fire."

Eula sat, holding the drink clasped in both hands to warm them. Paul took a chair next to her. "I've been thinking," he said, "when summer comes and the crops are sold, you and I are catching a boat to Fort Benton whether you've heard from Rafe or not. I can't stand to see you growing more drawn every day."

Eula jumped from her chair, spilling her drink, and wrapped her arms around her father's neck. "Oh, Papa, thank you. We may not find him—but at least we'll be trying. And by then you may be right. I may not want him—but I think I'll not change."

"Honey, we would have gone before now, but I had to see if you'd outgrow this. I thought it might be infatuation for a long time. Rafe *is* a good-looking devil. He seems the kind of man who would care well for his woman. Now I'm convinced you'll never turn loose." He nodded, "Rafe's your man."

Crazy Horse sat across the fire from Gunn, studying the smoke drifting toward the hole in the top of the tepee. Gunn waited, knowing that his friend would soon turn his attention back to him. While waiting, he thought about what he wanted to propose.

Crazy Horse lowered his gaze and looked directly at Gunn. "All right, Wambli Sapa, besides wanting to get in out of the snow, you have another reason for wanting to talk."

Gunn allowed himself a faint smile. He had learned that fooling Crazy Horse was a hopeless task. He nodded. "Curly, Mountain Cat tells me that where the Stillwater runs into the Yellowstone, there's a trading post. It's run by a white eye by the name of Muldoon."

Crazy Horse nodded. "He sells the Lakota long guns and rotten whiskey."

"Yes, and our people always get cheated. Why do you allow him to stay there—unharmed?"

Crazy Horse shrugged. "He does not harm the buffalo. He does not take up much land—and we need rifles."

"Curly, he doesn't just cheat the Lakota; he cheats all of the Teton Sioux. And he is taking something much more precious from you than pelts—he's taking your warriors from you."

"He has none of my warriors."

"Curly, he doesn't have to have them there with him. He's robbing them of their desire to fight—they trade that off for the rotgut he sells them."

Crazy Horse's eyes sharpened. He stood and walked clockwise around the tepee, then again sat cross-legged across the fire from Gunn.

"Wambli Sapa, since you came to us, you have taken many Crow scalps, taken many Crow horses, and captured young women. You are a warrior. But you only have two white-eye scalps on your lodge pole. Why do you now want to make war on the whites?"

Gunn stared at the fire, wishing he had one of the fine Havana cigars he'd sent upriver with Jake. Before answering, he pulled his bowie knife and honed it carefully on a piece of fine-grained sandstone. He wondered if he wanted to get rid of Muldoon because of the unprovoked fight at Fork Lincoln, and again the sneak attack on his and Bavousett's camp. He admitted that that might be part of his reason, but what he couldn't get out of his mind was the sodden, pitiful state he'd seen once proud warriors reduced to because of Muldoon's greed.

He tested the edge of his knife on the flat of his thumb, ran it down the hair on his arm, and noted that it shaved smooth. Gunn shifted his eyes to look into Crazy Horse's. "My brother, I want you to believe this: Muldoon is a much worse enemy of our people than the Crow. He is like the white man's sickness we call small pox. He has created a need among our people for things he can give us, and he exacts an extremely high price for it. We must rid our lands of him and his kind."

Crazy Horse's eyes bored into Gunn's. After seconds in which Gunn could almost visualize the workings of the war chief's mind, he nodded. "The warriors will follow you. I will stay here. Choose the men you want."

Gunn felt as men must feel when their king has tapped them on the shoulder and dubbed them knight. This trust Crazy Horse had just shown him was tantamount to being selected for one of the secret warrior societies.

Gunn stood. "We leave in the morning." Without further conversation he left the tepee.

He spent the remainder of the afternoon going from one tepee to another. He selected men carefully, wanting only the best. When the gray, snow-driven clouds darkened, Gunn had ten men he felt would follow him wherever he led. He then went to the tepee he shared with Bavousett.

"Where the hell you been?" The old mountain man asked. "You done let yore supper git cold—an' I ain't gonna het it up fer ye."

Gunn suppressed a smile. "Didn't ask you to, you cantankerous old goat." He placed the kettle close to the fire and said, "I've been putting together my own war party. Crazy Horse said I could take my pick."

"Pick fer what? Ain't no self-respectin' Injun gonna go out in this here weather an' fight nobody."

Gunn went about gathering his trail gear and packing it into a bedroll. "Didn't ask you." He saved readying his rifle and pistols until later.

Bavousett watched the preparation from under shaggy eyebrows. "Well—I gotta say you shore enough act like you gonna fight somebody, less'n of course you're fixin' to leave this here comfortable home we got for ourselves."

Gunn glanced at the stew kettle he'd put close to the fire. Steam wafted lazily across its surface. He squatted and ladled himself a helping. "Yeah," he said, "I'm leaving—but only for a few days. Crazy Horse is letting me take a party out to wipe Muldoon's trading post off the face of this territory. I already picked my men."

Bavousett stood and paced back and forth a few times, then turned on Gunn, his eyes spitting fire. "Ain't I good 'nuff to travel with you? Ain't I done showed you how to do nigh onto ever dang thing you need to know? Ain't I wet-nursed you through yore city slicker ig'orance? Now here you go an' set up a war party an' you ain't gonna let me go."

"Didn't figure you'd want to get out in this cold. Figured you'd want to stay by a nice warm fire while I was dumb enough to go out there and freeze my gonads off." Gunn stopped tying his blanket and looked directly at Bavousett. "You saying you will go with me?"

"Go with you—go with you?" Bavousett said, his voice rising with each word. "Why, dang it, if you don't let me go, I'll follow along behind like a whipped pup. Dang tootin' I'm goin'. Pshaw. This here weather's like spring thaw—ain't gonna slow me down one dang bit."

"We leave first thing in the morning." Gunn chewed a large chunk of buffalo jerky that the stew had failed to soften, then said, "You willing to take orders from me on this trip?"

"Shore I'll take orders from you. You done come to be a purty good warrior—course they's still a many o' thing I could learn ye. But reckon if ye're about to mess things up, you might listen to me."

"Old man, I won't ever stop listening to you. You've probably forgotten more about this country than I'll ever learn. When we draw close to Muldoon's place, I want you to sketch me a map of the layout." Gunn sat and cleaned and oiled his weapons. Finished with that, he turned into his robes, but sleep did not come easily. He found himself thinking more and more of Eula than of Jake—and he felt guilty for it.

True to her word, Jake had not tied any strings to what they had together. His thoughts shifted to Eula. She would be well into her sixteenth year, and as spunky and beautiful as he knew she must be, there was every chance that one of the gay blades of New Orleans had claimed her. That thought caused his chest to tighten. He clenched his fists, then realized that he had no claim on her. He had never said anything to her to suggest that he wanted more than friendship from her. Too, she might not want him—or he might not have the feeling for her he thought he did. Finally he pulled the buffalo robe tight around him and went to sleep.

When he stuck his head outside the next morning, snow was falling, and it must have been falling most of the night. Gunn guessed that the ground had about a six-inch blanket. Through the heavy flakes the acrid smell of smoke wafted past, telling him he was not one of the first out of his warm robes.

He drew his head back in and saw that Bavousett had stirred from his cocoon and was fixing breakfast.

By mind-mourning Gunn and his war party were several miles from the encampment. Despite the fact that the Sioux did not like to fight once they had gone into winter camp, Gunn heard not one warrior grumble about the conditions. They all wore buffalo coats, leggings, and had their heads tightly bundled in furs.

The snow stopped after the second day, but the hard freeze that gripped the land didn't abate. The warriors and horses plodded on. They kept their morale up by joshing about who would take the most scalps and rifles. Gunn had already told them he intended to destroy all of the whiskey in the post.

The sixth night, Gunn called his men around him to lay out his plan. "No war paint. They will have more men than we do, so we will go into the post five at a time. Mountain Cat and I will go in last. Muldoon knows us and we don't want him warned. Big Beaver, go to the counter and ask for whiskey. I think all in there will be looking at you. While that's going on, Mountain Cat and I will slip in. Carry your weapons under your robes—in your hands. When I fire, you all start firing. *Do not set fire to anything until we have a chance to take what we want.* We'll use their horses to pack what we take."

Gunn looked at Bavousett. "You figure there will be any men there that don't need killing?"

Bavousett shook his head. "Them kind'll be holed up in their cabins with their women—they got better sense than some I know, who goes ridin' round the country in weather what ain't fit fer nothin'."

"All right. Nobody but us walks away from that post. Let's eat and get some sleep. We hit them about mid-morning."

CHAPTER
TWELVE

FROM BEHIND A tree about twenty yards from the front of the post, Gunn watched his warriors ride toward the hitching rack. Five came from the east and five from the west.

They straggled to the door, each beating his shoulder with one hand as though to bring circulation back into it, his other hand hidden under his robe.

When they had crowded through and into the room, Gunn and Bavousett sprinted for the door, and stopped, one on each side of the doorjamb.

"What you Injuns want? Nobody but a damn fool rides around in this weather."

"Whiskey," Big Beaver said from deep in his furs.

Gunn nodded to Bavousett, and they both pushed the door open and entered. Gunn wanted Muldoon for himself but didn't stop to look for him. He pulled his .44 and put a bullet through a bearded giant lying on a bale of furs just inside the door. The acrid smell of gunsmoke mixed with the stink of unwashed bodies, old furs, and the myriad of odors that could be expected in a general store.

Every warrior there must have had a yell pushing at his throat when Gunn threw his first bullet. Shots sounded in every corner of the big lodge. The log walls pushed the bedlam back upon them. Time seemed to slow. Gunn methodically thumbed shots at the scurvy lot, trying to get their pistols out. Only a few had a chance to fight back—and they blindly pulled trigger into the dense black gunsmoke. The rest died with the first volley.

Slugs tore at Gunn's robe. A glance through the murky light showed all of his men still standing—but now using knives.

Gunn fired at two more of Muldoon's men. The heavy slugs tore into them, knocking them onto their backs, handguns hanging from their lifeless hands.

Gunn searched through the thin light for Muldoon. His men were taking scalps. Revolver in hand, Gunn walked to each corpse, prodded it with his foot in order to see its face, and when certain it was not Muldoon, moved to the next. The trader was not in the room.

Gunn ran to the rear window. Muldoon, a large wooden box under his arm, stumbled and staggered toward the edge of trees bordering the clearing.

Gunn vaulted through the window. "Muldoon," he yelled.

Looking like a huge bear, Muldoon stopped and faced Gunn. "You gonna sic yore Injuns on me?"

Gunn slowly shook his head. "Nope, this is gonna be my pleasure, Muldoon. You've sold your last jug of rotgut to my brothers. How do you want it—guns or knives?"

Muldoon stared at Gunn before answering. "Why're you fightin' yore own kind? You ain't no Injun."

"You're wrong, Muldoon. I'm half Lakota Sioux, and I don't like what you and *your* kind are doing to my people." Gunn slowly pulled at the thongs holding his robe together. "You're wrong about something else, Muldoon. Don't ever classify me—in any way—as being of your kind. Now—how do you want it?"

"I ain't never seen no damn Injun what was any good with handguns. I'll take pistols." Muldoon threw back his coat, hooked it behind the .44 he had strapped to his leg, and swept his hand toward his holster.

Gunn threw back his robe and drew. Muldoon, despite not waiting for Gunn to get his coat open, was too late. Gunn's first shot took him in the right shoulder, and his second in the left—the box he carried dropped to the ground.

Muldoon tried to make his maimed muscles raise the pistol again, but it was no use. His arm dropped to his side, and his .44 slipped from his fingers.

Gunn walked toward him, stopped, took careful aim, and fired again. Muldoon's left leg flew from under him, a .44 slug through his knee. Muldoon turned half around, caught his balance, and faced Gunn. Another shot and Muldoon's right knee went the way of his left. He fell in a great lump in the snow.

"Muldoon, you're not going to sell whiskey to even one more Indian—nor are you going to sell them rifles, nor are you going to pick fights with men you think to make sport of. I'm gonna leave you here—no horse—no shelter—no legs. If you survive, which is doubtful, I'll find you and kill you."

Gunn holstered his pistol and walked to stand over the stinking hulk of a man. He drew his bowie, slipped it in one smooth motion around Muldoon's scalp—and snapped the dripping mess from Muldoon's ivory skull. "Many men have lived after losing their hair. I never heard of one living after losing their legs, arms, *and* scalp." Muldoon didn't answer—he had fainted.

Gunn went through Muldoon's pockets, collected his weapons, picked up the heavy box Muldoon had carried, and went back inside the trading post. His men were gathering the things they wanted to take back to their encampment. They had not touched the scalps of the three men Gunn had killed. He took them.

"Bavousett, see if there's a freight wagon in the barn. With a wagon we can haul blankets, food, guns, and ammunition. There should be about twenty horses out there too. Some of that twenty must be broken to harness. I'll take this box of Muldoon's for my part of the plunder."

"What's in that there box?"

"Don't know—haven't looked."

Bavousett cast Gunn a sour look. "Boy, youd've made old Blackbeard seem like a milksop a few years back, but reckon that would've been a considerable waste. Ain't never seen nobody what was more of a Injun than you."

Bavousett's words stuck with Gunn, and that night lying in his robes, he thought about them. He had done things that no civilized man would ever think of. Had living with the Indians done this to him? He decided that the Indians had little to do with what he was. He continued his self-examination. His father—the father he knew—and his mother had been gentle people. They had loved and cared for him—but there was a side to them he never saw. Were they as savage as he? He thought not.

Living with his uncle had hardened him, then the years at sea had disciplined him to do what must be done. He had always tried to do what he thought was right, and his old captain had guided him along those lines.

What would Jake—or Eula—think of the things he had just done? Gunn was certain Jake could accept his actions. He lay there and knawed at the question of Eula. He had told her many of the things he had done at sea, and he had told her about killing the man in Barataria. She had not drawn away from him. He decided that she too could accept him for what he was. The woman he finally took as his wife would have to be strong. The frontier would demand that of them—whether he lived as a white or Indian.

Before going to sleep, he realized that he had solved another problem that had worried him. He had never once thought of marrying one of the women in Crazy Horse's band. His only thoughts had concerned Jake and Eula. He knew then he would return to the white man's world. He loved this life and the people he had come to know so well. He would stay with Crazy Horse until the grass and trees turned green again. Then he would leave.

The People welcomed Gunn and his men back. The cold and snow didn't hamper their rejoicing. After dividing the spoils of the raid, the women prepared food and fed them as heroes.

After the celebration Gunn and Bavousett sat alone in their tepee. Bavousett cocked an eye at Gunn. "When you gonna find out what's in that box o' Muldoon's?"

"That's gnawing your guts, isn't it, old man?"

"Well, gosh ding it, sure it is. Looks to me like you'd be havin' a hissy to find out yourself."

Gunn stood. "All right, I'll look. Don't want you stewing so hard. At your age you might just stew away to nothing."

"Ain't nuthin' wrong with my age. I can still outfight any danged tenderfoot like you," Bavousett said, all the while moving closer to the box Gunn had placed by his sleeping robes.

Gunn squatted by the stout wooden box and studied the cheap padlock thrust through the hasp. He pulled his Colt from its holster.

"Hot dang it. You ain't gonna shoot the damn lock off. Every danged Injun in this here camp'll be in here quicker'n spit soon's you fire."

Gunn slanted the old trapper an acid look. "I'm not dumb as you. I'm gonna knock it loose with the butt." While still talking, Gunn reversed his pistol and swung the handle against the lock. It came open.

Bavousett moved closer.

Gunn reholstered his pistol, walked back to the fire, and sat. Bavousett's face sagged; his mouth hung open. "Wh-what the unhinged hell are you doin'? Ain't you gonna look inside—see what you done took from that skunk?"

"Oh hell, Bavousett, it's not going anywhere." Gunn slumped down, acting as if he thought to sleep awhile, but looking at Bavousett from under his brows.

The old man reached for the box, drew back his hands as though they'd been burned, scratched his beard, and looked toward Gunn with a disgusted look. "Danged contrary varmint. How in the tarnation can you just sit in this here tepee alongside that there box, 'thout knowin' what's inside it?"

"I don't find it troubling at all. Fact is, I've already guessed what's inside."

"Well gosh dang it—tell me, Black Eagle—tell me. I ain't gonna sleep a wink till you do."

Gunn laughed and stood. "Reckon I better show you. It would bother my conscience to know I cost you a night's sleep."

He had thought to drag the suspense further, but he couldn't do his old friend that way—besides, he wanted to know what he had taken, also.

He flipped the lid back and heard Bavousett gasp. There were perhaps twenty small buckskin bags filled with something—and they were lying on top of a pile of double eagles. Gunn couldn't even guess at the worth of what he looked at. He lifted one of the bags and, from its weight, thought it contained gold dust. What he gazed upon represented perhaps years of Muldoon skinning the Indians out of pelts for watered-down whiskey and then turning the pelts into gold in Saint Louis. Gunn felt dirty just looking at it.

He peered at Bavousett. "Old man, there's enough money

here, if split fifty-fifty, for you to come down outta those mountains and live comfortably the rest of your life."

Bavousett fidgeted, looked in the box, then shifted his gaze to Gunn. "Yeah, but it ain't split fifty-fifty—an' even if it wuz, don't reckon I want to leave the mountains. I got me a good place up yonder below tree line, got me a good woman— Shoshone, she is. She takes good care o' all my needs an' I take care o' her." His eyes shifted back to the box, then back to Gunn. "They's times we could use a little extry money—but we ain't never really hurt none for nothin'. Reckon if you offered me som o' it, I'd turn it down. Might spoil me."

Gunn stared at the old trapper, and really saw him for the first time. He was a man free of want, free of living by any code but his own. He was happy with his lot in life. He had a woman he cared for—and obviously she cared for him. Simply put, Bavousett was a free man.

Gunn placed his hand on the bony old shoulder next to him. "Mountain Cat, whether you want it or not, half of this is yours. It'll make sure you never have lean times even if the trapping season is bad. Besides that, I'm gonna find me some land—a lot of it—and build me a ranch. If you and your woman ever grow tired of the mountains—or get too old to care for each other—come live with me. I'll fix a place for you."

"Sounds like you done made up yore mind about where you b'long in this here world."

Gunn stared at the fire a moment, then nodded. "Cat, I'm not sure where I belong. I believe I can fit into either world, but I've tried this one and I'm afraid of what I might become if I stay."

Bavousett filled his pipe, lit it, and studied Gunn for a long moment. "Boy, reckon I can tell you that. You stay with the Lakota an' you gonna wind up bein' one helluva war chief. In a few years you an' Crazy Horse would be maybe the best the Sioux Nation has—but then you ain't gonna be able to pick an' choose the whites you fight. Don't reckon you want that. On dark nights, in the loneliness of your tepee, all them white scalps of men who ain't never done nothin' to you would sit squarely on top o' yore conscience." He shook his head. "Nope, don't reckon you want that."

Gunn closed the box and hooked the broken padlock back

through the hasp. "Let's get some sleep. You and I have a lot of decisions to make, and I want to be wide awake when we make them." He crawled between his buffalo robes, pulled them up around his neck, and soon slept.

The next morning, after they had eaten, and Bavousett had gone to visit friends, Crazy Horse came to see Gunn, and it was obvious that something weighed heavily on his mind.

The war chief sat, letting the silence draw thin. When he finally peered at Gunn, his face showed a reluctance to speak.

"Go ahead, Curly. You have something that's bothering you, so let's talk about it."

"Black Eagle, I've thought about this and asked the spirits to help me. You are my brother, and what I'm about to say hurts. If you stay with the Lakota, you will share in our greatest victory—and in the passing of the Sioux Nation."

"What do you mean, brother?"

The somber Indian held up his hand to stop more questions. "The signs are all there. The buffalo are becoming few. We have to travel farther for our robes, tepees, and meat. When they are gone, our ways will go with them. The People will be prisoners in their own land. You can be a white man—or Lakota—but you can not be both."

Gunn packed a social pipe and handed it to Crazy Horse, who put fire to the bowl before continuing. "You are a great warrior. The People hold you as a friend—but I think you should go back to the whites."

Crazy Horse had given Gunn the opening he needed, but he felt a tightening of his chest and a lump in his throat. When finally he spoke, he knew he was trying to span the gap between two different cultures. "Curly, I have thought about this, and the only solution I've come up with is to get a ranch—in the Gallatin or Madison Valley—raising cattle. If I do that, there will be room and food there for the People . . ."

Again, Crazy Horse held up his hand. "No, my brother, I will lead the Oglalas as long as I can fight—but I will never lead them against you. You go make your ranch. You will not be harmed by us. How long will you stay with us?"

"I think when the trees again turn green I'll go."

Crazy Horse nodded. "When you are ready, I and ten of my

warriors will travel with you to where the whites are—then we will see our brother no more."

The lump in Gunn's throat threatened to burst and embarrass him. He had not cried in a long time.

CHAPTER
THIRTEEN

G ᴜɴɴ ꜱᴀᴛ ʜɪꜱ horse, surrounded by Crazy Horse, his warriors, and Bavousett. They were the same ten that had been with him for the attack on Muldoon's Trading Post.

They looked down at what looked like a bed of ants from their vantage point high on a hill, overlooking Alder Creek, only the ants were men and they were in the creek's waters. Occasionally the sun flashed a reflection from the pans they dipped for water to wash the gravel. Gold had drawn these men, hoping for quick riches. Virginia City, Montana Territory, sat at the south end of all the activity.

"Reckon this here's where you an' me part, young'un. My mountain ain't too fur from here—an' my woman's gonna think I done got myself killed if I don't git home soon." Bavousett's voice held mixed emotions—a reluctance to leave Gunn and a sense of urgency to get home and see his woman.

Gunn had pressed half of Muldoon's gold on Bavousett, but the old man had kept only about a quarter of it. He'd sneaked the rest back into the box while Gunn hunted for fresh meat. Gunn had found it that night and knew the old trapper wanted it that way.

"Go on. Go see your woman, and remember—I'll have a place for you when I get set up." He slapped Bavousett's horse on the rump, and while riding off, the trapper waved good-bye to Crazy Horse and his men. Gunn knew he'd see him again.

Gunn's next good-bye would be the hardest he'd ever attempted. He had lived with these men, fought by their side, visited them in their tepees, known their families. He stared at the sight below longer than needed, bracing himself for that which he hated doing. Unable to put off the inevitable any longer, he raised his gaze to sweep the men surrounding him. "You're my family," he said. "I will always be Oglala Lakota in my heart." He struck his breast. "Here, I will keep each of you."

Each of them handed him a pack wrapped in doeskin. Crazy Horse was last. He gave Gunn a long wrapped parcel. "You have learned to use the bow well, my brother. The bow maker and the arrow maker have made these for you—they are the best. Someday you may find the need for silent killing." Without further words the party kneed their horses around and headed back the way they had come. As soon as they showed him their backs, Gunn let the tears come that had been choking him for the last hour.

Laden with the eleven packs, Gunn pulled up in front of Frank McKean's Anaconda Hotel. He had again donned the Western garb he'd worn aboard the ship in New Orleans. Wrestling with the extra packs, he finally made it to the front desk without dropping them. Then he unloaded Muldoon's box from the packhorse. When he returned to the desk, the clerk stuck a key in his hand. "Come back an' sign in after you get rid o' them bundles. Yore room's jest down the hall yonder." Gunn nodded and made his way back to his room.

He had thought to ask for a room looking out on the street, but gave that idea up when he saw that the hotel sported only one level.

Gunn stacked his bundles on the floor beside the door, twisted the key in the lock, and went in. It was the first roof he'd had over his head in almost a year, with the exception of Muldoon's Post.

Gunn deposited all of his gear on the bed, went back to the desk for the heavy box, and back in his room started looking through the things Crazy Horse and his warriors had given him. There were beautifully hand-worked beaded and quilled vests, leggings, buckskin pants, and moccasins. They still held a faint scent of the tepee fires. He had only to close his eyes and he was again in the encampment. He shook his head to clear the nostalgia. This wouldn't do. If he was going to miss it that much, he should go back. The last thing he unwrapped was the bow and quiver of arrows. He ran his hands over the wood, letting the work of art soothe him.

After storing his gear, he went to the desk and signed in. The clerk told him that the hotel had a restaurant, a saloon, and in the basement a bowling alley. "I'll settle for the saloon. Haven't had a drink in a year."

The clerk stared at him as though he were some sort of social misfit. "You joshin' me, fella? Durned if I ever seen a man what ain't had a drink in that long a time. Well, go on—go git it. I ain't one what'll stand 'tween a thirsty man an' a drink."

Gunn walked down the hall to the saloon and bellied up to the bar. The bartender brought him his rye and a glass of water.

Gunn tasted his drink and noticed that the room smelled like every other saloon he'd been in—sour sweat, cigar smoke, and alcohol. He thought to toss his drink down and go outside in the cool, pure air, but resisted the urge. He wanted to listen to the talk, see what was happening in the town. After he familiarized himself with the goings-on, he thought he'd try and find Jake. He had no doubt she was here somewhere.

On every side men talked of only one thing—gold. This claim was bringing in so much, another claim was about to play out, and still another had caused a killing. Someone had tried to jump it, and the rightful owner had shot the claim jumper while he stood in water to his waist. Most of the men Gunn listened to had claims on Alder Creek, which ran into Stinking Water River. Alder Gulch was where the gold was, if he could believe those he listened to. Then he heard another miner talking about a different subject.

"Yep, that there woman's a real looker all right, but I ain't gonna mess with her. Why, she damned near whomped John Peters to death—an' all he done was pat 'er on 'er fanny. Ain't nobody in this here town what's got enough guts or money to interest 'er."

Gunn put his drink on the bar. "You know what name this woman goes by?" he asked, although he felt certain he knew the answer.

The miner stared at Gunn a moment. "You a newcomer?" At Gunn's nod, he continued, "Well, she's a big woman, blond, a real looker. People call 'er Jake. I'll call 'er any danged thing she wants. That there's one tough woman."

"Know where I might find 'er this time of day?"

The miner shook his head in apparent dismay. "Man, I done told you—she don't let nobody mess with 'er." He took a swallow of his beer and again looked at Gunn. "If you really want to know, I reckon she's in 'er shop. She come in here 'bout eight maybe ten months ago an' sold a bunch of goods she brung in by freight wagons. She put up a shanty to sell 'em out of, and when they was all gone, she jest set in to bakin' pies, donuts, cakes, bread. Hell, that there women can fix the best eatin's a man ever wrapped his mouth around. Her shop's out the front door an' to your right 'bout a couple hunnerd yards."

Gunn tipped his hat and said, "Much obliged. Think I'll go see 'er." He downed his drink and left. On the way out he asked the clerk where the livery was located so he could stable his horses.

After taking care of them, Gunn headed toward the bake-shop. The wind blew out of the north, and Gunn hurried his steps. The chill wind had nothing to do with his haste, but the smell of fresh baked goods did. It told him that in only a few more steps he'd see Jake—a friend like few men would ever have.

When he went through the front door, Jake had her back to him. She strained to put a sack of flour onto a shelf a bit too high. Gunn masked his voice and said, "Need some waitin' on, woman—right now."

"Well, goldang ye, wait and shut up the sass or I'll throw ye out the danged door."

Gunn burst into gales of laughter. Jake dropped the flour bag and spun to face him. "Rafe—oh, Rafe, I knowed it wuz you soon's you laughed." She finished the sentence in his arms. "Lordy, how I've missed you." She stood back and looked him over, from head to foot. "'Bout give you up. Where all you been?"

"Not now, woman, let me hold you a minute. I've missed you too." He pulled her into his arms and held her close.

A miner came through the door, gawked a minute, and ran from the store. Gunn again laughed. He imagined the man would spread it up and down the street that a man was in Jake's shop, hugging her, and she hadn't whipped up on him yet.

Jake looked up at him. "What's funny?"

Gunn told her about the man. "From what I heard in the hotel saloon, there's not a man in town would dare touch you. The description I heard was that you were a mixture of mountain lion, she-grizzly, and timber wolf, all rolled into one."

"Aw hell, Rafe, ain't none of 'em smell good as you. Even now, I know you musta jest got off'n the trail, but you smell better'n any o' these here he-goats." She took his arm and headed him toward the rear of the shop. "C'mon, I got coffee made an' enough bear sign to founder ye."

"You think I want bear sign more than I want you?"

"Aw, hell, I shoulda knowed all you'd want would be to take advantage o' me—right off."

Jake poured coffee and set a plate of hot doughnuts in front of him. He pushed a chair under her, then seated himself.

"Well, Jake, lookin' at this, I reckon I'll wait a few more weeks for you—just keep feeding me like this."

"You try waitin' longer'n tonight, and I'll make sure you ain't able to eat—not ever again. Nope, you won't be able to eat *or* take advantage o' me. Fact is, reckon I'll shut down shop an' we'll go in my room in the back an' talk about what you been doin'. I need to show you how much money I done made you while you wuz out yonder gallivantin round the countryside."

Gunn pulled her close again. "No. You're not going to close your business, and talking about money is not what I'm interested in. I want to hear about *you*."

They talked long into the afternoon. Finally, Jake cocked her head and studied him a moment. "Trapper wuz by the other day. Said he'd been in a Crow camp an' all they talked about wuz a white Lakota what been givin' 'em hell for a good while—that wuz you, wasn't it Rafe?"

Gunn nodded. "Probably. Me an' the Crow got right well acquainted."

Jake toyed with a loose thread around one of the buttonholes in her blouse, then looked at Gunn straight on. "You goin' back to 'em, Rafe? What I mean is—you made up your mind what you are? You a Injun or white man?"

Gunn shook his head. "I don't think I'll ever have the answer to that. I know I can fit into either, and in my heart—I think I'll always be both. However, I've decided to stay in the white man's world. I've given it a lot of thought, and Crazy Horse put the clincher on it. I'd like to do both—but that isn't possible. I never took a white man's scalp—a decent white man's, that is—or the scalp of a Sioux, so I can stay here with a clear conscience."

Jake stopped toying with her blouse and stared at him. "Reckoned you'd finally do that. I'm glad. Even if you take off for the other side o' them mountains, I s'pose you'll stay a white man this time."

Jake tried several times to get him to take a look at the books she had kept on the sale of his goods, but Gunn didn't want to take time to look at them. He wanted to walk out on the town and see what made it tick. He stood and told Jake that he'd be back after a while.

"You gonna wear your guns? I got a feelin' them friends o' yours from down the river are hangin' round here somewhere."

"The Cajuns? You seen 'em?"

"Naw. Ain't seen nothin, but reckon I done learned to tend to my feelin's. You keep yore eyes peeled for any varmints like that while you're out—you are comin' back tonight, ain't you? We got the books to go over an' . . . an', well, I got a pack o' letters for you. They done come all the way from N'Orleans, written in some woman's handwritin'. Come by here, an' stead o' stayin' here, we'll go to my cabin up yonder on the side of the hill."

Gunn grasped her shoulders. "Jake, every mule team in this territory couldn't keep me away from you. Yeah, I'll be back. Just want to see what the town's like." He tugged his hat down on his head and left.

Out on the street Gunn realized that this was his first look at a real frontier town, and everything in it was alive. The smell of freshly turned earth, coffee brewing, horse apples in the street, and occasionally a faint scent of tobacco smoke; and the rough-clad men, laughing, cursing, drinking; and the warm feel of his fingers brushing the walnut butt of his handgun; and the incessant noise of jackhammers, sledges pounding, dredges clunking as they lifted tons of ore bearing gravel from the creek; all of this screamed into his brain that he was in the real West.

Gunn turned into the door of the first saloon he came to. When he bellied up to the bar, he realized how different he was from the rest of the customers. He dressed differently, carried his gun differently, and he looked different. He admitted this to himself through no feeling of ego—just fact.

More than one pair of eyes took in his tied-down holster— and the men closest to him gave him a little more room. Gunn had the urge to go to his room and leave his gun there—but Jake's words about the Cajuns canceled that thought.

One man at the bar whispered, such that Gunn had no trouble hearing, that Gunn looked like the same type as "Blackjack" Slade, whom the vigilantes hung in March of '64. Gunn had no idea who Slade was, but there sure as hell wasn't anybody going to hang *him,* vigilantes or not.

One of Virginia City's early sheriffs, Henry Plummer, had been hanged in January 1863, along with two others. Plummer was not only sheriff, he also headed up the road agents preying on gold shipments. Gunn got the idea that the vigilantes dealt out justice more than the courts.

Listening to stories of hangings, shootings, and fistfights, Gunn soon felt better about having his gun at his side—he bought a bottle of rye whiskey and headed back to Jake's.

As soon as he came through the front door, he smelled food cooking—smelled like some sort of stew, and even with all the doughnuts Jake had fed him, his mouth watered.

"Get yore self in here and set, 'fore this here supper gits spoiled. Been settin' here awaitin', and I'm hongry too."

"Jake, after smelling it, I don't believe you could hold me away from it."

"Don't worry, big man, if I'm gonna keep yore strength up, I better feed you. With what I got planned for ye, ye're gonna need all the strength I can pile on ye." She was already dishing up a large bowl before Gunn could take his seat. "After we eat, we'll head up to my cabin." She cast him a look that could have been either a warning or an invitation. He'd have been right either way he took it.

During the meal Jake told him that she hadn't been up to her cabin in two weeks. "Just been stayin' here in the store. Usually

pretty late when I finish bakin', an' not wantin' to have to kill
any o' these varmints hereabouts, I just bunk here in the back
o' the store. I got yore letters, an' the books I been keepin' on
the goods you brung up the river. They're in the back room
yonder."

Gunn didn't say it, but he pitied any man who might try to
molest Jake.

"Jake, don't think I oughtta stay at your place. The whole
town'll talk. I'll kill the man who says anything about you."

"Rafe, you done knowed me nigh on to a year now—
countn' the time you an' Bavousett spent with Crazy Horse.
You figger I give one happy damn what any o' them hooligans
say 'bout me? I know you an' me ain't gonna last forever with
each other. Know them letters you been gettin' come from
some woman—probably a woman deservin' of you. So whatever happens, you an' me—well, I figger to really give 'em
something to talk about." Jake took a spoonful of her stew and
chewed it thoughtfully. "Ain't hearin' no but's, if's, or an's
outta you. We're goin' to my cabin after you're done puttin'
that there food away. We'll talk 'bout what money you
made—an' them letters—tomorrow, or the next day, or
whenever I free you up for other things."

CHAPTER
FOURTEEN

JAKE APPROACHED THE door of her cabin with pride. She looked puzzled when the latch string wasn't hanging out, then stepped aside for Gunn to look. He slipped his knife blade between the door and the jamb, pushed the bar up, and shoved the door open.

Gunn took her elbow and led her into the room with him. He squinted into the darkness trying to find the lamp, then struck a lucifer—the room was a wreck.

Broken furniture lay scattered about, legs broken off the table, chairs smashed; pots, pans, and dishes lay strewn across the floor. The dishes were in bits, with dried food caked to the pieces. The smell was enough to gag a buzzard—rotten food, stale whiskey, and dirty bodies. A lamp stood on the mantel above the fireplace. Gunn struck another lucifer and lit it.

"Oh, Rafe, this ain't the way I keep house—you gotta believe it, Rafe. They wan't a speck o' dirt in here last time I wuz here."

Gunn grasped her shoulders. "Shhh now, pretty woman, I know you wouldn't keep a place like this. Let's see what more damage has been done, then we'll see about fixing it." He took her arm and steered her toward a door at the rear.

"That's my bedroom, Rafe. I had it fixed all pretty so when you showed up you'd be proud o' me."

Gunn carried the lamp in his right hand, and the sight it showed them was every bit as bad as the front room—but in the bed lay two of the dirtiest white men Gunn had ever seen. They snored as though they'd never had sleep before. And beside the bed a dozen or more empty whiskey bottles lay.

Gunn stared at them a moment, then turned to Jake. "You get

on back down to the store and go to bed. I'll take care of these
two and straighten your cabin up a bit. I'll be down when I
finish."

"Ain't goin' no place. Want to watch what you do to
them—an' when you get through, I'm gonna commence to
change their way o' livin'.''

Gunn walked to the edge of the bed, grasped the mattress,
and upended it. The two slobs rolled to the floor, thrashed
about, tangled in their own arms and legs, sputtered a couple of
times, and started cursing.

"What the hell you doin', Stone? How we git on the floor?"

"You musta done it, you crazy bastard—oooo, jeez, my
haid's gonna explode any minute, Mike. Where's the whiskey?"

Gunn looked down at them a moment then pulled his .44 and
fired a shot into the floor between them. "Get up, trash. You're
gonna clean this place up so it's just the way you found it."

The one called Stone twisted and looked up at Gunn. "Who
the hell are you? What you doin' in our place?"

Gunn stared a moment. "What are *you* doing in this cabin?"

"Ours. We found it—nobody livin' here so we moved in," the
one called Mike answered. "Git outta here an' leave us be."

Gunn kicked Stone, the one closest to him. "Get up." When
they stood, Stone towered above Mike by a good foot—and
was about six inches taller than Gunn. They sported only
grungy, gray long johns.

Still holding his .44, Gunn said to Jake, "Go through the
pockets of their overalls and see if they have any dust—if you
can stand to touch the filthy rags."

"You ain't goin' through our clothes. Got no business here
anyhow." Mike stepped toward Gunn.

Gunn fired another shot. It grazed the side of Mike's foot.
"The next one's going through your foot. Stay where you are."
Mike danced on one leg.

Jake walked to Gunn's side hefting a doeskin bag in each
hand. "If I had a reckon, I'd say I'm a-holdin' 'bout a thousand
dollars in dust right here."

"Might not be enough to cover what they broke of yours—
but it's a start. Now, go downtown and buy some lye soap. This

place is gonna shine when they get through with it. Buy a table, chairs—anything you see that they broke."

"I ain't doin' no woman's work," Stone said.

"You're right," Gunn said. "You're not gonna do woman's work, you're gonna do *your* work. While you work, these handguns are gonna be on you every minute."

He tossed Jake his left-hand pistol. "Hold up going downtown. Stay here and keep that .44 on one—I'll watch the other. If he even hesitates, put a slug through his brisket. You watch the short one. Have him take this mattress out and burn it. You'll have to buy more ticking and round up corn husks to fill it with." He turned to Stone. "Start sweeping everything in here out the door."

A couple hours later, the cabin swept out, Jake had returned from town, and Gunn had the two intruders on their hands and knees scrubbing the floor with two fine-grained bricks.

"What they doin' now, Rafe?"

"At sea, that is called holystoning. It cleans a deck cleaner'n anything you ever saw. When they get through with that, they'll scrub it with some of that lye soap you bought."

"My gawd, Rafe, I thought I had this here place shiny clean, but you done showed me things 'bout cleanin' makes me think I didn't know nothin'."

"It has often been said, Jake, that sailors have the cleanest bodies and filthiest minds of any who live."

The two louts had been griping nonstop ever since Gunn started them on the job. Now Stone looked up from scouring the floor. "I'm gonna catch you 'thout them guns, an' when I do, I'm gonna beat you to death."

"When you take on that job, bring a lantern and your supper—it's gonna take you a while."

Another hour and they had finished the inside work. Then Gunn took them outside, still in their long johns, and had them build a fire and burn everything they had removed from the cabin—including their clothes.

"You sending us outta here broke, no guns, an' no clothes?" Mike asked.

"You hit the nail on the head, bucko," Gunn said. "And I'll tell you something else, if I ever see you within a hundred yards of this cabin—or Miss Jake—I'll kill you. Now get."

"Naw, mister, I'm gonna do the killin'—after Stone beats the hell outta you," Mike said, then walked toward town.

Gunn turned his attention to Jake. "You find any stuff to replace what they broke?"

"Yeah, Rafe. I knowed where to find it, same place as I found it in the first place. 'Fore I went shoppin' I took that there dust by Fred Bohn's assay office. He gave me fourteen hunnert dollars fer it. Old Man Newbanks down at the store sold me every thing I needed for four hunnert dollars. Soons he gits his wagon back from makin' 'nother delivery, he's gonna send my stuff up to me."

"You made a clear thousand dollars for them wrecking your place then."

"You gonna make me keep it? I oughtta give back what's left to them as owns it."

Gunn shook his head. "No. You're keeping it. Maybe that'll make that trash come after me sooner—I want to get it done."

Jake studied him a moment. "Rafe, times like this you act more Injun than white. I b'lieve you're hopin' fer a slam-bang, knockdown screwdy-roo."

Gunn's face felt stiff. "Damned if I know what a screwdy-roo is, but if it's an eye-gouging, biting, scratching, knuckle-and-skull fistfight, you've nailed it down pretty tight. Fact is, tomorrow I'm goin' looking for them."

Jake jerked her head in a nod. "Figgered as much. You gonna go git that pretty body o' yores all bruised an' busted up 'fore I ever have a chance to wear it down to a nubbin'.'"

They sat on the front stoop waiting for the wagon to bring Jake's furniture.

"Goldang it, if I'd a brung the books an' your letters from the bakeshop, we could a been goin' over them right now."

"No hurry, Jake. We have other things to keep us occupied for a while."

Jake looked at him, with a soft smile.

Three days later they had gone over the books and caught up on conversation—as well as other things. Jake had made Gunn a rich man—even if he had not already had the gold from Muldoon's box.

Every morning Jake had gone to her shop and sold her baked

goods while Gunn slept. He had also read the letters she had kept for him. They were all from Eula, and reading them in the sequence she had written them, he sensed her maturing. He put off answering them—not an easy thing to do, because he knew he wanted her, loved her—he thought, but he loved Jake too, but not in the same way.

That night, sitting by the fire, Gunn poured Jake and him each a drink. When they finished the first, he poured another.

Jake slanted him a knowing look. "Rafe, you're either tryin' to git me drunk and take advantage o' me—or you're gonna tell me somethin' I don't want to hear."

Rafe shook his head. "Maybe—I don't know. But, all that money you made for me I want you to keep, except what the goods cost me. You did all the work. Even hauled the stuff up here by mule team. I want you to keep it."

"You know I ain't gonna do that, Rafe. I built this here cabin outta that money. I kept the bakeshop. I done got more in life than I ever figgered to have." She studied him a moment, then asked, "What you doin', Rafe, tryin' to git rid o' me?"

He felt his face flush and was glad the firelight flickered dim enough to hide his feelings. He wanted both Eula and Jake, but he wasn't one of those saints from over Salt Lake City way—he couldn't have two wives—wouldn't if he could. He wouldn't do that to either Eula or Jake. He made up his mind.

"No, Jake. I'm not trying to get rid of you. Was just thinking to ask you to marry me."

Jake sat still enough to be chiseled from stone. She stared into the fire so long Rafe wondered if she'd heard him. Finally she shook her head, still looking into the fire. "Reckon I knowed you wuz gonna ask me that. Don't b'lieve they's anythin' I want more—but, Rafe, you don't love me with the kind o' love needed for gettin' married. Don't reckon I have that kind o' feelin' for you neither. What we have is special— real special. Yeah, we love each other, but our love is more like the respect two good men have fer one 'nother—and, yeah, we love each other's bodies. Lordy, don't reckon I ever thought a man could do to me what you do. All I got to do is look at you an' I melt—but, Rafe, that ain't love. It's hunger, pur-dee simple man-woman hunger. Ain't enough to marry up with a person."

Gunn felt that a weight lifted from his shoulders—but he couldn't let it rest. "Jake, you and I could make a good life for ourselves. We'd be a team, Jake. And we'd have each other."

She shook her head. "Naw, now, don't you go makin' it harder than it is. Yeah, we'd make a good team—might even own half this here town 'fore we got through, but after a while that's all we'd have. Wouldn't have no kids. Doctor done told me I can't have any—don't know why. Our fire for each other would burn down to ashes. We'd just be business partners."

She poured them another glass of rye whiskey. "Let's git snot-flyin' drunk an' you take advantage o' me all night long—or maybe I'll take advantage o' you."

Gunn gulped his drink, trying to drown his disappointment, and sat staring into the bottom of his empty glass. Maybe Jake was right, but he hated like hell to turn loose. If he wrote Eula a letter asking her to marry him, he and Jake would be through with the man-woman thing. He wouldn't continue it, and he knew Jake wouldn't either. "Pour me another drink, woman. If we're gonna get snot-flying drunk, let's get after it."

CHAPTER
FIFTEEN

GUNN SAT ON the edge of his bed in the hotel cleaning and oiling his guns. Finished with them, he honed his knife. He had enemies and he wanted to be ready for them. In addition to the ones he'd made up at Jake's cabin, he felt that the Cajuns were close by. Just a feeling, but his time with Bavousett and the Lakota had not been wasted.

He still had not written Eula.

He kept telling himself that he had not written her because he had trouble to take care of first—but was that the real reason?

He had not been back to see Jake, but he still wanted her, and he knew she wanted him just as badly. He had thought of what she had said on their last night together—and thought maybe she was right. But sitting here, he imagined the woman scent of her, the taste of her lips, and the velvety feel of her skin. Now he was just putting off cutting the final cord—he would never forget her, wouldn't even try, but they both deserved something that would last.

He put on his guns and headed for the street. He had a knuckle-and-skull fight to take care of.

He went in several saloons and saw nothing of the two he looked for. He went in the Olive Branch last. Only two men stood at the bar, and they weren't the ones he looked for. "You seen two men, one a half a head taller'n me and the other about six inches shorter? They go by the names of Stone and Mike," Gunn asked the bartender.

Before he could answer, the man next to Gunn said, "They're down at their diggin's. Probably come in here 'bout sundown—usually do."

Gunn asked for a beer. He didn't want but the one. Too many wouldn't mix with the job he had to do.

"What you want them for?" the man next to him asked. "If you want to buy their claim, I hear it's about played out."

"Don't want their claim. Stone made a threat to beat me to death—and Mike staked out the right to kill me with guns if Stone failed at the job. I figured to save them a lot of time looking for me."

"Mister, you took on a job I don't reckon nobody else around here would have on a bet."

The bartender cut in, "I'll tell you one thing, you ain't about to fight 'em in here. Take it outside—or I'll blow hell out of all three o' you."

Gunn stared at him a moment. "I'll tackle 'em outside, then if you want to try to make good on blowing me to hell—have at it. It's been tried before." He walked toward the door, and as he did, he heard the man he'd been standing next to say, "Bartender, if you got any sense at all, you won't tackle that man. He looked mean plumb to the core."

Gunn sat outside jawing with the spit-and-whittle bunch until the sun had almost disappeared behind the Pioneer Range. About half of the red ball still showed when he saw the two he looked for walking toward the saloon.

He stepped off the boardwalk into the fine dust of the street. "You made a brag, Stone. Make good on it."

Stone stopped short, and his gaze swept Gunn from head to toe. "Shuck them pistols."

Gunn had already unbuckled his gunbelt. He wrapped it around the holsters and handed it to one of the men he'd been talking to on the boardwalk. "After I finish with your friend, Mike, you said something about killing me. How you want it—guns or knives?"

"Pistols—but they ain't gonna be 'nuff left o' you to buckle a holster on when Stone gets through."

The man Gunn had handed his gunbelt to said, "You try to take a hand in that fight, Mike, an' I'll kill you myself. Stand clear."

Gunn breathed easier. He had been worried that Mike would do something to turn the tide for his friend. He looked at the man and nodded. "Thanks, friend."

Stone stood about ten feet from Gunn. He flexed his arms, then stood on tiptoe a couple of times to loosen his leg muscles. He was still the filthiest son of a bitch Gunn had ever seen—but he was also the biggest, and every time he moved, his muscles bulged the clothes covering them. Gunn exhaled slowly and hoped what he'd learned about fighting in New York, and the mayhem he'd learned at sea, would be enough. He stood relaxed. Stone planted his feet and rushed.

Gunn stepped aside and swung when Stone tried to change his course. His fist connected with Stone's cheek. Blood spurted. Stone shook his head and plowed in again, swinging. His right caught Gunn high on the shoulder.

Gunn spun and fell. Before he could regain his feet, Stone ran at him, jumped, and came down feet-first where Gunn's chest had been. At the last moment Gunn rolled to the side and came to his feet.

Before the goliath could face him again, Gunn clubbed him with a right and a left, one to the ribs and one to the kidneys. Stone's face turned the color of putty. Gunn stepped in swinging—a right, a left, and a right to Stone's heart. Stone gasped and backpedaled.

Gunn bored in swinging. Abruptly, Stone stopped, planted his feet, and landed a solid blow to Gunn's gut. It knocked him down. He'd learned from the last time he was on the ground. He no sooner hit the dirt than he rolled to get out of the way of Stone's feet. He tried to suck air into his lungs to keep from vomiting. If Stone hit him a solid blow like that again, he might not be able to get up. This time he made it back to his feet. Somewhere in the back of his mind he sensed that a crowd had gathered—but they gave the fighters plenty of room. That blow had told him he could not trade blows with the huge man.

Gunn used his boxing skills now. He moved in and slugged Stone with a left above the right eye. Blood streamed into Stone's eye and down his face.

Gotta get the other eye, Gunn thought—his lungs working better now. If he could partially blind Stone, maybe he could get enough punches in to stop him—for good.

Gunn feinted with his left, Stone dropped his guard to block the punch, and Gunn landed a wicked right to Stone's left eye. Gunn backed off, waiting for the blood to flow. It came fast.

The big man blindly swung a right. Gunn grabbed his arm and spun, throwing Stone against the side of a tethered horse. The horse shied and Stone fell. Gunn aimed a kick at the filthy head—and missed. Stone grabbed Gunn's leg and twisted. Gunn spun with it and saved getting his knee wrenched.

They gained their feet. Stone swiped at Gunn's eyes with dirt-filled sleeves—what was left of them. The dirt mixed with blood further blinded him. He swung that huge right and hit Gunn over the heart. Gunn's mouth dropped open. He felt as if he might black out—as if there were no air left in the world.

Gasping, he stepped to the side and avoided another punch, which surely would have been the end of the fight. Stone was stumbling and swinging blindly. Gunn carefully stayed out of reach of the clublike fists and peppered Stone with blows designed to open a cut every time they connected. He had Stone bleeding from his mouth, nose, cheekbones, and eyes.

Gunn swung once again at each eye, then moved his attack to the body. He was only now aware that he couldn't see out of his left eye—it was swollen shut.

He put everything he had into a punch to Stone's heart that stopped his flailing—then he hit him again in the same place.

Stone stood there, his feet planted solidly in the fine dust, his mouth hanging open—working like a fish sucking for air.

Gunn dropped his right to below Stone's belt and then brought it up in a blur of a punch. It landed, sounding like a sledgehammer against soft stone, right on the point of Stone's chin.

The punch knocked Stone back two steps. He caught himself and stepped forward.

Fall, you bastard. What the hell's holding you up? Gunn thought. He had never hit any man that hard before.

Stone took two more rubber-legged steps toward Gunn. First his knees folded from under him, moving ahead of his body—then he fell. Gunn walked to the horse trough and washed his face. It felt like a piece of raw beef. Getting his breath, he walked to the boardwalk and held out his hands for his gunbelt. If he had to fight Mike with pistols, he'd better do it before his hands stiffened from the beating they'd taken.

He buckled his belt and tied down his holsters before looking to find Mike.

Mike leaned against a post on the boardwalk.

"You made your brag too, Mike. I'm better with these .44's than I am with my fists. Step away from those people, and let's see the color of your guts."

Mike wore his pistol shoved into his belt. He held his hands well clear of it. "Ain't no way, fella. I wuz just lettin' my mouth overload my donkey-brayin' ass. I ain't fightin' you with guns er nothin' else. Let me take care of my partner."

Gunn eyed him a moment and said, "Do it." He stepped toward the boardwalk—and saw one of the Cajuns. His hand went to his holster, but the Cajun disappeared around the corner of the building.

He—and Jake—had been right. His New Orleans enemies were close—too close. Fear washed over him. How could he fight men when he didn't know where they were—or from where they would attack? He took a deep breath and willed himself to relax. Now he would have to rely on his Lakota training and instincts.

He turned toward the hotel, and with his first step he became aware of pain. His chest hurt, his arms felt leaden, as if he had a sack of grain tied to each hand, and his head ached—the fight had made him half a man. Until he cleaned up and rested, he would not be able to fight anyone, much less three Cajuns.

In his room he propped a chair under the door handle and secured the window lock, then he peeled his clothes off and swabbed gently at his cuts and bruises. After ministering to his hurts, he lay down and napped awhile, then he took a bath and put on fresh clothes. Only then did he pull himself out of the stupor the fight had left him in.

He had to find the Cajuns, but he couldn't go out the door and search aimlessly like a fool. They wanted him, and they would wait for the right time and place to attack. They knew where he was, and Gunn knew they had the patience of outdoor men everywhere. He had to avoid setting a pattern of eating, sleeping, walking about the town. They would come to him, and he had to ensure that he made it hard for them to select a place to hit. Too, he thought they would wait until he was alone. That meant they would try to get him out of town somehow. He shrugged. What the hell, he was part Oglala Lakota—a fight out away from town would be playing the game by his rules. He smiled to himself, feeling this challenge wash away the effect of the fight.

Gunn knew it was time he wrote Eula. It was not something to be put off any longer. It was her he wanted to marry, and Jake had made it plain that she would not take a divided love—she wanted all of him or none, and he could not give her that. He wrote Eula that the Cajuns had followed him here to Virginia City, and that as soon as he took care of the trouble with them, he would head for New Orleans. He asked her to marry him, knowing the answer would be yes from the tone of the letters Jake had saved for him.

Gunn left his room and went to the hotel porch. Before stepping outside, he searched the street in both directions and, not seeing any of the Cajuns, sat and talked to the guys in the spit-and-whittle club. The man who had held his pistols during the fight asked Gunn if he thought to stake a claim.

"No, I have a little money put back and figure to raise cattle, or maybe open a store." The store bit was an outright lie. Gunn knew he was no more cut out to be a storekeeper than to be a seamstress. "You see three men, mostly stick together pretty tight, dark black hair, slim as a stiletto, except one, who's stocky, hanging around here?"

The man nodded. "Ain't seen much of 'em, but yeah, they're around." He rubbed his jaw and peered down the street. "Funny thing 'bout 'em. They ain't miners, trappers, or townspeople. They don't do nothin'. Seems like they're lookin' fer somethin' or somebody—friends o' your'n?"

Gunn allowed a slight smile. "Friends? No, I don't think anyone would call us friends, but we have something in common. They want to kill me, and I want to keep them from doing it."

The miner eyed him a moment before saying, "Man, you ain't been in town but a few days, but you do have a way about you of garnering trouble to yourself—or maybe it just follows you around."

Gunn laughed. "Yeah—I reckon that last is right, it follows me around. Been following me for some time now." It was then that he saw the tallest of the three staring at him from the corner of a building two doors down. He raised his hand, smiled, and waved. The Cajun disappeared around the corner.

CHAPTER
SIXTEEN

GUNN STOOD. "SEE you around," he said to the miner and casually stepped off the boardwalk. He angled across the street to where he'd seen the Cajun. Although he tried to create the attitude of indolence, his mind raced.

The Cajun would be long gone, but he would have left sign—and Gunn believed he could pick up enough of it to tell him in what direction his enemies had set up camp. He didn't believe they would have built a cabin, but they might have taken over an abandoned one.

At the corner of the building, he leaned a shoulder against it and studied the spot in which the man had stood. There were a pair of boot prints, much smaller than most around there would make. He walked between the buildings and saw that there had been but little foot traffic there. The Cajun's tracks were easy to follow—almost as though he hoped to be followed.

The urge to run after the man gripped Gunn—but he squelched the idea. That was exactly what they wanted him to do, he thought. If they could lure him after them—get him out of town—he'd be playing the game by their rules. He'd be a fool to fall for that.

Reaching the back of the two buildings, he stopped short before stepping into the open. A great pile of boulders lined the banks of Alder Creek. Gunn gave them more attention than he normally would have, and when he felt sure he had nothing to fear from that direction, he moved from the buildings into the field behind the boulders.

The tracks became harder to follow. Where there had been dust, he now walked in clumpy short grass. He searched the area ahead as closely as he did the ground at his feet. If they were waiting for a clear shot at him, this was where they would take it. A hot brassy taste flooded his tongue. There were no trees lining the creek—they had long ago succumbed to the shovels and picks of the placer miners. Gunn grunted his satisfaction. The tracks were easy to follow again—as though his quarry had tried to make it easy for him.

He followed for another hundred yards or so, long enough to convince himself that south of town was where they had holed up. He stopped, searched ahead, and saw many places from where a rifleman could train his sights on him. He decided to continue the search another time—a time of his choosing. He had twisted to turn back when he felt a streak of fire run across his ribs, accompanied by the flat report of a rifle.

Gunn threw himself sidewise, rolled, and put a small land swell between him and the gunman. He cursed himself for leaving the hotel without his long gun. His handgun was next to useless at this range.

Warm, sticky fluid soaked his shirt. He shoved his hand inside his coat. A crease along his ribs burned as if a hot branding iron had been dragged across his side.

He took stock of his surroundings. The swale he lay in ran toward the creek. Although shallow, it might protect him as far as the bank, and there he could drop into the creek bed, which he could follow to the north end of town, and get back to the hotel.

He thought of standing and charging the spot where the shot had come from. He shook his head. That would be a dumb move. If the Cajun had not run like hell as soon as he fired, Gunn knew he would be playing right into his attacker's hands.

Gunn pulled his .44 and slithered toward the creek bank. While crawling, he pondered heading south when he got to the water, but discarded the idea—he didn't have the proper weapons.

His side hurt more all the time. The first shock of the impact had worn off and, with it, pain flooded the area. He changed course slightly and poked his head above the roll in the land. A bullet kicked dirt into his face. He flattened against the ground and rolled to the bottom of the swale. Now he got serious about reaching the creek. He stretched almost straight and, without raising his body but inches from the ground, dragged himself as fast as his elbows could pull him.

Although a shallow wound, the cut across his ribs bled heavily now. He would have to gét back to town and get it bandaged before he weakened. The Cajun had given him a good idea bout the direction he had to search, but he would look for them like a Lakota—and kill like a Lakota.

He still had about twenty yards to go—and about a quarter of that distance was across level ground. He slowed, stopped, and flattened against the earth. The smell of dust and the sunbaked grass made him choke back a sneeze, causing his side muscles to pull tight, knot, and blind him with pain.

Gunn studied that flat area. He would be a prime target during those few yards, and a good rifleman would have no trouble putting lead into him. But from what he'd seen of the Cajuns' marksmanship, he didn't think they were that good. Regardless, he'd have to chance it.

He inched to the spot he figured was his last chance to stay hidden, got to his hands and knees, and launched himself toward the creek bank. Dirt exploded to his side and then against the bank just as he dived over the lip. Two shots and neither of them touched him. He lay half in the cold water, panting and sweating, little of it caused by exertion. He'd thought he had been scared before, but what he had felt then was nothing to what he felt now.

He couldn't stay here. He stood and, bent almost double, ran toward the north. When he thought he was about at the end of town, he came out of the creek bed, expecting to draw fire, and braced for it, but all was quiet. He ran to the rutted road and turned toward town, intending to go to his room and wrap his wound.

When he came to Jake's shop, he hurried to get past it—and almost made it.

"Where the hell you goin'? Won't you even stop and say howdy anymore?"

He stopped and leaned against the wall, feeling that his legs would fold under him. "Hi, Jake. Didn't figure to bother you. I need to get to my room."

"Oh damn, now you gone an' got yourself hurt. That there hurt you got is bleedin' right fierce." She hurried to his side, put her arm under his, and pulled him to lean against her. "Here, let me help you git yoreself to the back of the shop. Seems like you always need tendin', an' ain't got sense enough to stay outta trouble. C'mon now, don't argue. Jake's gonna fix you up again."

Gunn didn't argue. His jaw muscles clenched so tight he couldn't have gotten a word out if he'd wanted to.

Jake led him to the back room and, after making him comfortable, pulled a bottle of rye whiskey, about half-full, from the shelf above her head. She then opened a drawer and pulled a flour sack from it. "Warshed these sacks an' jist got 'em dry this mornin'—make good bandages."

Gunn sat there without uttering a word. She cleaned the long gash with the whiskey left in the bottle from which he'd last helped her drink. She clucked like a mother hen each time he winced. Finished cleaning it, she wrapped his side tightly. "Need it to be good an' tight. Probably cracked a rib along with cuttin' yore pretty hide." She patted the bandage when she finished, and said. "There, that ought to hold you till you can get shot up or cut again."

"What makes you think I got shot?"

"Well, hell, Rafe, I done tended more gunshot wounds than you ever seen. Shore now, that there's a gunshot I jest tended."

Gunn nodded. "You're right, Jake. One of those Cajuns just about had me where he wanted me. If they don't kill me first, I found the direction to look for them. I'm tired of having to sneak around everywhere I go. Gonna hunt *them* now. Hell, I still don't know what they want me for—but whatever it is I'm gonna kill them."

"If they don't kill you first."

"Anyway, thanks, Jake. Seems like I'm always thanking you for something. If I started right now trying to repay you for all you've done for me, it would take the rest of my life."

"You don't owe me nothin', Rafe. Jest doin' for you has been my pay—but, pshaw now. Let's don't git into that kind of talk or we'll be right back to doin' what we said we wasn't gonna do no more."

Gunn stared at her a moment, shook his head, and stood. "Better be getting on back to the hotel. Need to pick up my rifle and a little gift Crazy Horse gave me."

As soon as he stood, Jake backed off a couple of paces as though she feared being too close to him, but then she reached to the shelf behind and took down two glasses. "One for old times sake, Rafe?"

He nodded, still looking into her eyes. "One for old times sake, Jake." Just looking at her about tore his guts out, and he realized that the want in him wasn't just physical.

She poured each of them about a half glassful, then they touched glasses, drank, and Gunn hurried from her shop—afraid to stay longer.

Outside he felt surprise that the sun had set. He headed for the hotel.

In his room, he cleaned and oiled his weapons again, although none showed a speck of dust—then he opened the doeskin sleeve Crazy Horse had handed him and slid the beautifully crafted bow from it. With the bowstring in place, he tested the pull. It was perfect, and sighting down the shaft of each arrow, he saw they were straight. Last, he whetted his knife.

He removed his boots, all his clothes, and put on buckskins and moccasins. Opening the door to his room a crack, he glanced down the length of the hall. Clear, he slipped to the back door and went into the darkness. He'd forgotten about dinner.

Staying to the backs of the buildings, he slipped past the church and left town. Wherever the Cajuns had holed up, he thought they would have a fire—and he would investigate every light.

Moving silent as an evening breeze through the night, he again felt like an Oglala Lakota, so much that he felt The People moving with him.

At first the fire or lantern light from different miner's shacks was plentiful. He slipped to each and studied those who sat by their fire, or read in the flickering light of candles or lanterns. None were those he looked for.

The tents and shacks thinned, and he guessed he was now over a mile from town. He checked three more places and was creeping steadily south toward the mountains when he saw in the distance a dim light. Gunn thought at first that it might be a star, but he realized that it was below the crest of the mountains in the background.

The only sound he made was a thin swish as his feet brushed through the dried grass. Soon the light showed to be a rectangle—another miner's shack.

He squatted in the darkness, thinking. If he used his rifle or pistol, they would assume it was him. He didn't want that— yet. He wanted to lessen the odds without announcing that he knew where they were. He thought on that a moment, nodded to himself, stood, and inched forward.

The shack loomed dark in front of him. Avoiding looking at the lighted window, he searched the periphery and saw no sign that they had posted a watch. He inched closer to the wall—then slid along it toward the window.

This was the first close, good look he'd had at them. Every other time he'd been this close, he'd been fighting for his life; now he saw them sitting relaxed by their fire.

A right handsome trio, he thought. They sat mostly with their backs or sides toward him, silently staring at the fire. After a while one of them stood, poured coffee, and sat.

Gunn felt no guilt when he nocked an arrow. He would kill any or all of them without warning. They had never warned him, and, too, he had fought with the Lakotas—they never warned an enemy. Surprise, and the battle was half-won. He'd kill only one of them now.

He chose the one with his back to him. The expanse between his shoulders made a better target. He pulled the fletch to his cheek, sighted, and turned it loose.

Gunn waited only a second, long enough to see his arrow bury itself in the Cajun's back.

All hell broke loose in the shack—cursing, yelling to douse the fire. "Indians" was one word Gunn heard before he drifted out of hearing. He circled to the side with the fireplace—and waited, certain they would give the side with the window their attention.

He hated that his brothers would take the blame for the attack, and then was amused at the thought that the Cajuns *had* suffered an Indian attack.

"Shut the damned window," one of them yelled. Gunn heard it slam into place—then total silence.

He stood there in the darkness and waited, sure that eventually they would come outside, when no shots were fired and no more arrows poured into their room from the doorway. He was also sure that what he was about to do was damn foolishness.

After a few minutes, one of them said, "They're gone. Let's us take a look outside."

"Mon, I ain't goan out there wit no Indians."

"Aw, come the hell on."

There was a moment of silence, then the reluctant one said, "Awright. You go first."

Gunn waited for them to clear the door and circle to the window side, then he ran toward it, .44 in hand. They would not be gone long. Fear would drive them back inside. He had to do his work and be gone before that happened.

Inside he pulled his knife and stripped the scalp from the one he'd killed. This little touch should convince them that they had been attacked by Indians. He tried to pull his arrow free. It hung up on a bone or something. He couldn't pull it out. He glanced at the door, knowing he was pushing his luck. He tugged at the arrow one more time, then turned and bolted from the shack. He rounded the corner just as the two came growling back toward the door.

A shot that came nowhere close, and one of them said, "What the hell you shootin' at? Wan't nothing there."

"I seen somethin', swear I did."

"You din't see nothing—git on inside."

Gunn stayed close enough to hear them trying to care for their brother—and blaming red-skinned savages for his death—then he took a wide loop around the shack and headed back toward Virginia City. On the way back he buried the scalp, which he had no use for.

The time back to town seemed far shorter.

In his room he washed up and changed into Levi's and a flannel shirt, strapped on his guns, and became aware of the smells wafting to him from the kitchen. Steak, onion, and stew smell caused saliva to flow around his tongue, and his stomach to remind him that he hadn't eaten since breakfast. He headed for the dining room.

Finishing his third cup of coffee after eating a steak that covered his plate, Gunn considered his options. He couldn't go to the law—there wasn't any—but if there had been, they wouldn't have understood that the Cajuns were bent on killing him, and that they would do it where blame could not be placed. This was something he had to take care of himself.

He thought of Jake and wanted to go to her, but he shook his head. He had written Eula and posted the letter.

CHAPTER
SEVENTEEN

EULA AND HER father rode in the bed of a freight wagon only one day north of Virginia City. They had docked in Fort Benton two weeks earlier and paid a freighter to take them to Alder Gulch. Paul had promised her they would search the towns of Nevada City and Virginia City for Gunn, and if they failed to find him, they would return to New Orleans.

"Papa, you've never said it straight out—but you think I'm foolish for coming all the way up here to find a man who may not love me—or, being honest, a man I may not love, don't you?"

Paul stared at the mountains a moment before answering, then he looked her in the eyes. "Eula, I don't know. I only know I couldn't stand to see you make your daily trek to the edge of the river and stare upstream. I don't know whether you were searching for the dream of Rafe—or for the real man. I only know we had to put it to rest once and for all."

"You won't be angry with me if it doesn't work out?"

"Little one, have I ever been angry with you? No, I just want to see you happy, and if it takes a four-month trip to do that—then so be it. We'll find him. I think he's a good man, a strong man—but I'm not sure the life he'll lead will be for you."

The wagon bumped and lurched across a deep chuckhole. Eula grabbed for the seat to steady herself, then said, "Papa, if he's the one, whatever life he chooses will be good for me—I'll stand by his side no matter what."

Paul snaked his arm around her shoulders and pulled her to him. "Ah, little one, I never had a doubt about that. If I had, we would never have made this trip." He squinted his eyes against the sun glare, to see the head of the wagon train. "Looks like the wagon master is signaling for a stop—probably for the night."

"Well, I don't have the things to prepare you a meal like Mama Jory would, but a good cup of coffee, New Orleans style, with lots of chicory, will be good." Eula waited for the big Studebaker wagon to stop, climbed down, and excused herself to go into the brush to take care of her personal needs.

When she came back, Paul had a fire going, and she prepared their meal, such that the provisions they had would permit. She opened an airtight of peaches, made a few biscuits from the starter she never allowed herself to run out of before adding to it, and put a couple of strips of venison close to the fire to broil.

While they ate, the wagon boss came by and told them they would reach Nevada City about noon the next day, and that it was only a couple of miles from Virginia City.

Paul looked at Eula. "Butterflies, little one?"

She nodded. "A little nervous now that this search is about to end. He may not even be there—we'll just have to wait and see."

Paul laughed. "Whatever's meant to be, will be. Just don't make yourself sick worrying about it."

"No. I'll not do that. I'll know as soon as we meet—we'll both know." She cut another bite from her steak and sat chewing it, thinking. This was the most beautiful country she had ever dreamed existed. Rafe would probably end up ranching. Yes, she would like that; she would like anything a man she loved chose to do. Rafe was a man who would do anything well, a man who was tough and hard enough to overcome any obstacle. Thinking of him, she had sometimes wondered if perhaps he was too hard—but then this country required a bit of steel in a man. She sighed, and stacked the dishes for washing. They had sat long by the fire, and it was time to sleep.

Forty miles to the south, Gunn's thoughts had shifted to the Cajuns. He couldn't go out two more nights and eliminate them one by one. It wouldn't be that easy—they would keep watch now. He had no doubt that they would continue to try to draw him away from town—one of them dead wouldn't change that. The vigilance committee in town wouldn't permit a gunfight in the city.

Gunn finished his meal and went to his room. He'd sleep on it.

He spent a sleepless night, and when the sun came up, he was no closer to knowing how to get rid of his nemesis than he'd been the night before.

Eating breakfast, he decided to get out of town. He wanted to see that valley across the mountain to the east. If it was all he'd heard, that was where he wanted to build his ranch. While gone, he would try to get some fresh meat for Jake—she couldn't object if he just dropped it by her shop. And out by himself he might think clearer. He went to his room for his rifle.

While saddling his horse, he compared the scents he'd known at sea with those that surrounded him. Here there was the smell of tanned leather, a hint of cured-on-the-stem hay, horse droppings, occasionally tobacco wafting by, and the tantalizing aroma of coffee brewing. He had liked the sea with its fresh salt air, but this was where he belonged.

He mounted and rode toward the east, careful to skirt the area the Cajuns had holed up in. A steady climb out of Virginia City took him into the clear crisp air of the Gravelly Range. When he topped out before descending to the Madison River, he stopped. As far as he could see the Madison Valley stretched to the south, and down its bottom the river wended its way to empty into the Missouri. Across the valley and on into the distance, the snow-peaked tips of the Absaroka Mountains towered.

Gunn breathed in until he felt his chest muscles protest. His time with the Lakota had given him a taste of the open country. He would never be happy in a town again. This country was his. He would build his ranch in that valley he looked upon, take his woman to it, and raise his children there.

Movement out of the corner of his eye. Holding the reins of his horse, Gunn threw himself from the saddle. Four majestic deer crossed the trail and bounded down the side of the mountain. Without thinking, he had brought his rifle to his shoulder and was squeezing the trigger when he relaxed his pull. He didn't want this hunt to end before it started. He mounted and kneed his horse down the trail, wanting to reach the river and ride its banks a ways—maybe find his homesite.

Now Gunn used all the care Cat Bavousett and the Lakota had taught him. Here the Crow and the Shoshone ranged, as well as the Teton Sioux. The Crow were the ones who caused him caution. If he met them, he wanted loyal men at his back, and for that, he knew he might have to pull in some of the Texas drovers he'd heard had come up the Bozeman trail with longhorns. They knew cattle and were as salty a bunch of men as could be found.

Before reaching the bottom, and while he still had the vantage point of elevation, Gunn studied the trees along the riverbank, and the long expanse of green grass, for movement. In the distance a large band of wild horses grazed. He brushed them from his thoughts—he looked for mounted horses.

The trees along the river held his attention the longest. If the Crow were not in sight, those trees could hide an army of them, and if they had seen him first, that was probably where they'd wait—letting him get closer.

His gut muscles tensed. His throat muscles tightened. He kneed his horse in a direct line for the trees. While still a ways out, he changed course to the south, thinking that if they were there, he might cause them to give away their position. Nothing happened. Abruptly he swung his horse to the north—that brought them out of hiding—three of them. Gunn kicked his horse into a hard run.

A quick look showed Gunn he was about two hundred yards from the bottom of an escarpment. In some distant past a pile of boulders had slid down its face and were strewn along the base, as though carelessly tossed there by some giant hand. He looked over his shoulder. His attackers had not gained on him. He guessed them to be Crow.

Gunn threw himself from the saddle, dragging his rifle from the scabbard as he fell. He slapped his horse on the rump, urging him and the packhorse farther into the rocks.

He rolled to the shelter of the largest boulder close to him, brought his Henry to his shoulder, and fired. The lead rider fell. The warriors were firing now, and weren't missing by far. Rock fragments sprayed Gunn's face. He hunkered closer to the ground and fired again. He missed—but caused the Indians to split, one going to each side. If they left their horses and hid in the rocks, he was in trouble up to his neck. There was no way in hell he could watch both directions.

He fired at the one to his right and saw him grab for his horse's mane. A solid hit—but the warrior spilled off his horse close to another pile of rocks and snaked his way into the space between them. Gunn turned his attention to his left in time to see that one go to ground.

Now they would play a waiting game. Gunn was sure they thought they dealt with a white man—and white men were famous for having little patience. But he'd seen a few Crow who couldn't bear to wait.

He lay there, studying the boulders to his left. That Indian lucked out, he thought; he had rocks all around him. Gunn twisted to study the position of the warrior he had hit—it looked about as secure as that of the other Crow. If his bullet had done much damage, maybe he could afford to give most of his attention to the healthy one.

He rolled to his back and scanned the face of the cliff, hoping to see a way to escape up its face. After a moment he shook his head. Even a mountain goat couldn't have scaled that granite wall.

The instant he gave up the idea of using that as an escape route, he saw an outcropping that seemed to hang from the cliff's face with a precarious hold.

His gaze slid down the cliff to its base. That outcropping was almost straight above where he gaged the healthy warrior to be. He nodded. Maybe it would work.

Several minutes passed during which Gunn divided his time between checking the position of the two Indians and looking over every inch of the outcropping.

Finally he chose a split in the strata that ran almost perpendicular to the ground. He aimed his Henry at the crack and fired, quickly jacked shells into the chamber, and fired twice more.

With his last shot a large granite shard broke loose and slid down the rock face, bringing with it an avalanche of talus. Gunn shifted his attention to where he judged his healthy adversary waited.

The talus and small piece of cliff gained momentum, picking up tons of more debris.

At first the rockfall was light, then it grew heavier. It flushed the man from his hiding place. A brown arm showed—then the warrior stood and charged Gunn's position. Gunn fired, levered another shell into the magazine, and fired again. At the instant the first bullet hit, Gunn saw its twin puncture the Indian's breastbone. The Crow jerked to one side and fell. Either of the holes Gunn had seen open the Indian's chest would have been fatal.

He twisted to give the other Crow his attention, in time to see a brown streak coming through the air at him, holding as wicked-looking a knife as Gunn had ever seen. Gunn rolled back against the rock, his hand groping for the knife in its sheath at his back. The Indian's dive landed him alongside.

Gunn's knife came clear at the moment he rolled to cover the warrior. Gunn swept his blade toward the Indian's throat. The Crow blocked his slice with his own knife. It was then that Gunn realized the Indian used only one hand. His whole left side was covered with blood. Before Gunn could draw back his weapon and slice again, the warrior fell to the side. The bullet Gunn had fired at him as he rode in had finally done its job—but he had died fighting.

Gunn stood and looked from one Crow to the other. He had it in his mind to take their hair. He stepped toward the first one he had killed, frowned, shook his head, and stooped to jab his knife into the sand several times to clean the blade. He would not take their scalps—it was time he stopped being a Lakota— unless he needed to be again sometime in the future.

It took almost an hour, and backbreaking, sweaty work, but when Gunn picked up the last large rock an dropped it over the niche he'd put the two Indians in, he felt that animals would not get at them to chew on their bones and strew them across the grassy glade where they rested.

If this episode were any indication, Gunn knew he was going to have to fight for every day he spent in this valley. His gaze swept the riverbank and ranged across the rich grass-covered land. He felt his chest swell. He swallowed twice to rid his throat of the lump formed there. This was home—he'd fight the whole Crow Nation for it if he had to—and he'd probably have to.

Two days later Gunn finished dressing an elk, packed it on his spare horse, and headed back toward Virginia City. He'd done all here that he planned.

CHAPTER
EIGHTEEN

GUNN, KNOWING JAKE would be at her bakeshop, stopped by her cabin, built a fire, and rigged a pole from which to hang the fresh meat. He split enough firewood to finish drying the strips into which he'd cut the elk, and took a couple of good-sized roasts in and put them in her cooler, which wasn't much more than a hole in the wall behind a cupboard, to let the cool outside air in. Then he went around back and sat close enough to the fire to knock the chill from him.

He'd not had a cigar in a couple of weeks and thought to enjoy one while the tantalizing smell of the drying meat tickled his nostrils. That thought didn't hold for long. He groped in his coat pocket and found only broken leaves remaining of what had been a cigar when he left his room three days before. He shrugged and leaned against the wall. To hell with it, he thought. He didn't need to smoke anyway.

Every hour or so Gunn replenished the wood on the coals, watching the strips of meat dry and become winter food. They would make a good stew when introduced to water again. He fell asleep.

"Gol dang you, Rafe Gunn. What you tryin' to do, make a milksop outta me?"

Gunn stirred and cracked one eyelid to slant a look at Jake who stood, hands on hips, staring down at him.

"You think I cain't take care o' myself?"

Gunn tried, but couldn't control the grin. Damn, he thought, it's good to hear her chewing on my butt. "Yes'm, reckon you can take care of yourself anywhere—but I killed an elk out yonder in the Madison Valley. Figured it'd spoil if I didn't do something with it. Couldn't think of anyone who liked to eat more'n you—'less it was me. So I fixed it for winter eatin'."

Jake's face softened. "Aw now, Rafe. I thank you, I truly do, 'ceptin' you an' me agreed to stay away from each other."

Gunn rolled to his side and stood. "So we did, Jake, and I'll not break that agreement. I meant to be gone before you closed the shop and came home. I'll be going now."

Jake stepped toward him, quickly, then backed off. "Reckon it'd be best you did, big man. Where you're concerned, I ain't got much sense. My big old body sorta soaks up my brain." She kept her distance, and Gunn didn't make it more difficult for either of them.

Jake ran her hands down the front of her skirt, gathered a ball of it into her hand, and worried it into a wrinkled mess. "I . . . I, well, thank you for the meat an' fixin' it up good for winter."

"You're welcome, Jake. Next time I'll make sure I don't fall asleep and let you catch me here."

"Ain't gonna be a next time, Rafe."

He tipped his hat and walked toward town. Even knowing the Cajuns were close by, Gunn settled into a funk, not aware of his surroundings. He found himself wishing he hadn't written Eula the letter. He didn't know whether he loved Eula or not—but he was beginning to think, despite what he and Jake had agreed to, that staying away from each other might not be all that easy. They could never become just business partners. "Aw, hell," he muttered. He looked up and saw he was about to walk past his hotel. He changed course and went to his room.

Three days in the country, with only the cold river to bathe in, made his first priority a hot bath and shave—then a drink, and a meal *he* hadn't cooked.

He cleaned and oiled his weapons, then took care of himself and went to the saloon.

Gunn headed for a table. At the bar he would be forced to talk to the men around him, and he didn't want talk.

After ordering his drink, he studied the people. Most were drummers, gamblers, and a few of the town merchants. At the bar stood a man with his back to the room—a back and stance that were vaguely familiar. Gunn's drink came, and while drinking it, he thought about the Cajuns. What did they want with him? His mind backtracked to New Orleans and could think of nothing he had ever done to gain their enmity.

His thoughts shifted to Jake, then Eula. He compared them, and still neither of them came up short. The thought of Eula sent currents of warmth and desire through him, and he tried to bring her memory into sharp focus—it didn't work. Her image came through as in a heavy fog. When he'd met her, she was the first woman he'd ever had a chance to know. Was that the reason she stayed so close in his thoughts? He glanced at the man whom he'd thought familiar a few moments ago. He still had the nagging feeling that he should know him.

Gunn tossed off the rest of his drink, shrugged, and stood. The only way to tell would be to look at his face. He walked up and stood behind the man. At that instant, recognition came.

"Paul, what in the devil are you doing here? Where's Eula?"

Gunn grasped Paul's hand, then they clasped each other in a bear hug.

"Rafe Gunn. We've been looking for you." He glanced from Gunn's boots to his face. "You're looking fit. You'll have to tell me all that's happened since you left New Orleans—it sure as hell hasn't hurt you any."

"Where's Eula?"

"She rented a horse and took a ride to the south, or east, of town a couple hours ago—should be back soon. If she knew I'd found *you*, she'd be here now."

Gunn frowned. "Paul, you shouldn't have let her go. There are all kinds of people out here—not the typical Westerner—and those Cajuns have followed me here. They're living in a cabin south of town. If she doesn't show pretty soon, we better look for her."

"Aw, she'll be all right. She has a handgun with her—and you've seen how well she shoots. Grab us a table and I'll get the drinks."

Gunn did as Paul suggested, but he couldn't get rid of the queasy feeling in his stomach. The Cajuns had seen him with Eula; they would know her—and he didn't like it.

While he and Paul talked and sipped at their drinks, Gunn kept glancing at the door, wishing Eula would look over the batwings and signal them that she was there. He brought her father up to date on the things that had transpired since his leaving New Orleans. He had about gotten to where he'd left

Fort Lincoln with Bavousett when a boy of about fourteen pushed through the doors and looked around.

The boy seemed to be looking for someone in particular. He had to be, Gunn thought, because he wouldn't have been allowed in there otherwise.

He was a skinny kid, dressed in hand-me-downs much too large for his slight frame. He turned his head from one side to the other, looking at each person, then he went to the bar and said something to the bartender.

The bartender pointed toward the table at which he and D'Anville sat. The boy came over.

"Mr. d'Anville?"

Paul nodded. "That's me, son. What can I do for you?"

"Nothin' fer me, sir. I wuz told to give you a message. Two men, black hair, 'most as skinny as me said to tell you they had yore daughter, an' fer a Mr. Gunn to come alone for her or they'd kill her. Seems they have it in mind to trade her for Gunn. I ain't s'posed to tell nobody but you this message. Said fer him to just ride out south o' town—that they'd find him."

Gunn drew a silver dollar from his pocket and tossed it to the kid. With one hand the kid caught it and tossed it back. "They done paid me, mister. Thanks anyway."

Gunn took the coin in midair and dropped it into the kid's pocket. "Thanks, youngster. You earned this. We'll take it from here."

The doors closed behind the boy, and Gunn said over his shoulder to D'Anville, "Now you know what I was afraid of. Those men are intent on killing me."

D'Anville sat staring into his drink. "What'll we do, Rafe? She is all I have in this world."

"First off, I'm gonna give you the hardest job either of us will have."

"Anything, Rafe, anything you say."

Gunn tossed off his drink and ordered a couple more.

"Gunn, we haven't time for a drink. We have to get going. My daughter's life is in danger."

D'Anville had stood while talking. Gunn waved him back into his seat. "Sit down, Paul. I'm gonna find Eula—and I'll do it alone. I know how to hunt them—you'd only get us all killed. Now, sit there and drink your whiskey—don't talk; I've got to think."

Gunn took a swallow of his whiskey, not feeling the burn of it slide down his throat. He stared at the far wall, not seeing it. Those Cajuns would not harm Eula; he was convinced they were not the kind. In their own way, he thought them honorable men—and that honor was what had kept them on his trail for so long. *He* was the one they wanted, and they were using Eula as the lure to get him into their trap. All right, he would go after her, but he would call the shots—he would not dance to their tune.

His eyes focused on D'Anville. "Paul, I'm going to find Eula and bring her back to you. You're gonna sit here and wait. After I leave, give me six hours, and if I'm not back by then, tell the bartender what has happened. He'll get the vigilance committee to take a hand. He'll know how to do it. Now, I'm telling you—don't jump the gun. If you do, a lot of innocent people will get hurt. Now the hardest part—I'm not leaving here until it's full dark. That's gonna be hard—the waiting—but it's the only way to play this hand. I'm going to my room and make a few preparations. You can come with me if you like."

D'Anville nodded, tossed off his drink, and stood.

In his room Gunn motioned D'Anville to the room's only chair. "Sit there while I get ready. That bottle on the table is pretty good whiskey. Help yourself."

While he changed into buckskins, checked his guns, knife, and the shaft of each arrow, Gunn kept thinking that if he'd not gone to take a look at the Madison Valley, he would have been here when Eula and Paul arrived, and this would not have happened to her. He gnawed on that thought for a while and shrugged. If hell—if he'd not gone to sea in the first place, none of this would be taking place. You had to play the cards the way they fell.

He felt D'Anville's gaze boring into him. "What's the matter?"

D'Anville shook his head. "Nothing, but in the last few minutes I've seen you change from a Westerner to an Indian— and it seems to fit you well. I can't hear you move. The only way I would know you were here if I weren't looking at you is the smell of leather."

Gunn pinned D'Anville with a stare. "Paul, I *am* Indian, or had you forgotten? There are times—like this—that I believe I'm more Indian than white, and you'd better be glad that I am."

D'Anville returned his stare and said, softly, "I wonder how Eula will handle that."

"You'd better thank the Everywhere Spirit that she'll be alive to handle it."

After dark, as he'd done before, Gunn slipped out the back door of the hotel. When he went by the door to the kitchen, the aroma reminded him that he still hadn't eaten.

He had put up a good front to D'Anville, showing more confidence than he really felt. But he was going against two very dangerous men—men who felt they had "right" on their side, and that always made for a more formidable enemy. Gunn mentally shook his head. He would not allow self-doubts— they might make the difference between winning and losing.

Silently he skirted the town, taking care to avoid the soddies, cabins, and shacks, whether they showed a light or not. He'd been on the trail about an hour when out of the darkness a soddy materialized before he could change his course to go around it. A dog bounded toward him, a continuous string of barks breaking the silence.

Gunn froze. He didn't dare run—that might cause the dog to attack. Instead, deep in his throat he made a mewling sound— then squatted and called in a soft, deep voice, "C'mon, pup, here now, I'm your friend." He held his hand out slowly to entice the dog closer.

The animal dropped close to the ground and inched forward, his bark now only a whine—he wanted to be petted. Abruptly the night's stillness was broken. The door to the soddy swung open, and a man stepped into the night. "What the hell's wrong with you, dawg? Somebody traipsin' around here in the dark?"

The hound had crawled under Gunn's hand and lay there trying to lick the sleeve of his shirt. Gunn gently massaged the hair at the base of the animal's skull. Neither of them made a sound.

The man stepped back through the doorway, grumbling about the stupid hound he'd taken in.

Gunn patted the pup, stood, and moved into the night. He'd gone only a few steps when he became aware that the dog followed him. He raised a hand to shoo the animal back to his home, but stopped short. Hell, the hound wouldn't make any more noise than he himself made. "C'mon, fella, we can be partners for tonight."

The dog moved to Gunn's side and trotted along happy as a

hog in a mud wallow. Poor devil probably never had a kind word before, Gunn thought.

The two moved as shadows through the night—then it began to rain, a slow, cold drizzle that would soon soak Gunn's buckskins, and then they would weigh heavy on his shoulders. It wasn't the added weight that worried him. Wet leather, moving against his sides, or against his trouser legs, would squeak—not much noise, but enough to warn a watchful enemy.

When Gunn estimated he was close to the Cajun's cabin, he circled, wanting to approach it from the blind side, the side on which the chimney stood.

The pup stayed with him. He was still a pup, although Gunn thought he was almost full grown.

The cabin showed no lights, not even the flicker of a fire. Abruptly it loomed in front of him, black against the lighter dark of the night. Gunn inched his way toward the rough log structure, moving his arms and legs slowly to help eliminate the sound his clothes might make. He had almost reached the wall when the pup ran ahead of him, and around the corner.

"Hey, dawg, wheah you come from?" Again Gunn heard the pup whining deep in his throat. The Cajun must have been petting him. "You gonna haveta git gone now. I got work to do."

Damn, Gunn thought, he had to kill that man, and there he was petting a wet, bedraggled pooch. Why couldn't he talk to them—find out what they had against him—and maybe let the whole thing drop? He knew that wouldn't work as soon as the thought entered his mind. Those men had trailed him a long way, and one of them had paid his life for it.

Gunn took advantage of the few moments the Cajun petted the dog, knowing the man wouldn't have all of his senses tuned to his surroundings. He moved quickly to the corner of the cabin—and almost stumbled over the man squatted by the pooch. Gunn hoped the other one wasn't close by.

He pulled his knife and swung—he missed. The Cajun came up off the ground in one smooth motion. The two locked arms around each other, each straining to break his knife arm free. The Cajun, although of slight build, was wiry, his muscles seeming to be of steel.

The fought silently, as men will do when their life and breath hinges on it. Gunn hoped the other Cajun didn't hear them.

Gunn pitted muscle against muscle. It seemed his tendons would tear themselves out of his arms. The Cajun swung one foot behind Gunn's leg and tripped him to the ground—the slim, black-haired man on top. Gunn's enemy now had his blade in hand. He raised it to plunge in into Gunn's chest. At that moment—the dog chose sides.

With a growl deep in his throat, he darted in and grabbed the Cajun's free arm in his jaws. It gave Gunn the break he needed.

He moved his knife between them and thrust upward—straight into his enemy's gut. At the same time he grabbed the man's slim neck with his left hand and squeezed to shut off the groan that was inevitable. The Cajun stiffened, every muscle tense—then he relaxed on top of Gunn.

Gunn lay there a moment, panting, then carefully moved the body off of him. He listened for any sign that they had been heard. Silence, dead silence, shrouded him. Where was the other man?

He sat there in the mud, stroking the dog's neck. He wanted to say thank you, but didn't dare utter the words, for fear of being heard.

He sucked in a deep breath and stood. He crept to the cabin's wall and leaned against it, trying to see to each side. He had to locate the last of his enemies.

The one he killed had been on the door side, and Gunn had come in on the fireplace side. He knew the remaining Cajun *had* to be on the side opposite the door.

Gunn thought about entering the cabin and freeing Eula—he had no doubt they had her trussed up in there—but he discarded that thought. The Cajun could trap him inside and burn the cabin—or be free to move around outside as he wished, with all the windows and doors to fire through. Gunn shook his head. He might get Eula killed that way. He had to find his enemy and fight him outside.

Gunn slipped along the chimney wall toward the back. The pup followed.

He reached the corner of the small building, squatted, and peered around it. His gaze swept across the wall and back again, then he searched farther out, and then again. He looked until his eyes played him tricks—every darker object became suspect; he had to stop his search at every blot and strain to see any movement. The dog had wandered off.

While with his brothers, the Lakota, Gunn had learned the value of patience. He started his search at the wall again. He had not looked long when he saw movement about twenty yards out. He tensed and drew his .44, studying the spot. Rain dripped from his forehead into his eyes. He brushed the drops from his brows and squinted to see better. His gaze covered the area like an artist's brush. The pup was casting about, his nose to the ground.

Gunn exhaled slowly. If anyone stood out there in the rain, Gunn felt the dog would have announced him, or the person would have greeted the pet with a curse, or a greeting of some kind.

Despite thinking that the man had to be there somewhere, Gunn rounded the corner and slid along the back wall. He had reached about the halfway point of it when his cold, moccasined foot came down on a stick. It popped with a noise that seemed as loud as the gunshot that followed it.

A blow like a sledgehammer hit Gunn in his leg, slamming him against the rough logs. Two more shots followed. Gunn fired at the powder flash, then bracketed it with a shot to each side. He heard a groan.

Gunn's whole left leg was numb. He dreaded the pain that would follow, but for now he had other worries. Was the man out there dead? Was he badly wounded? Was he just waiting for Gunn to move so he could get in another shot?

Gunn felt warmth flowing down his thigh. He hoped the bleeding didn't weaken him before he could be sure the fight was over. He kept his eyes pointed at the spot where he'd seen the gun flashes. There wasn't anything standing. He searched the ground, and there saw a darker shadow.

He pinned his gaze to it, watching for movement. He groped around at his feet until he found a short length of wood, and then tossed it to the side, toward where his adversary had gone down, hoping to draw fire. No movement.

Only a fool would have walked straight in on the man—Gunn circled, thinking to come on him from the back. Another groan, followed by raspy breathing. It came from where he thought the man had fallen. He circled farther and then, with no more noise than the tiny droplets of rain, closed in on the wounded man.

When within four or five feet of him, Gunn saw that he lay on his back, his arms stretched over his head—hands empty.

Gunn walked to him and stooped. "Where you hit?"

"Doan know. Hurt—hurt lak de devil."

"Stay still. I'll get you inside out of this rain and see if I can patch you up."

"Woan do no good. Ain't gonna last that long."

Gunn studied the man and knew he told the truth. His entire chest, looking black in the night, was soaked with blood. He wouldn't last long—but Gunn had to know why the Cajuns had hunted him.

"Before you go, tell me why you men have been chasing me. As far as I know I've never harmed any of you."

"Barataria—you killed our brother. Now, with me, you have killed us all."

"Lie still. I'll get you inside."

"Too late. I-I'm . . ." His head lolled to the side, his eyes wide, staring—at nothing.

Gunn squatted there a moment. This man and his brothers had been good, tenacious enemies. A man was lucky when he could count men like these as his adversaries. He stood and went to the cabin.

He groped around in the dark, found a lantern, and lighted it.

The first thing he saw was Eula, tied hand and foot to the bunk against the wall.

His knife made short work of the lashings. Next he removed the gag tied around her head.

"Where you been so long, Rafe? I've been lying here waiting." Then she threw herself into his arms. "Oh, you beautiful man, I knew if I ever got myself into real trouble, you'd show up."

Gunn grasped her shoulders and held her at arm's length. "Hello, pretty lady, this was my trouble—not yours." He glanced at his watch and saw that he had two hours before D'Anville roused the vigilantes. He didn't have time to bury the two brothers.

"Stay where you are until I get the two men I killed in here out of the rain. We'll send someone out from town to bury them. Gotta get you into town so your father won't worry any longer."

"You've seen Papa?"

Gunn nodded. "I've seen him."

He left and soon returned carrying the brother he'd killed in front of the cabin. He repeated the trip and carried the last of the two to the cabin.

While walking, he thought that Eula had fulfilled the promise of beauty he had seen in her as a girl. She was perhaps the most beautiful woman he'd ever seen. His wound stopped those thoughts. It shot pain the length of his leg and into his hip.

Inside he dropped the last of the brothers and slit his trouser leg. It was a soggy mess, what with the blood and the rain.

"You're hurt. Oh, why didn't you say something?"

Gunn glanced at her. She had pulled a drawer open and was searching through it. A clean shirt came to hand, and she began tearing it into strips. "This'll have to do for bandages until I get you to a doctor."

Gunn's throat swelled with pride. Eula hadn't paled, nor had she shrunk from doing what had to be done—she stepped right in to clean and dress the bullet hole. And despite the pain, when her cool, strong fingers touched his flesh, his muscles tightened—just the feel of her sent waves of warmth through him. She would make one helluva frontier wife.

Finally she patted the bandages and looked him in the eye. "Hurt?"

"Feels better."

"We'll get you into town." She stepped back and looked questioningly at him. "Rafe, you haven't written. Have you even thought of me since you left?"

He nodded. "More than you can imagine, Eula. I just posted a letter to you a couple of days ago, tellin' you I was going to come to New Orleans this fall—to see if you'd grown up. Now I know."

He wanted to take her into his arms—but held back. She was breathtakingly beautiful, and she could stand the sight of blood—but was that enough? He didn't know this woman who stood in front of him, and she didn't know him.

She stood there, obviously waiting to be kissed. Gunn turned toward the door. "Let's get someone out here to bury these two. They are worthy enemies."

CHAPTER
NINETEEN

THREE O'CLOCK IN the morning, and the town still roared when Gunn and Eula slogged down the street, cold, wet, and as scruffy-looking as the hound that followed them. Gunn grinned to himself. He'd found himself a dog—or had the dog found him?

"We'll get you to the doctor, then I'll find Papa."

"No. We'll find your father first. He'll be near crazy with worry by now."

Eula looked from his eyes to his legs. "The bleeding seems to have stopped—at least it's not soaked through your bandage. All right, let's find Papa."

At the hotel Gunn peered over the batwing doors, checked the people in the saloon, shook his head, and said, "Not in there. We'll go to your room—or mine."

They found D'Anville in Gunn's room. Without a word he gathered Eula into his arms. The look he cast Gunn over her shoulder said all the thanks a man could have put into a volume.

"At least *you're* glad to see me, Papa. Rafe never even kissed me after he took care of his enemies—but you're going to take care of that right now, aren't you, Rafe?"

Gunn held his arms wide, and she stepped into them.

He felt all the fire of desire pulse through him. He held her tightly, felt her strain against him, then relax and partially withdraw. He waited for the feeling he had when with Jake. He wanted to feel protective—and to feel the need to provide for this woman the rest of his life—not just desire. The feeling didn't come.

178

Eula stepped back and stared him in the eye. "You didn't feel it either, did you, Rafe?"

He shook his head. "No, little one. It seems that we're destined to be good friends the rest of our lives. Somehow I think having you for a good friend will be more than most men and women ever have with each other."

"*That* is a promise, my handsome friend, and you'd better come to see us." She looked at her father. "Papa, looks like I've dragged you across half this nation of ours chasing a dream. It was a beautiful dream—but that's all that it was. I suppose we can go home now, anytime you're ready. Somehow I feel empty inside." Abruptly she looked at Gunn's leg, which he favored by letting his other one hold his weight. "Oh, Rafe, I've been so thoughtless." She glanced at her father. "Papa, see if you can find a doctor."

"No," Gunn cut in, "you bandaged it well, it's not bleeding, and it doesn't pain much. It'll wait until morning."

He limped to the bed and sat on its edge. "Eula, we've just made some very important decisions based on what we expected from one kiss. Don't you think we should give it a chance—see each other for a couple of weeks and then make up our minds?"

Eula stared him straight in the eyes. "Rafe, I'm not willing to try to kindle a flame under wet kindling—and I don't believe you are either. Neither of us felt what we hoped for in that kiss. If even a tad of the emotion we wanted had been there, I'd say yes, let's try—but, Rafe, it just wasn't there."

Gunn wanted to protest, wanted to try to regain what he'd dreamed of so many nights, but he knew it was a futile hope. Eula was right. Even while he held Eula in his arms, the feel and thought of Jake had been between them. His dream from this night on would be of only one woman—but she didn't want him.

She didn't want him? How the hell did he really know that? She would have to tell him one more time, and she'd better make it a strong denial, as only Jake could, or he'd hog-tie her and carry her into the hills. He realized he'd been staring at the wall while thinking and brought his gaze back to them.

"Whoa, now," Gunn broke in. "There's something you both can do for me." He stood, went to the nightstand, and poured

D'Anville and himself a drink, then looked questioningly at Eula. She shook her head.

"What I was about to say is that there is a woman here who thinks I'm to marry the lady who has been mailing me the letters from New Orleans. I want you to tell her differently. Sit down and make yourselves at home while I round up one other person."

D'Anville took a swallow of his drink and asked, "When you gonna get this other person?"

"Right now."

"Now, Rafe? Hell, it's four o'clock in the morning."

Gunn glanced at his watch. "Well, so it is. But this can't wait. Like I said, make yourselves at home—I'll be right back."

Gunn returned about half an hour later escorting a grumbling, sleepy-eyed man with him. "C'mon, we're gonna call on a lady."

"Rafe, you're not going to wake a lady up this time of day, are you?"

"Trail along, little one, and see."

Their first stop was at Jake's bakeshop. No answer. Gunn motioned them to follow him, and he led them up the hill to Jake's cabin.

Gunn sucked in a deep breath and let it out slowly, then he had his three companions stand to the side of the door. "Stay here. This woman is just as likely to fire a shotgun blast through the door as she is to answer my knock. Ready?"

At their nods, Gunn pounded on the thick pine planks that served as the door and quickly stepped to the side. "It's me, Jake. Don't do anything like blast through that door."

"What the gosh-dinged hell are you doing here this time o' night, Rafe Gunn? You drunk? Git gone now or I'll shore 'nuff blast yore sorry ass off."

Gunn glanced at Eula, who stood wide-eyed and more than a little scared. He spewed a laugh from between tightly pressed lips. "Jake, I'm not drunk—and I'm not sorry assed. Open the door. I've someone I want you to meet."

"Gol danged you, I'll meet 'em after sunup. Now, git gone."

"Not gonna leave till you open up and see who I brought to see you."

The bar across the inside scraped the rough panels. The door swung open. Jake stood there in a heavy flannel nightgown that reached to the floor. She had thrown on a wrap and clutched it together tightly over her breasts.

When she saw Eula, she opened her mouth for what Gunn was sure would be another scathing comment. "What in the sopped-up hell are you doing traipsing around with the likes of Rafe Gunn, girl? You look like one o' them fillies what's been brung up knowin' to leave the likes o' him alone."

Eula had opened her mouth to say something when the whole scene apparently tickled her funny bone. She laughed, and then laughed some more, until she clutched her sides in pain.

"What the blasted hell are you laughin' at, woman? Ain't funny draggin' a pore defenseless female outta bed this time o' day."

Before anyone could think of an answer, Gunn reached through the doorway and pulled Jake out—and into his arms. "Woman, don't you say another word. I want you to meet the D'Anvilles, Eula and her father, Paul. This sleepy-eyed gent is a preacher. He's gonna marry us."

"I done told you—we ain't gettin' married. Don't want no man what loves another woman. Besides, we don't think o' each other like a man an' woman's s'posed to if they gonna git hitched."

Gunn still held her tightly in his arms despite her squirming to be let loose. "Jake, you speak for yourself when you say we don't love each other. I love you. I want to marry you—but well, hell, if you don't want *me,* don't reckon there's anything I can do about that." He turned her loose.

Jake looked at him a moment. "You mean that, Rafe?" She looked at Eula. "You the one what's been writin' Rafe them letters he got all winter?"

Eula nodded.

"You ain't gonna fight to keep yore man?" Jake continued.

"Jake, he's not my man. We found that out tonight. We're good friends, that's all." Eula grinned like a young imp. "And besides, Jake, there is no way I would try to hold a man against you. You're the most fearsome female I've ever seen. Probably the only one who could make this man toe the line."

Jake looked from Eula to Gunn. "That true, Rafe? All them things I said to you 'bout us bein' just partners—well, I only said them so you could go off an' be happy 'thout feeling sorry fer me. Ain't wantin' nobody to feel that way 'bout me. Course I love you—want you, an' . . . an', well, don't reckon either one o' us'll ever be just partners." She looked at each of them. "Come on in. Reckon I got the fixin's fer some breakfast. Put the coffee on, Rafe."

"Gonna get put in double harness first, woman—then we'll eat, if this preacher'll put his sleep off a little longer."

Gunn looked at Paul. "You're gonna be both the best man *and* give the bride away. Eula, you be the maid of honor, and Preacher—you start saying those words over us. Tie the knot as tight as you can."

"*I'll* take care o' that there knot, big man, don't you worry none. Ain't no way you gonna slip away from me." Jake cast Gunn a prayerful look and said, "'Less you want to."

Gunn again folded her in his arms. "No way, woman. I'll never leave you—for the Sioux or those mountains you've been trying to send me over." He waved them into a semicircle around the preacher and said, "Let's do it."

SPECIAL PREVIEW!

One was a Yankee gentleman, the other a Rebel hell-raiser. They met in a barroom brawl, and the only thing they had in common was a price on their heads—and an aversion to honest work . . .

Texas Horsetrading Co.

Gene Shelton, acclaimed author of *Texas Legends*, brings you a rousing new epic novel of the Wild West.

Here is a special excerpt from this authentic new Western—available from Diamond Books . . .

THE LAST THING Brubs McCallan remembered was a beer bottle headed straight for the bridge of his nose.

Now he came awake in a near panic, a cold, numbing fear that he had gone blind. Beyond the stabbing pain in his head he could make out only jerky, hazy shapes.

Brubs sighed with relief as he realized he was only in jail.

The shapes were hazy and indistinct partly because only a thin, weak light filtered into the cell from the low flame of a guttering oil lamp on a shelf outside the bars. And the shapes were fuzzy partly because his left eye was swollen almost shut.

Brubs leaned back against the thin blankets on the hard wooden cot and groaned. The movement sent the sledgehammer in his head to pounding a fresh set of spikes through his temples.

"Good morning."

Brubs started at the sound of the voice. He tried to focus his good eye on the dim form on the cot across the room. He could tell that the man was tall. His boots stuck out past the end of the cot. He had an arm hooked behind his head for a pillow, his hat pulled down over his eyes. "Mornin' yourself," Brubs mumbled over a swollen lower lip. "Question is, which mornin' is it, anyway?"

"Sunday, I believe. How do you feel?"

"Like I had a boot hung up in the stirrup and got drug over half of Texas." Brubs lifted a hand to his puffy face and heard the scratch of his palm against stubble. "And like somebody swabbed the outhouse with my tongue. Other than that, passin' fair."

"Glad to hear that. I was afraid that beer bottle might have caused some permanent damage."

Brubs swung his feet over the edge of the cot, sat up, and immediately regretted it. The hammer slammed harder against the spikes in his brain. He squinted at the tall man on the bunk across the way. "I remember you," he said after a moment. "How come you whopped me with that beer bottle?"

"I couldn't find an ax handle and you were getting the upper hand on me at the time," the man said.

Brubs wiggled his nose between a thumb and forefinger. "At least you didn't bust my beak again," he said. "That would have plumb made me mad. I done broke it twice the last year and a half. What was we fightin' about?"

The tall man swung his feet over the side of the cot and sat, rubbing a hand across the back of his neck. "You don't remember? After all, you started it."

"Oh. Yeah, I reckon it's comin' back now. But that cowboy was cheatin'. Seen him palm a card on his deal." Brubs snorted in disgust. "Wasn't even good at cheatin'."

"How do you know that?"

"If he'd been any good I wouldn't of caught him. I can't play poker worth a flip. Who pulled him off me?"

"I did."

"What'd you do that for? I had him right where I wanted him. I was hittin' him square in the fist with my face ever' time he swung. Another minute or two, I'd of had him wore plumb down."

"I didn't want to interfere, but I saw him reach for a knife. That didn't seem fair in a fistfight."

Brubs sighed. "You're dead right about that. That when I belted you?"

"The first time."

Brubs heaved himself unsteadily to his feet. It wasn't easy. Brubs packed a hundred and sixty pounds of mostly muscle on a stubby five-foot-seven frame, and it seemed to him that every one of those muscles was bruised, stretched, or sore. Standing up didn't help his head much, either.

The man on the other bunk raised a hand. "If you don't mind, I'd just as soon not start it again. I don't have a beer bottle with me at the moment."

"Aw, hell," Brubs said, "I wasn't gonna start nothin'. Just wanted to say I'm obliged you didn't let that cowboy stick a knife in my gizzard." He strode stiffly to the side of the bunk and offered a hand. "Brubs McCallan."

The man on the cot stood. He was a head taller than Brubs, lean and wiry, built along the lines of a mountain cat where Brubs tended toward the badger clan. The lanky man took Brubs's hand. His grip was firm and dry. "Dave Willoughby. Nice to make your acquaintance under more civilized conditions."

"Wouldn't call the San Antonio jail civilized," Brubs said with a grin. The smile started his split lower lip to leaking blood again. He released Willoughby's hand. "We tear the place up pretty good?"

"My last recollection is that we had made an impressive start to that end," Willoughby said. "Shortly thereafter, somebody blew the lantern out on me, too."

Both men turned as a door creaked open and bootsteps sounded. The oil lamp outside the cell flared higher as a stocky man twisted the brass key of the wick feeder with a thick hand. The light spilled over a weathered face crowned by an unruly thatch of gray hair. "What's all the yammering about? Gettin' so a man can't sleep around here anymore."

The stocky man stood with the lamp held at shoulder height. A ring of keys clinked as he hobbled to the cell. His left knee was stiff. He had to swing the leg in a half circle when he walked. The lamplight glittered from a badge on his vest and the brass back strap of a big revolver holstered high on his right hip.

"You the sheriff?" Brubs asked.

"Night deputy. Sheriff don't come on duty for another couple hours. Name's Charlie Purvis. If you boys are gonna be the guests of Bexar County for a while, you better learn to keep it quiet when I'm on duty."

"We will certainly keep that in mind, Deputy Purvis," Dave Willoughby said. "We apologize for having disturbed you. We will be more reserved in the future."

Burbs glared through his one open eye at the deputy. "What do you mean, guests of the county?"

"In case you boys ain't heard," the deputy said, "that brawl you started over at the Longhorn just about wrecked the place. I don't figure you two've got enough to pay the fines and damages."

Dave sighed audibly. "How much might that be, Deputy?"

"Twenty-four dollar fine apiece for startin' the fight and disturbin' the peace. Thirty-one dollars each for damages. Plus a dime for the beer bottle you busted over your friend's head."

"What?" Brub's voice was a startled croak. "You gonna charge this man a dime for whoppin' me with a beer bottle?"

The deputy shrugged. "Good glass bottles are hard to find out here. Owner of the Longhorn says they're worth a dime apiece."

Brubs snorted in disgust. "Damnedest thing I ever heard." He glanced up at Willoughby. "Good thing you didn't hit me with the back bar mirror. God knows what that would of cost. You got any money, Dave?"

Willoughby rummaged in a pocket and poked a finger among a handful of coins. "Thirty-one cents."

Brubs sighed in relief. "Good. There for a minute I was afraid we were plumb broke." He fumbled in his own pocket. "I got seventeen cents. Had four dollars when I set in on that poker game."

"Looks like you boys got troubles," Purvis said, shaking his shaggy head. "Can't let you out till the fines and damages are paid."

"How we gonna pay if we're in jail?"

Purvis shrugged. "Should have thought about that before you decided to wreck the Longhorn. Guess you'll just have to work it out on the county farm."

"Farm!" Brubs sniffed in wounded indignation and held out his hands. "These look like farmer's hands?"

The deputy squinted. "Nope. Don't show no sign of work if you don't count the skinned knuckles." Purvis grinned. "They'll toughen up quick on a hoe handle. We got forty acres in corn and cotton, and ten weeds for every crop plant. Pay's four bits a day." He scratched his jaw with a thick finger. "Let's see, now—fifty cents a day, you owe fifty-one dollars. . . . Works out to be a hundred and two days. Each."

Dave Willoughby sighed. "Looks like it's going to be a long summer."

Purvis plucked a watch from his vest pocket, flipped the case open, and grunted. "Near onto sunup. You boys wrecked my nap. Might as well put some coffee on." He snapped the watch shut. "I reckon the county can spare a couple cups if you two rowdies want some."

Brubs scrubbed a hand over the back of his neck. "I'll shoot anybody you want for a cup of coffee. Got anything for hangovers? I got a size twelve headache in a size seven head."

The deputy chuckled. "Sympathy's all I got to offer. Know how you feel. I been there, back in my younger days. Busted up a saloon or two myself. You boys sit tight. I'll be back in a few minutes with the coffee."

Brubs trudged back to the cot and sat, elbows propped against his knees. He became aware of a gray light spreading through the cell and glanced at the wall above Dave's bunk. A small, barred rectangle high above the floor brightened with the approaching dawn. "Well, Dave," Brubs said after a moment, "you sure got us in a mess this time."

Willoughby turned to face Brubs, a quizzical expression on his face. "*I* got us in a mess? I was under the impression that you started the fight and I was an innocent bystander."

Brubs shrugged as best he could without moving his throbbing head. "Don't matter. Question now is, how do we break out of here?"

Willoughby raised a hand, palm out. "Wait a minute—you can't be serious! Breaking out of jail is a felony offense. We would be wanted criminals, possibly with a price on our heads. If you're thinking of escape, even if it was possible, count me out."

Brubs prodded his puffy eyebrow with a finger. The swelling seemed to be going down some. "I ain't working for the county, Dave. 'Specially not on some damn farm." He squinted at his free hand. "These hands don't fit no hoe handle. That's how come I left home in the first place."

Willoughby strode to his own bunk and stretched out on his back. "Where's home?"

"Nacogdoches, I reckon. Never had a real home to call it such." He raised his undamaged eyebrow at Willoughby. "You sure talk funny. Since we're tradin' life stories here, where you from?"

"Cincinnati."

"That on the Sabine or the Red River?"

"Neither. It's on the Ohio."

Brubs moaned. "Oh, Christ. I'm sittin' here tryin' my best to die from day-old whiskey, I got my butt whupped in a saloon fight, I owe money I ain't got, I been threatened with choppin' cotton, and now it turns out I'm sharin' a room with a Yankee. If I hadn't had such a damn good time last night, I'd be plumb disgusted."

A faint smile flitted over Willoughby's face. "I suppose it was a rather interesting diversion, at that." He winced and probed the inside of his cheek with his tongue. "I think you chipped one of my teeth. For a little man, you swing a mean punch."

The creak of the door between cell block and outer office brought both men to their feet. Brubs could smell the coffee before the deputy came into view, carrying two tin cups on a flat wooden slab. Purvis crouched stiffly and slid the cups through the grub slot of the cell.

Brubs grabbed a cup, scorched his fingers on the hot tin, sipped at the scalding liquid, and sighed, contented. "Mother's milk for a hungover child," he said. "If I was a preacher I'd bless your soul, Charlie Purvis."

Purvis straightened slowly, the creak of his joints clearly audible. "You boys'll get some half-raw bacon and burnt biscuits when the sheriff gets here. Need anything else meantime?"

"I don't reckon you could see your way clear to leave the key in the lock?" Brubs asked hopefully.

Purvis shook his head. "Couldn't do that." He pointed toward a dark smear on the adobe wall near the door of the office. "Just in case you boys got some ideas perkin' along with the headaches, study on that spot over there. That's what's left of the last man tried to bust out of my jail." He clucked his tongue. "Sure did hate to cut down on him with that smoothbore. Double load of buckshot splattered all over the place. Made a downright awful mess. Why, pieces of that fellow were—"

"I think we understand your message, Deputy," Willoughby

interrupted with a wince. "If you don't mind, spare us the gory details."

The deputy shrugged. "Well, I'll leave you boys to your chicken pluckin'. Sure don't envy you none. It gets hotter than the devil's kitchen out in those fields in summer."

Brubs moaned aloud at the comment.

"Is there somebody who could help us?" Willoughby asked. "A bondsman, perhaps, or someone who would loan us the money to get out of here?"

Charlie Purvis frowned. "Might be one man. I'm not sure you'd like the deal, though."

"Charlie," Brubs said, pleading, "I'd make a deal with Old Scratch himself to keep my hands off a damn hoe handle."

The deputy shrugged. "Same difference, maybe. But I'll talk to him." Purvis turned and limped away. The door creaked shut behind him.

Brubs stopped pacing the narrow cell and glanced at the small, high window overhead, then at the lean man reclining on the bunk. "How long we been in this place, Dave?"

Willoughby shoved the hat back from over his eyes. "I'd guess a little over half a day."

"Seems a passel longer than that."

"Patience, I gather, is not your strong suit."

Brubs snorted. "Buzzards got patience. All it gets 'em is rotten meat and a yard and a half of ugly apiece." He started pacing again.

"Relax, Brubs," Willoughby said, "you're wasting energy and tiring me out, tromping back and forth like that." He pulled the hat back over his eyes. "Better save your strength for that cotton patch."

Brubs paused to glare at the man on the cot. "You are truly a comfort to a dyin' man, Dave Willoughby. Truly a comfort."

The clomp of boots and the squeak of the door brought Brubs's pacing to a halt. Sheriff Milt Garrison strode to the cell, a big, burly man at his side. The big man seemed to wear more hair than a grizzly, Brubs thought. Gray fur covered most of his face, bristled his forearms, sprouted from heavy knuckles, and even stuck out through the buttonholes on his shirt. For a moment Brubs thought the man didn't have eyes. Then he realized they were the same color as the hair and were tucked back under brows as thick and wiry as badger bristles.

"These the two Charlie told me about?" The hairy man's voice grated like a shovel blade against gravel.

"That's them." Milt Garrison leaned against the bars of the cell. "Told you they didn't look like much."

"Well, hell," the hairy one said, "if they're tough enough to wreck the Longhorn, maybe they'll do."

"Boys, meet Lawrence T. Pettibone, owner of Bexar and Rio Grande Freight Lines. He's got a deal to offer you." Garrison waved a hand toward the prisoners. "The short one's Brubs McCallan. Other one's Dave Willoughby."

Lawrence T. Pettibone nodded a greeting. "I hear you boys run up a pretty big bill last night. How bad you want to get shut of this place?"

"Mighty bad, Mr. Pettibone," Brubs said.

"All right, here's the deal. I won't say it but once, so you listen careful." Pettibone's smoky eyes seemed to turn harder, like a prize agate marble Brubs remembered from his childhood. "I need two men. You boys got horses and saddles?"

Brubs nodded. "Yes, sir, Mr. Pettibone, we sure do. Over at the livery."

Pettibone snorted. "Probably owe money on them, too."

"Yes, sir. I reckon we owe a dollar apiece board on the mounts."

"You savvy guns?"

Brubs nodded again. "Sure do. I'm a better'n fair hand with a long gun, and I can hit an outhouse with a pistol if it ain't too far off."

"How about you, Willoughby?"

Willoughby's brow wrinkled. "Yes, sir, I can use weapons. If the need arises." His tone sounded cautious.

Pettibone grunted. Brubs couldn't tell if it was a good grunt or a bad grunt. "All right, I guess you two'll do. I was hopin' for better, but a man can't be too picky these days." He pulled a twist of tobacco from a shirt pocket, gnawed off a chew, and settled it in his cheek. "I need two outriders. Guards for a shipment goin' to El Paso day after tomorrow. I'll pay your fines and damages. You ride shotgun for the Bexar and Rio line until you work it off. At a dollar a day."

Brubs sighed in relief. "Dave, that's twice the pay the county offered. And no hoe handles."

"Mr. Pettibone," Willoughby said, "may I inquire as to why you are short of manpower?"

Pettibone twisted his head and spat a wad of tobacco juice. It spanged neatly into a brass cuspidor below the lamp shelf. "Bandits killed 'em last run. Blew more holes in 'em than we could count. Stole my whole damn load."

"Bandits? You mean outlaws?"

Pettibone sighed in disgust. "Now just who the hell else would hold up a freight wagon? A gang of Methodist preachers?"

Willoughby shook his head warily. "I'm not sure about this, Mr. Pettibone. It's one thing to work for a man. It's another matter to possibly have to kill or be killed in the line of work."

Pettibone's gray eyes narrowed. "Suit yourself, son. It don't matter to me. But I need *two* men. Charlie said he figured you two come as a package. Guess I'll have to find me a couple other saddle tramps." He turned and started to walk away.

"Mr. Pettibone, wait a minute," Brubs called. He turned to Dave. "You leave the talkin' to me, Dave," he whispered. "I'm gettin' out of here, and you're goin' with me."

The big man turned back.

"My partner here ain't no lace-drawers type, Mr. Pettibone," Brubs said earnestly. "He's a top hand with a gun and got more guts than a bull buffalo. He just went through some stuff in the war that bothers him time to time. Don't you fret about old Dave." He clapped his cell mate on the shoulder. "You just get us out of here, and we'll make sure your wagon gets through."

Pettibone glared at the two prisoners for several heartbeats, then shrugged. "All right. You're hired." He jabbed a heavy finger at Brubs. "I want you boys to know one thing. I ain't in the charity business. You duck out or turn yellow on me and you'll wish to high hell you were back in this lockup, 'cause I'll skin you out and tan your hides for a pillow to ease my piles, and every time I go to the outhouse I'll take it along to remember you by. Savvy?"

"Yes, sir," Brubs said eagerly. "We savvy. You're the boss."

"Good. Keep that in mind. I'll pick you boys up tomorrow afternoon." He turned to walk away.

"Mr. Pettibone?"

"Now what, McCallan?"

Brubs swallowed. "Reckon you could get us out today? No disrespect to Bexar County or this fine sheriff here, but this ain't the most comfortable jail I ever been in. I sure would like to get my stuff in shape and take the kinks out of my sorrel before we move out."

Pettibone glowered at Brubs for a moment. "Damned if you boys don't try a man's patience something fierce. All right, I'll get you out now. You got any place to stay?"

"No, sir, Mr. Pettibone."

Pettibone's massive chest rose and fell. Brubs thought he saw the hair in the big man's ears bristle. "You can bunk in at my place. Cost you a dollar a day apiece. I'll add it onto what it's going to cost me to spring the pair of you. Damn, but the cost of help's gettin' high these days." Pettibone turned to the sheriff. "Cut 'em loose, Milt."

Brubs heaved a deep sigh of relief as the key turned in the cell lock and the barred door swung open. He knew it was the same air outside the cell as in, but it still smelled better. He and Willoughby fell into step behind the sheriff and Pettibone.

Brubs and Willoughby waited patiently as Lawrence T. Pettibone frowned at the column of figures on Sheriff Milt Garrison's ledger. "What the hell's this ten cents for a beer bottle?"

"Dave busted one over my head, Mr. Pettibone," Brubs said.

Pettibone snorted in disgust. "Damnedest thing I ever heard," he growled. "Chargin' a man for bustin' a beer bottle in a saloon brawl."

"Sort of the way I figured it, Mr. Pettibone," Brubs said earnestly. "Pricin' a man's fun plumb out of sight these days."

"I ain't payin' for no damn bottle," Pettibone said. "No way I can figure how to get ten cents worth of work out of two guys on a dollar a day."

Brubs dug in a pocket and produced a coin. "Give me a nickel, Dave. We'll split the cost of the bottle."

Pettibone finally grunted and pulled a wad of bills from a pocket. Brubs's eyes went wide at the sight of the roll. It was more money than he'd seen in one place since the big horse race up in Denton. Pettibone licked a thumb and counted out the bills, sighing as he caressed each one. Pettibone acted like he was burying a sainted mother every time he put a dollar on the desk, Brubs thought.

Garrison gathered up the bills, dropped the money in a tin box, and scribbled a receipt. He handed the paper to Pettibone, then retrieved the prisoners' weapons from a locked closet. "Guess you bought yourself some shotgun riders, Lawrence," he said.

Pettibone cast a cold glance at Brubs and Willoughby. "Don't know if I bought a good horse or a wind-broke plug," he groused. "I sure as hell hope they ride and shoot better than they smell. You boys are a touch ripe. There's a big water tank out by my wagon barn. Wouldn't hurt either of you to nuzzle up to some soap. Now, strap them gun belts on and let's go bail your horses out of the lockup."

Willoughby paused for a moment, rotated the cylinder of his Colt, and raised an eyebrow. "Should we go ahead and load the chambers now, Mr. Pettibone?" he asked.

Pettibone groaned aloud. "Fools. I just bought two idiots with my hard-earned money. Dammit, son, what good's an unloaded pistol?" He watched in disgust as Willoughby thumbed cartridges into the Colt and reached for his Winchester rifle. "I guess you boys got plenty of ammunition?"

"I got ten rifle cartridges," Brubs said, shoving loads into his scarred Henry .44 rimfire long gun. "Maybe a dozen for the pistol."

"I have half a box of .44-40's," Willoughby said. "Same caliber fits both my handgun and rifle."

Pettibone snorted in disgust. "Damn. Now I've got to lay out some more hard cash on you two. My men don't ride with less than a hundred rounds each. Come on—we'll stop off at the general store down the street."

The two men fell into step behind Pettibone. A few minutes later the hairy one emerged from the store, four boxes of ammunition in a big hand. "I'll add the cost of the shells to your bill, boys. Fifty cents a box."

"Fifty cents? Mr. Pettibone, that's a dime more than I paid anywhere," Brubs said, incredulous.

"Call it a nuisance fee," Pettibone growled, "because you

boys are nuisances if I ever seen 'em. Course if you'd rather work it out with the county—"

"No, sir," Brubs said quickly. "I reckon that's fair enough. We won't nuisance you no more."

"I doubt that." Pettibone spat a wad of used-up tobacco into the street. "Let's get home before you two drifters cost me my last dollar."

"Mr. Pettibone?"

"What now, McCallan?"

"Any chance we could get a bottle of whiskey added to our bill?"

"No, by God!" Pettibone bellowed. "Don't push your luck, boy, or you'll be behind a hoe handle all summer!"

"Yes, sir," Brubs said. "But it was worth a try."

A half hour later, Brubs and Willoughby rode side by side behind Lawrence T. Pettibone's buggy. Brubs forked a big, rangy sorrel, and Dave rode a leggy black that looked to have some Tennessee racing stock in his bloodline.

"Brubs," Willoughby said quietly, "I have the distinct impression that our new employer is somewhat thrifty with his funds."

Brubs flashed a quick grin. "I reckon he can squeeze a peso until the Mexican eagle looks like a plucked crow."

Lawrence T. Pettibone's combination home and wagon yard and adjoining stock pastures spread over most of a section of the northern outskirts of San Antonio.

Brubs had to admit he was impressed. The corrals were sturdy, fenced by peeled logs the size of a man's thigh, and watered by a big windmill that creaked as it whirred in the southwest breeze. The barn was as solidly built as the corrals, expansive and well-ventilated. The main house was big, and built of real cut lumber, not adobe or split logs.

Brubs was even more impressed with what came from inside the big house.

Pettibone pushed the door open, growled at Brubs and Willoughby to wait on the porch, and went inside. He was back a minute later with a stiff-bristled brush and a bar of lye soap in hand, and one of the prettiest girls Brubs had seen west of Savannah trailing behind.

The girl was blond. Palomino hair tumbled past her shoulders, dancing gold in the warm afternoon sunshine. The pale rose housedress she wore wrapped itself around a figure that made Brubs want to paw the ground and snort. Her eyes were big, blue, and had a smoldering look about them above a perky, upturned nose. She looked to be about twenty. This, Brubs knew instinctively, was one hot-blooded woman. He swept the battered and stained hat from his head.

"Boys, this here is Callie, my daughter," Pettibone said. "Callie, these two bums'll be riding shotgun for us a spell. Don't shoot 'em for prowlers until I get my money back out of 'em. The little feller's name is Brubs McCallan. The tall one's Dave Willoughby."

Brubs bowed deep at the waist, then grinned at the blonde. He wished for a moment he had just had a bath and shave; some women were mighty picky about that, as if it made some sort of difference. "Mighty pleased to make your acquaintance, Miss Pettibone," Brubs said. "A pretty girl does brighten a poor saddle tramp's day."

"Lay a hand on Callie and I'll kill you," Pettibone said. It wasn't exactly a threat, Brubs noted. More like a statement of fact.

Brubs tore his gaze from the girl and glanced at his cell mate. Willoughby had removed his hat, but merely nodded a greeting. He did not speak.

A second woman, a Mexican somewhere in her late twenties, appeared at the door. She was a bit thick of hip and waist, her upper lip dusted by scattered but distinct black hairs. Overall though, not bad looking, Brubs decided. Away from the blonde she might even be pretty.

"That's Juanita. She's the cook and maid." Pettibone held out the brush and lye soap. "Long as I'm makin' introductions, this is stuff to clean up with. Put your horses in the barn and yourselves in that water tank out back, or don't come in for supper."

Brubs hesitated, reluctant to leave the warm glow that seemed to spread in all directions from Callie, until he realized that Lawrence T. Pettibone was glaring a hole through him. Brubs quickly replaced his hat, turned away, and mounted with a flourish, swinging into the saddle without touching a stirrup.

He wasn't above showing off a bit when a pretty girl was watching. He kneed his sorrel gelding around and set off after Willoughby who was already leading his leggy black toward the barn thirty yards away.

"Man, ain't she something?" Brubs said as he reined in alongside Willoughby. "I ain't seen a filly like that my whole life through. Prime stuff, that Callie."

Willoughby cast a worried glance at Brubs. "You heard what Pettibone said, Brubs. You'd better leave the girl alone."

Brubs chuckled aloud. "Just adds a little spice to the puddin', my Yankee friend. You see the way Callie was lookin' at me? Her eyes got all smoky-like."

"I saw the way Pettibone was looking at you." Willoughby swung the corral gate open.

"Ah, that inflated tadpole ain't much to worry about," Brubs said.

"I worry about a lot of things, Brubs. One of which is that if you try messing around with that girl, somebody is likely to get hurt. Like you and me."

Brubs reached down and cuffed Dave on the shoulder. "Don't you fret, Dave. You just watch ol' Brubs work that herd, you'll learn somethin' about handlin' women."

"And that," Willoughby said solemnly, "is exactly what's bothering me. I'm beginning to wonder if perhaps Brubs McCallan wasn't put on this earth just to get one Dave Willoughby killed."

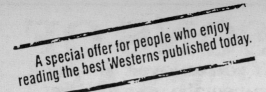

A special offer for people who enjoy reading the best Westerns published today.

WESTERNS!

NO OBLIGATION

Mail the coupon below

To start your subscription and receive 2 FREE WESTERNS, fill out the coupon below and mail it today. We'll send your first shipment which includes 2 FREE BOOKS as soon as we receive it.

Mail To **True Value Home Subscription Services, Inc. P.O. Box 5235**
120 Brighton Road, Clifton, New Jersey 07015-5235

YES! I want to start reviewing the very best Westerns being published today. Send me my first shipment of 6 Westerns for me to preview FREE for 10 days. If I decide to keep them, I'll pay for just 4 of the books at the low subscriber price of $2.75 each, a total $11.00 (a $21.00 value). Then each month I'll receive the 6 newest and best Westerns to preview Free for 10 days. If I'm not satisfied I may return them within 10 days and owe nothing. Otherwise I'll be billed at the special low subscriber rate of $2.75 each, a total of $16.50 (at least a $21.00 value) and save $4.50 off the publishers price. There are never any shipping, handling or other hidden charges. I understand I am under no obligation to purchase any number of books and I can cancel my subscription at any time, no questions asked. In any case the 2 FREE books are mine to keep.

Name _____

Street Address _____ Apt. No _____

City _____ State _____ Zip Code _____

Telephone _____

Signature _____
(if under 18 parent or guardian must sign)

Terms and prices subject to change. Orders subject
to acceptance by True Value Home Subscription
Services, Inc.

11337-9